We Meet Again

We Meet Again

An Anthology

G. B. Carmichael

Lineage Independent Publishing

Marriottsville, MD

https://lineage-indypub.com

Table of Contents

FOREWORD

Writing anything for publication is challenging, and G. B. Carmichael has certainly risen to that challenge. In this *magnum opus, she presents* an extensive body of work that includes two novellas, a wide range of short stories, and a few poems thrown in for good measure. This is her second anthology and fourth book overall.

Life was the inspiration for every story or poem in this anthology. Sometimes playful, occasionally lusty, always cheeky, and thoroughly captivating, the stories will engage the reader in thought-provoking and sometimes visceral ways. The first novella, "We Meet Again," discusses the legacy of former slaves in the United States.

Later, Carmichael brings World War I and World War II into the reader's focus in short stories such as "The Dancer" or "The Miracle of World War I." In a couple of other stories, she tells the stories of adults suffering from depression or dealing with seemingly insurmountable situations (hence the "trigger warning").

One of my favorites is "The In Between," which captures the everlasting nature of love. The story speaks volumes in just a few short pages, and I suggest that it is a "tissues to the ready" tale. Another of my favorite stories took me back to Liverpool in approximately 1960. You'll just have to find it. It's short – but sweet.

The stories as a whole are a cross-section of life on this earth – and sometimes what comes afterwards.

I am honored to be the editor and publisher of this anthology and look forward to G. B. Carmichael's future works.

Michael Paul Hurd

Author/Editor/Publisher

Lineage Independent Publishing

We Meet Again! (A Novella)

Celestine's Story

Celestine hurried up the narrow street. She wasn't one hundred percent sure it had been *him*, but just the possibility filled her with terror. Panic now laid waste to any logical thought other than escape.

She passed over Magazine Street, up the roads leading to Lafayette Square, and boundless options for escape.

Just one more block and the question of "Was it or wasn't it?" would not matter.

She was crossing the Camp Street intersection, when from a darkened doorway she'd barely passed, someone swiftly stepped up behind her. His left hand covered her mouth as the right arm encircled her waist and lifted her backward into the shadows.

"We meet again, lovely Celestine." His voice was the devil's, every word dripped venom and evil. Her bladder involuntarily voided in a fight or flight response; sadly, she could do neither.

Daniel FitzAlan, known by all simply as 'FitzAlan' was the overseer at the Magnolia Grove Plantation that stood in between St. Peter's and St. Charles, northwest of Saint Louis, in Missouri. A grand Italianate-style mansion, it boasted seventy-five rooms, including a gaol, and was owned by Danny's boss, sugarcane planter Andrew James Jackson, who'd had it built in the 1830's.

Celestine had been born there fifteen years previously. Her mother, Khadija, still cried for her home somewhere on the African continent.

Her father was either Danny or her owner, Andrew Jackson. Both had frequently taken their pleasure with her mother before whipping the skin off her back for being slow to respond to an order given in her bed or out in the fields.

This was not an unusual occurrence in those dark days.

*   *   *   *   *

Khadija had been caught in a raid on her village when she was about seven. Her mother and baby brother had been sold on the block in Saint Louis's Market Street; she never saw them again. Soon after, she was sold to the Magnolia Plantation.

Celestine had heard the stories, her mother's not much different from so many of the plantation's slaves. The only thing Khadija could recall with certainty was her name. The boss man, though, had decreed her new name to be Betsy from the day she arrived at Magnolia Grove.

When Betsy was delivered of her beautiful daughter, she promised herself to raise her child to be ready to run if ever an opportunity presented itself to them.

Every week she wrapped bread and fruit in her kerchief and hid it by the edge of the field, near the gates of the plantation's backroad.

Sometimes, as Celestine grew and the master visited her mother's cabin, she would make him laugh and he'd press a nickel into her tiny hand before sending her to a neighbour, or to play outside. Betsy saved every one of them. Even one dollar might be the difference between death and freedom. There were worse things than death awaiting many of the caught runaways. She'd heard tell of slaves being given to the dogs to tear to bits, and hanging was always a favourite. (did you know, readers, that the word picnic, comes from "pick a piccanniny and hang him," a suggested invitation for a day out's entertainment for Southern folk back then?)

As a small child, Celestine played and was schooled with the master's children in the big house nursery suite. The boy, Rhett, and she were fast friends and fished and swam in the bayou. She had good memories of those innocent summers. It was Rhett who'd asked his father where Betsy had been born. Celestine had told him she wished she knew what country was her mother's native home. He had promised to ask if she'd get him one of her mother's famous biscuits.

* * * * *

Gabon sits on the coast of Africa. Equatorial Guinea and the Congo were neighbours. Many of her peers on the plantation claimed heritage from these places and others were from Cameroon and Angola. The slavers had raped their way down the west coast of Africa.

When Celestine learnt all of this, she sought out the older women who spoke of Gabon as their homeland. She sucked every snippet of memory of their culture, history and of the land itself; she needed to understand her heritage. She begged lists of names for girls there and popular family names.

Eventually, she decided upon "Alvi." Once she was free, no-one would ever call her by her slave name again. She would be Alvi Koumba, a free woman of Gabon. She spent many hours daydreaming of her life when she was eventually free.

* * * * *

When Rhett was fifteen, two years Celestine's senior, his father gave her to him as a birthday gift, to learn the ways of men's pleasure. Over the previous two or three years

Celestine had watched the changes transform her childhood friend. Each trip home from his school, she noted a little more of her friend had disappeared.

Now he was a young facsimile of his father and she was just a slave, his slave, and he used her as such.

Around this time, Celestine began to notice the male slaves speaking in whispers round the evening fires. She sat quietly on the edge of the gatherings and listened. She heard talk of a man they called "Old Abe" who was causing a ruckus up north and calling for the end of slavery; they were talking of the war that had been raging on for near two years.

The year of 1863 began as every New Year's Day did, with them having to clear the detritus and debris from the New Year's Eve ball which the master hosted annually. However, the day ended very differently for the master, and every slave-owning man in the south.,

Mr. Lincoln, "Old Abe," the President of America, had declared that morning that all slaves, including those held by rebel state men or women, were declared free from that day. The third year of the civil war began with a noble declaration in the North and was answered with a furious rebel yell in the South.

The whispers around the fires were soon about places like Shiloh, Yorktown and Sharpsburg, or Antietam as it's called in the North. They told of the bloodshed and bitter fighting. Things were not going so well for the Confederate States. More men would flock to the ranks, including the boss man and his son Rhett and many slaves, who were forced into the army of the south. Forced by their owners to fight to secure their continued enslavement.

The overseer, Daniel FitzAlan was now in charge of the day-to-day running of the plantation under the Mistress.

Melanie Jackson, nee Bouvier, was a bored socialite, ten years her husband's junior and Daniel was a devil, with the looks of a dashing vagabond: wild black hair, turbulent blue eyes and a heart as black as his stallion. It wasn't long after Rhett and his father left for the war that the whispers between mouth and ear began. Talk was of the mistress's sojourns to her boudoir with the dashing overseer every afternoon. Those two hours or so of calm on the plantation was a blessing on all the staff. There was nary a one who was not afeart of the overseer.

*　　*　　*　　*　　*

By the March Celestine had decided it was time to run for freedom. Khadija refused to be included in the plans; she blamed her age and pointed out that she didn't have the education her daughter had been accorded and it might be the reason that would get them caught. The girl begged, but her mother would not be swayed. She did promise, though, to come as soon as Celestine sent word that she had work and a home for her mother to come to. Finally, Celestine acquiesced: as soon as Mr. Lincoln had these rebels whipped, her mother would join her.

The following week Celestine waited till the moment Mr. FitzAllan had rounded the back of the big house and she took off running. It was early in the year of 1863 that she, Alvi, declared herself FREE!

She took the most illogical route. An old captive Iroquois Indian had told her of a secret path through the swamp to the south of the boundary of Magnolia Grove. They'd expect a runaway to head to the northern states or at least toward the Union troops.

She travelled at night, and she'd learnt from her eavesdropping where the safe houses were rumoured to be. The railway she'd heard spoken of was the freedom railway. An "underground" network all across the country, homes where there was help to be found for the likes of Alvi. Now she thought herself free, she would use her slave name no more.

For three days, she travelled south, then in Mount Vernon, Illinois, where a "friend" arranged a ride northeast towards her final destination.

From there she was to go to meet a contact in St Louis on the north side of Lafayette Square, where another helping hand would see her along the next part of her journey to Hagerstown and freedom.

Sadly, the short walk from the south side outskirts of Lafayette square. to the north side where her contact awaited her, was where she thought she'd spotted Daniel FitzAlan.

She'd retraced her steps and made her approach via another route. She was just approaching the last intersection before the road led into Lafayette Square when, unseen by Alvi, a man stepped up behind her. Reaching from the darkness of a doorway and without warning, his right hand clamped over her mouth while is left simultaneously encircled her waist, lifting her off her feet. Alvi's blood ran cold as the devil's voice whispered in her ear, *"We meet again, Celestine!"*

FitzAllan!

After dragging her into the alleyway, he put her feet back on the ground and, turning her to face him, he punched her hard on the side of the head. Everything went dark and her knees buckled. If she fully lost consciousness, it was but fleeting.

Daniel had underestimated this young girl. He assumed he had her senseless and malleable. Instead, she grabbed the small roll of coins from her pocket and, closing her fist tightly round them, smashed nickel and knuckle into his nose. It stunned him long enough for her to notice the large rock being used to hold the rubbish lid in place. Using both hands and every ounce of strength, she delivered a blow that ensured her the time to make it to her meeting and escape. She stuffed the coin roll back in her pocket and divested Daniel of his money pouch, then took to her heels as if Lucifer himself was on her trail.

By late June, she'd made it to Hagerstown. Here Alvi first set eyes upon black men in blue uniforms. Free men and black. Here she became a camp follower.

*　　*　　*　　*　　*

She'd been standing on a street corner agog at the sight of these saviours, line upon line of black and white soldiers all fighting to make her free. It was so wondrous to her that she didn't notice the sister mulatto standing beside her. This light skinned woman was beautiful. Her skin like a milky coffee and her hair, much like Alvi's own, only longer, was piled high and tied with a brightly coloured kerchief. She smiled; her full red lips looked luscious against her bright white teeth.

"What's the matter, chile,' you never saw a woman smile afore?"

Alvi paused, then offered out her hand, "Excuse me forgetting my manners, Miss. I was admiring your hair style. My name is Alvi. Alvi Koumba."

"Why hello, Miss Alvi, I am Miss Désirée." They shook hands in the genteel fashion of the day.

They fell into easy conversation about the troops in all their splendour, and the emancipation bill (though Alvi did not know then, that was what the declaration had been called). She soaked up every snippet, any piece of information might be vital.

Miss Désirée told her that she was travelling with the troop's supply train, helping in the cookhouse. Alvi asked was it possible for any woman to travel with them.

"Well now, honey, you gotta have something to trade for a place or you gotta work. You got anything to trade, chile?"

Alvi paused, thinking what was clear but unsaid in Desirée's words. She concluded that as it had been taken from her by force before, she reckoned for freedom, she could tolerate being some soldier's woman till she reached the north.

"Yes'm. I got me some trade goods, an' I ain't been a chile since I was thirteen years old."

Désirée led her into the camp. Her newly rouged lips and primped hair piled into her own kerchief, she was a sight to behold. Not a man failed to notice as she sashayed alongside her new friend.

A week later, Alvi contemplated the past months. She'd ridden in her first locomotive, travelled almost seven hundred miles, went alone through swamps and slave country, and had made friends and found a new version of herself that would not be easily recognisable by her mother. Having detrained in Columbus, they were joined by the 2nd Massachusetts Regiment, who were newly come from the battle at Fort Wayne. They were headed northeast to a place named Gettysburg. There was thirty-three miles to their destination.

*   *   *   *   *

Alvi had gleaned a broad knowledge of herbs and healing from all the women at Magnolia Grove. It stood her in good stead and had won her a place working in the hospital tent under the regimental surgeon. The fact that she could read and write and knew her numbers turned her into an invaluable assistant even when surrounded by the slaughter of battle.

The first three days of July taught her many life lessons. She found herself to be stoic, calm in the midst of panic, and with a depth of compassion she'd have never anticipated in herself. Even the Confederate white soldiers appreciated the care and compassion she showed to those who previously would have valued their dog higher than her life.

Alvi saw hundreds of men die, suffering the damage of shot and shell. She also witnessed their true heroism in the face of not only impending death, but in the face of a life in ruins, with bodies and minds broken. Faces of soldiers damaged by artillery or a surgeon's knife as he battled and sliced, to save their life but not their looks.

It was here the 54th Massachusetts Regiment joined the depleted numbers she'd previously travelled with.

She was no longer an ignorant girl by July 7th when they left Gettysburg and headed South through Washington and Richmond, crossing then from Virginia into North Carolina.

It was on the 7th that she met Julius Cade, a sergeant in the newly formed 54th. They'd only received their colours in the May and here they were: the first ever Black regiment in the union army.

Their white officers were held in high regard by the private soldiers, especially their Colonel, Robert Gould Shaw. He was the son of a prominent Bostonian family who were staunch supporters of the abolitionist bill.

Initially, Colonel Shaw was reluctant to accept this commission for he feared they'd never allow his men to see action, but at last accepted the post.

Julius and Alvi both were hit by the thunderbolt, "love at first sight" and the regimental Chaplain reluctantly agreed to marry the pair on the 11th of July. Each night, the pair lay together under the stars planning for their life when the war ended. They figured they'd have enough of a nest egg of saved pay, especially as Alvi was now on the hospital payroll as a surgeon's assistant. They reckoned Kansas or Colorado, a small piece of land where they could settle, raise a family, and have Alvi's mother come live with them.

Alvi had never known such joy: she asked herself sometimes was it right to be so happy when the country seemed hell bent on destroying itself, and all in it.

Julius had only one gripe, despite their uniform, and finally the arrival of their weapons, it would seem that the powers that be held little confidence or trust that the black soldiers would hold the line in the face of the enemy's guns.

It gnawed at his pride and every man jack in the regiment felt the same. Had these men not more reason than anyone to want to wipe the slave-owning grey coats from the face of the earth? However, changing men's thinking takes time. Waiting for this change was affecting the morale of the 54th.

On the morning of the 16th, Julius expected a day no different from the previous ones. There had been no portent to hint at the significance this day would have on him and history.

Near Grimball's Landing, they were out foraging when they happened upon a skirmishing party of the 1st Carolina Regiment. There followed the drawing of first blood by the 54th. They prevailed with panache and valour. Robert Gould Shaw's confidence in his troops was proven and then some. The word of their success and courage heated the telegraph wires up and down the country. Everyone in the 54th claimed it was a glorious day for the forwarding of the cause of the North and freedom for all enslaved men in every state. They enjoyed the notoriety and glory for forty-eight hours, never realising it had signed the death warrant of many celebrating that day.

Colonel Shaw soon received orders that he and his men should assist in the razing of a small town they passed through. Shaw didn't hold with making the women and children suffer more than they had to, surrounded by war. He and his men felt the shine of their pride and honour dull at having such a terrible task. Shaw sent word to his commander in chief, asking if this was general orders issued or just a vengeful act by an officer Shaw's senior. He never received a reply to this communication.

Instead, he received orders for what appeared to be a suicide mission. He was to have the dubious *honour* of leading the attack on a position to the south of their encampment. He would be in overall charge of the 54th, and units from the 3rd New Hampshire's, 6th Connecticut,

9th Maine, 48th New Yorkers and the 76th Pennsylvania regiments. It was conferred as a great honour, but Shaw suspected it was to punish them for showing these pompous asses at HQ and Washington that his men were equal to any in the Union army, his men having distinguished themselves so well in their first major engagement and earning their unique place in history.

* * * * *

On the morning of July 18th, 1863, Alvi drew Julius into a warm embrace, saying he'd best be home on time for supper as she had something special she wished to discuss with him. She had confirmed her suspicions: she was pregnant with their first child.

Julius kissed her tenderly and swore she was the prettiest thing he'd ever laid eyes on. His embrace was so fierce she felt his foreboding that he did not expect to return to her. All day she prayed he'd be proved wrong.

Alvi watched from a distance the charge of the 54th across open ground to attack the parapets of Fort Wagner. She witnessed the decimation of this historic and brave regiment. Some six hundred troops had taken the field; Colonel Shaw and 280 men were killed, wounded or unaccounted for. Forty-two percent of the regiment, including her Julius, were gone, gone into the annals of history and glory, and the arms of the Lord.

Alvi took his pay and the paltry gratuity given to the black widows, a lesser amount than that sent to the women of the white soldiers. Was Colonel Shaw's widow's grief and loss greater than that of Sergeant Cade's wife? Alvi realised that even though more enlightened than the men of the South, racism was still alive and well in the North.

She stayed with the troops, working until she was eight months gone and could hide her condition no longer. The surgeon she worked under in the hospital tent had guessed her secret but waited for Alvi to come to him.

He was a good man, who, upon his father's demise and his inheritance of the family estates in the North, had freed all the slaves, offered them employment, a home, and a decent living if they wished to stay under his employ.

He gave Alvi the name of his estate manager and the address of his home in Sherborn, Massachusetts. She took the travel pass and bought a ticket to Boston. She walked the last twenty-six miles to Sherborn, safely arriving at Major Belkin's home.

A tall black man in a black frock coat, tan breeches, a white shirt, and black boots was about to mount a roan stallion of about seventeen hands, clearly a well-bred animal. At first, she considered the possibility that he might be a carpet bagger.

"Good morning, Ma-am, can I assist you?" his voice held none of the southern drawl that most other black man she'd ever known used. He was no runaway.

"I am a friend of Major Belkin. He said to come here and to give this letter to a Mr. Jacob Bell."

"Well, I am Jacob," he said, accepting the envelope Alvi had drawn from her valise.

"You are his overseer?" her surprise on show.

"That I am!" Jacob replied laughing. "And you are?"

"Oh, Lordy! Forgive my manners. I am Widow Cade. My husband was killed at Fort Wagner. I was a hospital orderly under Major Belkin of the same regiment as my husband."

"Come, let's get into the house, Mrs. Cade, I'll have cook to fix you some refreshments whilst I read the instructions you bring from the Major."

Alvi sat at the long refectory table in a light, clean and airy kitchen that led out into a well-tended herb garden. She could see past the wall enclosing this kitchen garden to an orchard where what looked like peaches the size of a new-born child's head hung, nearly ready for picking. It seemed like the land of milk and honey to this child of slavery. She could build a home here, she thought to herself.

Jacob sat opposite and read the letter. In it, he was instructed to give Alvi one of the old butler's cottages that were empty. Belkin also suggested that he no longer needed a valet while he was at home and could hire in additional help if or when visitors needed it.

Belkin's wife had died during the delivery of their third child. Their current mammy was now getting on in years and Major Belkin felt that Alvi might prove an excellent doctor's assistant – once delivered of her own child, of course.

He had offered her a full-time position made up as a part time help to Mammy Rebecca but also to be the resident nurse to the whole household. This would give her a home, a decent position, and a way to care for her child to boot.

*   *   *   *   *

The war raged on all over the country and many a mother, wife, sister, and daughter were in the black garb of mourning. The streets of both the North and the South were filled with pale faced wraiths whose eyes were dulled with the grief and broken hearts. Tales also reached their ears of the writ issued against runaways captured in Union blue. They would face capital punishment.

They also heard that the body of Colonel Shaw, Julius's commanding officer, had not been returned as was the custom for a fallen enemy officer. The Confederate officer at Fort Wagner sought to cause insult to the memory of a gentleman officer by burying him with his black troops.

The Shaw family responded with the greatest dignity stating, "Our beloved son would have had it no other way and would have declared himself proud to lie with his brave troops."

* * * * *

On the ides of March, 1864, Alvi was confined to her bed with the onset of labour. Mammy Rebecca declared all was progressing normally and Solomon Cade was delivered by Mammy Rebecca in the early hours of March 13th. Both mother and son were hale and hearty. Mammy Rebecca had delivered more babies than she could count in her sixty-three years, but never a free child. Rebecca's father was also from Gabon, and in gratitude for Mammy's care, Alvi named her son for Mammy's father. Solomon Cade of Gabon blood was a free born child. Alvi was content.

The many months following Solomon's birth brought blessings to look back on. Solomon uttered his first words, took his first steps, saw and played in the snow that first Christmas. The war had drawn to a close as the spring of 1865 arrived. The south surrendering in Virginia at Appomattox Courthouse on April 9th.

Robert E Lee gave up his arms to Ulysses S Grant with the stoicism of the fine soldier he was. And Grant was a noble opponent who allowed Lee his sword and his dignity.

In the September of that year, Alvi and Jacob Bell had taken Solomon into Boston. They were to meet the train from Saint Louis bringing Khadija for a long-awaited reunion with her beloved daughter. The letter had arrived a week previously with her travel details. The trio left early to avail themselves of the opportunity to pick up some supplies for Doctor Belkin's surgery and some items for two of his children due to leave for boarding school in a few weeks.

Jacob and Alvi were easy in each other's company and little Solomon adored the tall athletic overseer. He toddled behind Jacob like a shadow. Many a near spill had occurred as Jacob turned to almost fall over the toddler on his heels. Alvi secretly suspected Jacob was sweet on her; she herself acknowledged her attraction to this kind, handsome man. Who wouldn't be, she thought, but made no move to encourage Jacob. She wasn't ready yet for making space for a man in her heart, one that still held the ghost of Julius.

In Boston, the three moved through the busy thoroughfare, browsing, and making their purchases. Solomon, now toddling, could not be contained or stilled. As the appointed time for Khadija's arrival approached Jacob led them to the corner of Providence and Carver Street, then showed them across the road into the public gardens. It would allow Solomon to let off some steam and the train depot was just across the road.

Jacob, Alvi and Solomon chased each other all over the park, Solomon laughing and screeching as all toddlers do. After a demand to play cowboys and Indians, Alvi cried off and headed for a bench to rest and anticipate seeing her mama again.

She had been sitting in quiet contemplation for maybe ten minutes when she was grabbed from behind, and like a rerun of a nightmare, evil dripped in her ear:

"Celestine, we meet yet again."

He must have hit her with a cosh of some ilk, for her world turned black.

*   *   *   *   *

She came to in a dirty stable that had seen better days. The roof leaked and what remnants of straw that still lay on the flagstone floor was rotten and stank. She tried not to think what the odours might be.

Back in the park, Jacob rounded a small copse of rhododendrons with Solomon tucked under his arm; he was brought to pause as there was no sign of Alvi. He thought it unlike her to leave without a word, but assumed she was impatient and had gone to meet her mother's train.

"Come on then, boy. Let's go collect our two women of Gabon."

Jacob couldn't see Alvi as the train pulled in. The steam and large crowds waiting to board mixing with those who were attempting to alight with bags and trunks made his task difficult. As it cleared some, Khadija was easy to spot, Alvi was so very like her.

As she stood searching the faces in the crowd Jacob approached her. "Miss Khadija?" he spoke confidently.

Assuming the pair had been sent by her daughter, Khadija replied, "Yes, and who might you be little one?" addressing Solomon who was perched on Jacob's shoulders. "And where is my daughter?"

"I am Jacob Bell, and this is your grandson, Solomon. I thought Alvi had left the park before us to be here to meet you alone first... I can't think where she might have gone!"

The trio returned to the park in search of Alvi, hoping to find her looking for them. It was Jacob who found Solomon's toy horse. It was broken and lay on the path leading to the Arlington Street exit. He left Solomon with his grandmother and raced up the path, his heart filled with fear. As he bounded through the exit gate he almost fell over an old soldier. Many like this chap, minus an arm and half a leg were reduced now to begging to survive.

"Sir," he asked, "have you seen a woman leave through here, wearing a black full skirt with – "

The old soldier interrupted him, " – with a scarlet petticoat?"

"Yes! Where did she go?" asked an anxious Jacob.

The soldier looked askance for a moment then said, "The fella carrying her took her up there and went into one of the old stable buildings."

Jacob ran, his heart pounding, for he loved this strong, independent woman. He couldn't lose her before he'd had the chance to tell her so.

*   *   *   *   *

Alvi's eyes slowly became accustomed to the dark and dingy shadows and then finally focused upon the dishevelled figure sitting on an old box.

"Mister FitzAlan, I'm at a loss why you are here and what you could possibly want with me. I am a free woman under the law now, so you can't possibly think to return me to Magnolia Grove. I understand there is a possibility that you sired me, however your behaviour and treatment toward me suggests no loving reunion is sought here. So, what do you want with me?"

Daniel laughed, "You are no kin to me, and the master knew that. I cannot father a child. The rifle butts of English soldiers who took some fun in beating a fifteen-year-old lad so bad it near killed him. He... I... lived, but will never be able to enjoy any progeny. So, no, I'm not your father. You can't imagine my delight when I heard a whisper that Betsy was travelling to meet her runaway daughter today. I just made sure I was here to meet you too.

"That stunt you pulled back in St Louis that gave you freedom took everything from me. I was humiliated for being bested by a lass and relieved of my position. The master and young master Rhett had been killed at Fredericksburg on May 3rd, just weeks after you ran. The mistress and the younger children were taken by the cholera barely a week after my return. They reckon the troops passing through brought it to the Grove, it took many in the surrounding area. So, no, I also didn't come to take you back, either.

"I came to kill you. I worked for that family for years and got what for it? Humiliation, and penury! Whilst you, black trash, inherits it all". Alvi was shocked into silence

Daniel continued, "Mr. Jackson had no other kin and Mistress had only one brother. He was killed in the attack on Fort Wagner, by that ridiculous regiment of trained monkeys, raised by those fools in the North. I will not let a pack of niggers and picaninnies inherit what decent hard working white folk worked to build and gave their lives to protect. You, little Celestine, will die here today in the dirt and filth where you belong. But I aim to have me some fun first though."

"I don't think so, sir. Please stand aside. I have no wish to shoot, but I most certainly will." Jacob Bell stood in the doorway, his face like it was set in stone.

"Alvi, are you alright? Can you stand"?

He chanced a swift look in her direction and was pleased to see her upright.

"Jacob, I am bound, tied to a hook on the wall. Do you have a knife or something to cut the binds"?

Jacob slowly bent his knees into a squat, never taking eyes off Daniel. He felt for the handle and pulled free his Bowie knife. He threw the sheathed knife to Alvi.

In that second Daniel made his charge. He barrelled into Alvi as Jacob's gun fired. Both fell hard, crashing back into the wall of the old stable stall. Jacob saw Daniel land on top of Alvi; he didn't know if he'd hit this vicious monster.

"Alvi! Alvi! Speak to me, woman! Are you alright?"

He flew to where both forms lay still on the floor, Daniel sprawled over Alvi's body as if in a lover's embrace. The sight infuriated Jacob and he hauled Daniel's still form off the woman that was his heart's desire. There was blood all over Alvi, but he realised quickly that it was FitzAlan's. The Bowie knife was embedded in the evil man's heart by its position. Daniel had caused his own death as he launched at Alvi the very moment that she'd drawn the knife to cut her bonds. Jacob's bullet had shattered FitzAlan's shoulder; he was glad he hadn't missed.

After what felt a lifetime, Alvi opened her eyes.

"Oh, woman, you scared me some. I thought I'd lost you, and I couldn't have borne that."

"Jacob, give me some air and some time. I know we are destined to enjoy a life together, but can we collect my mother first?"

Jacob laughed out loud, "What a woman you are, Alvi, or Celestine, no matter your name... I am forever your humble servant."

As they came out, the old soldier noticed Alvi's kerchief. It had been Julius's. It was part of his uniform not worn that fateful day. It was marked with the insignia of the 54th.

"Ma'am, are you alright? I wish I'd realised how much trouble you was in, even as an old cripple I'd have done something, for a supporter of the 54th. I'd have done something, I swear."

"Were you in the 54th, sir?" asked Jacob.

"I fought beside them some. I lost these," nodding to the empty sleeve and half a trouser leg empty too, "at Fort Wagner. I was with B Company. Never saw such raw courage in my life, like big black lions they were. I was hit in the second wave of the attack and was trying to drag my sorry ass back to the lines. There was a big bull of a Sergeant of the 54th who was hit, but mobile, and was also making for the lines when he saw me. Even wounded he picked me up and threw me on his broad shoulder. We was almost back when he was hit again. A shell shot took him; he was dead afore he knew he'd been hit. His fall threw me forward and I was knocked cold. When I came to, I took his cap and pips." He reached inside his tattered tunic.

"See, miss?"

Alvi's hand shook as she accepted the cap. Somehow, she knew before she lowered her eyes onto the blue service cap hat band. There in her hand was still visible despite the dried blood, Sergeant. J. Cade. 54th MA.

The old soldier was still crying when Jacob returned with the buggy to the park gate. Khadija was holding her grandson and embracing her daughter. Jacob paused for a moment, still reeling from all that had happened, how it had changed their path.

He'd purchased a warm serviceable coat and breeches for the former soldier, whose life had been saved by Julius Cade. The buggy got them all back to the farm in good time. As expected, Doctor Belkin supported their offer to the old soldier of somewhere to live until Alvi could settle the affairs at Magnolia Grove. She would never understand Mr. Andrew Jackson's decision to name her as his biological child and to give her her freedom and a bequest in his will. She was certain he never expected that she'd be his only living kin and would inherit it all. *"Life was strange for sure,"* thought Alvi.

Two years later, with money from the sale of the plantation, Alvi and Jacob were married in the grounds at Sherborn Farm. Doctor Belkin gave her away and Solomon was their ring bearer.

Later they left the farm for their own place, not too many miles away from the Belkin spread and the surgery. After all, Alvi was still working as his nurse aid.

Jacob ran their farm and former private Banks was employed in breaking and training of the horses they traded in as well as the beef herd that grazed on their acres of beautiful arable pasture. Solomon caused mischief and havoc to ensure nobody was ever bored.

Jacob and Alvi had two daughters in the six years after their marriage, first Rebecca and soon after, Khadija Grace. Both trained under Alvi and Doctor Belkin to be nurses and worked in the military hospitals in World War I, nursing and helping to train nurses for the military.

Solomon grew into a fine young man and married Marguerite, daughter of Doctor Belkin.

Sometime in the future Alvi would be buried on the land she owned; her headstone reads:

Here lies

Alvi Cade-Bell,

daughter of Khadija,

a free woman of Gabon

Private Banks

Theodore James Banks was born on a cold, dreich night in the one-bedroom home, that was the upper floor of the gable end of a terrace house on the end of the row in Main Street, Bannockburn, Scotland.

His mother, lived there alone, whilst his father was somewhere in South Africa, serving with the East India Company.

Lizzie Banks died alone, surviving the difficult but swift birth of her son only long enough to cut his cord and wrap him in his swaddling shawl, then drew him close to her as she passed out and bled to death.

Their neighbour, Nancy Wilson discovered the desperate and sad scene on popping in to see her chum to ask if Lizzie needed anything.

Nancy arranged everything from the funeral to the sending of word to the offices of the East India Company to return Corporal Banks to his newborn son upon the sad and sudden demise of his wife.

Six months passed before a reply came, if that were what it could be termed. It read:

Cpl James Banks was killed in action on duty against the Xhosa tribe, in the army of this company.

Pay owed to date of death; seven shillings and six pence.

Severance pay.

including death bounty for loss of life, Seven pounds.

Total seven pounds, seven shillings & six pence.

The chit for this amount can be redeemed at any bank.

Regretfully,

Pay Master , Cpt C. Jones

Cc British East India Company.

Nancy and her husband Edward had the child christened as Lizzie would have done, and he was their adopted son, for all intents and purposes. His name was as Lizzie had chosen on the day they'd scried her belly using Lizzie's gold wedding band, sure and certain ever after that she would deliver a son.

The Wilsons would raise Theo and love him as if he were their own.

His life was no better nor harder than most of the working class in Scotland at that time. He was always a calm, confident and oft times, as Edward was heard say, "a cheeky wee bugger." But cheeky or not, he had a good character and a big heart.

By the time Theo had reached eighteen, tales of the Americas had lit the fuse that lies in many a Scot's breast. Wanderlust. The warrior poet nation has borne many a travelling son and daughter. Dr. David Livingstone, John Rae, Thomas Abernathy to name a few. All fearless and determined explorers, though their first professions were Physician, Surgeon, and Seafarer.

Wherever you travel in this world, you'll aye find a Scot...

Theo's soul was cut from this cloth, and he hankered after going to the newly opening "Wild West."

Aged a month shy of his nineteenth birthday, he signed on as a rating on a ship bound for Canada's east coast, to what we know as Nova Scotia.

A year in the fur trade set him up financially to be free to head south. He saw the old year out and hailed 1854 at a Ceilidh where other ex-pat Scots and Irish knew how to party; the New Yorkers observed the total abandon these Gaels enjoyed in jealous affection.

As a more than competent horseman with a knack with the more tricky and stubborn mounts, he had no trouble finding work as a cowboy. Of course, this was nothing new to the Scot who'd seen and been part of the cattle and sheep droves from the highlands to the markets in the lowlands, all done traditionally on horseback. Even today evidence of those past times are remembered in the "Drovers Inn" at Inverarnan, Arrochar, near Loch Lomond, Scotland. Rob Roy MacGregor was said to have been a patron there before his death in 1734. The Chisholm Trail is a perfect example of both the wandering nature of the Scots and their part in the "Cowboy" narrative in the USA.

Theodore was loving the excitement and adventure, however there was one aspect of life in this new country that he despised, and that was slavery.

His own country had, along with their Hibernian cousins in Ireland, lost people to America, Australia, and Canada, and had experienced subjugation, domination, and yes, slavery! It raised Theo's dander to see a man whipped just because he was Black, and without recourse or protection under the law.

He was watching a Kentucky-born chap who was stirring the pot about slavery. Yes, Theo admired this Mr. Abraham Lincoln. The man was being attacked by different factions, for being an Abolitionist in the fifties and not being a more resolute one in 1860.

By 1861, that same Mr. Lincoln, of lowly birth in the wilds of Kentucky, took up residence as the sixteenth President of the United States. He was inaugurated on Monday, March 4th, 1861. By April 12th that same year, the country was forced into civil war by the seceded states who supported slavery.

Theo joined up that September. One of his Irish pals had seen Theo and made his farewells, saying he was away to the Irish Brigade. It was as near to a Scottish unit that Theo expected to find, so he left with Jimmy Lynch. They signed up with the 69th New York Infantry, nicknamed by General Robert E. Lee himself as the "Fighting 69th" for its tenacity in battle against his own Confederate forces. These Irishmen knew of repression, poverty and discrimination and abhorred the ideology of the Southern states.

He was there at Bull Run. Antietam in '62, where he received his first wound. He ended up back in New York in recovery and was almost ready to be returned to the 69th when he received a dinner invitation to the family home of another friend. This meal would have major repercussions in the life of the idealistic Scot. He was told it was a small party, his friend, his friend's wife, himself and another couple, a Mr. Robert, and Mrs. Annie Gould Shaw.

Leaving his friends home in the wee small hours of Feb 18th, 1863, Theodore pondered his decision to do as invited by Mr. (soon to be Colonel) Shaw, to resign from the 69th and join a newly formed controversial regiment of Black soldiers. The officers would be white, to pacify the doubters. It was the first time a Black man could enlist in the Union Army. Robert Gould Shaw would assume command on the ominous Ides of March, March 13th, 1863. The only Scot in a Black Regiment; another first, Theo suspected.

The history books say all that needs saying about attitudes, and indeed even in the North, there was reluctance to support Lincoln in this move. They doubted the moral fibre of the Black man: would he stand and fight, or turn tail and run in the face of the enemy?

Grimball's Landing showed their mettle and left egg on the face of the prominent citizen dissenters. And for having the audacity to prove these men wrong, they were assigned a barely veiled suicide mission under the guise of being granted the honour of leading the attack on Fort Wagner.

Theo had no illusions. He also had no doubt he'd not fail to fight to his last breath for these men beside him. Colonel Shaw led the charge. In such a short space of time much of this new regiment had entered the annals of history on the blood drenched space over which their bodies were strewn.

Theo was past the halfway point to the beachhead fortification in the second wave, when a musket ball shredded his shoulder and arm. Before he could properly assess the damage, a shell exploded, and his right leg now terminated just above the knee. He was sure he would bleed to death before he could get back to the Union lines. He was trying, and failing, to affect a tourniquet at his thigh, but with only one arm!

Then out of the smoke and dust, A big fellah from the first wave staggered towards where Theo lay. He, too, was injured and was attempting to secure his arm inside his shirt. His left arm, like Theo's, was just shredded meat and blood.

This lion stopped, squatted down and between them they tied off Theo's arm and leg in secure tourniquets, the kerchief of the 54th was stemming the arterial bleed in Theo's arm.

Then, this Sergeant picked him up like a sack of potatoes and threw Theo over his good shoulder. Theo passed out at that point, but not for long. He came to, hearing the password and answer call from his lines. He was astonished and was just giving thanks to his God when his saviour took another hit. This time he would have not had time to register the death blow impact before he would have been standing before his maker.

Medics had Theo to the surgeon tent in short minutes. He would live, but minus half an arm and one leg.

He spent the next two years either in hospital or Boston, trying to survive. Afterwards, he was reduced to begging on the streets. He was losing the strength to go on, and his humanity, too, was eroding; he hated himself all the more for that.

Then a miracle happened, and another chance encounter again changed forever the course of Theodore James Bank's life.

Khadija's Story

1871, Sherborn, Massachusetts.

Khadija watched as the horse whisperer, Theo Banks, navigated his newly acquired wheelchair from the bunk house to the corral, where a rowdy bucking stallion was snorting and blowing hard. He was telling the humans watching that they should be under no illusion. Putting a saddle or a man up on his back, would be no easy feat.

Theo was with young Solomon as they approached the fence behind which Hannibal, this beautiful horse, stood pawing the dust and eying them suspiciously.

Theo turned his back to the prancing animal and told Solomon to ignore the beast too.

Theo lay his hand along one bar of the fence; in his open palm a juicy red apple lay. It was about the tenth or eleventh day that he'd gone through the same ritual. A slight twitch of Solomon's eyebrow alerted Theo to the horse's approach.

Theo felt something moist and soft, heard a snicker, and the apple and horse were both gone in the time it took to register it was a muzzle. This ritual was performed for a further week, then Theo opened the gate, entering with Solomon. This time, Solomon held the apple in his outstretched palm. Hannibal had gone directly to Theo, but quickly spotted the apple in Solomon's hand.

He made a few feigned approaches, but finally his courage was found – or his caution overwhelmed – by his want for the delicious fruit. Now he was being hand fed by two humans. Theo offered his hand to the noble equine:

Hannibal was slow and wary, but he came. Theo gently laid his hand on the horse's muzzle. It was the start of a wonderful friendship.

Once Hannibal had been rider-trained, Jacob created a special saddle for Theo. The horse instinctively knew his rider was different and somehow fragile. He was gentle, measured, and always obedient for his friend. In later years, when Solomon rode him, then Hannibal could set his spirit free, and covered ground like a winter's gale. It was exhilarating for both horse and rider.

Khadija admired the spirit of the old soldier. His entry into their lives had brought many blessings. He was thoughtful, kind and made them all laugh till the tears ran freely and made their bellies jiggle with glee.

She was caught in her reverie by Theo, and was a little startled when his voice, so close to her ear, broke her train of thought.

"Khadija, where are you daydreaming yourself to be? Is this place and its people not good enough for you, woman?"

"Don't you be worrying none about my whereabouts, Theo Banks. It ain't no business of yours."

"Ah, woman, why are you always so harsh with me? Me, who asks you every month to marry me. It's been near on two years now. Every month I asks, and every month you ignore me. You waitin' on a better offer, woman?"

Khadija felt herself blush, "Now don't be teasing an old woman! T'aint kind. I've half a mind to say 'yes,' just to see the fear on your face." She felt an unexpected thrill as she put her daydreams into words."

Theo grinned, "Well now, Khadija, woman of Gabon, you go right ahead and just see if I'm serious or scared." He gave her a very impish grin, his eyes twinkling from the thrill of the flirtation.

If Khadija were honest with herself, she'd admit that she'd grown to love this man. Theo, who, despite his trials and pain, was content with his lot and never complained at the unfairness of his situation.

Then, like a bolt of lightning, it struck this beautiful woman of Africa, that she was no longer a slave. She needed no permission but her own to be happy. She loved Theo and life passed too fast to waste any more of it.

"Okay, soldier boy, you really want this woman as a wife? Then best you go ask my son in law if he gives you leave to ask me to marry your sorry ass." Khadija was having fun with Theo. She needed no permission from Jacob, but she like the idea of him having to ask for her, as he would have had to ask her father if she was still a girl.

Theo looked up, uncertain Had he heard her right?

"Did you just say 'yes' and tell me to go ask Jacob for your hand?"

Seeing her face and the shadow of doubt, she was questioning his sincerity now, and he saw her fear of rejection. All these fleeting glimpses told him he'd heard right.

"Woman, stay right there, I'll be back before you can say 'cotton ball.'"

That wheelchair raised dust as Theo hastened across to the ranch house, yelling for Jacob all the way.

The two met at the steps to the porch. Khadija watched for a minute, a minute that felt like an eternity. All sorts of thoughts whirling around in her head, the most prominent was "woman what have you done?"

A loud laugh erupted from Jacob. Khadija saw him slap Theo's back and then call for Alvi. There ensued another minute of discourse between the three before Alvi's head shot up as her eyes searched out the solitary figure of her mother. Alvi was carrying the second of her two children at this point, but she picked up her skirts and ran to her mother. Her signature scarlet petticoat was flapping round her knees as she flew to her mother's arms.

42

"Mama! Oh, Mama! I'm so glad for you both!" Alvi squealed in delight.

Jacob and Theo joined them, and each held the woman they loved as they laughed and cried together in a moment of untarnished joy.

Over a celebratory dinner that night, Jacob and Alvi called for quiet and declared they had an announcement to make.

"Theo, Mama, you are the only parents we have and as such, it's our pleasure to tell you that tomorrow we begin a house over by the river, on the other side of the bunk house. Theo, we shall draw the plans together to make it perfect for both your needs now and in the future." The aura of happiness was almost tangible that night.

Much later that same night, Khadija had a dream. She was back in her father's house in Gabon. Her father spoke to her, "Khadija Ondo, daughter of Grace Koumba and Blaise Ondo, who is the son of Jemuel Ondo and Amelia Moussavon, we send the spirits of all our forefathers to deliver our love and blessings to you. Till we meet again. Be happy daughter!"

Khadija woke with tears on her face but joy in her heart. The spirit of her father had reminded her of who she was. She felt pride, something she'd not felt since she was a little girl. Like a bolt of lightning, it struck this beautiful woman of Africa that she was no longer a slave. She needed no permission but her own to be happy. Khadijah loved Theo and life passed too fast to waste any more of it.

When the parson began the wedding ceremony, he asked, "Who gives Khadija Ondo to be joined with Theodore James Banks?" Khadija could never remember feeling happiness like this before.

Alvi beamed as she responded to the parson, "I do!" She then took her mother's hand, looked into her eyes, and said, "Seems to me, Mama, that it's 'bout time you got some happiness." Khadijah's age was unclear, but everyone assumed she was in her mid-forties,

Six months later Theo and Khadija moved into their beautiful one storey cabin and settled in happy contentment into married life.

In the spring of1890, Theo sadly passed in his sleep. The doctor's report from the city autopsy offices agreed with Doctor Belkin. A piece of shell that had been unable to be removed in the field hospital had moved over time, and that night it had entered his brain and caused his death. Khadija was devastated and in November of 1891 she, too, passed away. This time, Doctor Belkin said cause of death was a broken heart.

When Theo died, a graveyard was created on the hill behind their home, Khadija had planted flowers at his headstone which read:

Here lies Theo J. Banks, of Bannockburn, Scotland.

Survivor of the Battle at Fort Wagner."

Husband to Khadija Ondo

Jacob and Solomon had fenced off a large plot but when Khadija was laid to rest, her headstone was set close to Theo and reads:

Here lies Khadija Ondo Banks,

A free woman of Gabon.

Their legacy is ever growing in many unexpected ways.

Julius, Robert, and Tommy's Story

In 1889, Solomon was married to Marguerite Belkin, daughter of the good doctor who befriended Alvi after her husband, Julius, was killed at Fort Wagner. The young couple lived and worked with Jacob and Alvi on the farm.

In 1890, after Theo and Khadija had passed, Jacob and Alvi gave Solomon and his wife the cabin they'd built for the loving parents they'd had in Theo and Khadija. A second-floor addition was done just in time for the arrival of Alvi's first grandchild. Melissa Cade-Bell was born in the early spring of 1893, followed in '94 by twins: a daughter; Greta, then five minutes later a son; Julius Jacob Cade-Bell, named for Solomon's fathers.

Life in the Cade-Bell household was loud, busy, and happy. The years passed as they do, faster than the blink of an eye, the milestone markers of those years were happy ones.

When Melissa was twenty-one in 1914, she married a horse breeder from the other side of Boston. Greta, too, was affianced and planned to wed her beau, Robert Delany, a shipping agent, the following spring.

Melissa and her husband, Thomas Clancy, stayed at Alvi and Doctor Belkin's for a month a piece upon returning from their honeymoon in New Hampshire.

They were set to leave Alvi on Friday August 10th, for their new home and new life.

The fates however had their own ideas:

The Tuesday prior changed their plans, and those of millions across the globe. Britain had declared, that as of the fourth of August 1914, they were at war with Germany.

Over a dinner, that had been planned as a farewell to the newlyweds, the men talked of the war.

Jacob and Alvi were horrified to hear Julius, Thomas and Robert discussing the situation and considering travelling to England to join up.

Julius had been raised hearing the stories of the Glorious 54th Massachusetts Regiment's charge at Fort Wagner. How his granddaddy had saved a man's life at the cost of his own, and had been posthumously awarded the Medal of Honor, of which Julius was now the keeper. Theo had applied for it after hearing about how William H Carey had been presented with his. The first black man to receive this honour, Julius's was presented posthumously to his widow, Alvi.

His legacy had lit a fire in young Julius; Tommy and Robert were inspired by his service too.

Alvi and her daughters watched and waited and prayed, hoping it was just boyish dreams of derring do.

In 1915, after Greta and Robert's wedding the family were all gathered at dinner again. Once again the conversation had centered on the war and America's determination to have no part in the troubles of Europe. Solomon's son would be dissuaded no longer, and neither would Tommy nor Robert.

The September of that year saw the three set out for Canada. Three women, three wives, and a mother all held their breath, and felt they'd never draw another until their menfolk returned to them whole. Their aunts Khadija Grace and Rebecca Désirée, too, were itching to be allowed to go and help. Both were fully qualified nurses and had no ties that demanded them to stay at home.

Once in Canada, the trio of would-be soldiers encountered amused bewilderment at the recruiting station, but finally they were attested and set off to train with the Calgary Highlanders.

After basic training, they boarded a ship set for England. By December of 1915, they had arrived, had more training on Salisbury plains and were headed for the front.

They were to be the replacements for the 10th Battalion, the "Fighting Tenth" as they were now known. This was a unit made up from an amalgamation of the 103rd Calgary Rifles and the 106th Winnipeg Light Infantry. The 10th first set out in late 1914, so when the lads arrived to join them, this unit was already battle hardened and the new blood would need to prove themselves. At least they thought so.

The veterans of this battalion had survived their first engagement at the second battle of Ypres in the April of 1915. There, six thousand of the ten thousand in the division were the blood price spent in the face of Germany's first use of chlorine gas. It had routed two entire French divisions, but the 10th had held. On April 22, the 10th along with the 16th offered a counter-attack; this offensive at Kitchener's Wood was during the battle of St Julien. Of the 10th, 816 men went "over the top." Only 193 survived. The German advance was halted, earning the 10th battle honours.

In early September through October, the trio of Yankees saw their first action. They took part in a defensive deployment north of Albert, near Boiselle. It was mainly a successful first blood inasmuch as none of them were dead or injured.

On and on, again and again the hell continued during the Somme campaign; losses at Ancre Heights were described as modest. It was a different story in the massive offensive at Thiepval ridge, which claimed 241 men from their unit, and where again they earnt battle honours.

When Julius, Robert and Tommy managed to get to the rear, they met and always the conversation began with the news from home. The latest news was heart-breaking.

Each had received a letter informing them of the death of Aunt Rebecca.

Rebecca and her sister Khadija, known now by her middle name, Grace, were both trained nurses and volunteered as soon as the chance arose. It transpired that Rebecca had been caught in a shelling on the ships bringing wounded back from Le Havre to England. She was not meant to be on the ship but had told her colleague she wanted to get a particular patient's notes to an on-board doctor; his injuries were time critical. We don't know what happened exactly, but a when few German planes arrived, the ship slipped anchor and tried for open water.

Marked as a hospital ship, they believed the planes' target to be Le Havre, and assumed there was safety out in open water. We will never know the mind of the pilot, if it was an accident or deliberate, but the two bombs landed square on the ship.

Not all were killed, but most were either badly burned or injured if they had survived the initial attack. Grace had searched for her sister in the makeshift mortuary, but her body was never found. An orderly at the hospital promised Grace he'd go daily to check if any more bodies were recovered as she had been ordered back with her unit.

Each of the boys who had so eagerly sailed to war had changed in so many ways and on so many levels.

Their fastidiousness, and urge to stay clean and smart was swiftly lost in the blue clay, blood, and filth of the trenches. Shiny buttons, buckles and rifle barrels were dangerous, giving away their position.

Constant attention to the lice didn't last too long either; it was now 'just how it was!' They paid the little blighter's little heed now.

No longer did they salute an officer in the line. It was a perfect identification of targets for snipers on the other side of no-man's land, which in some areas, was only about 100 yards away.

Shaving was now a luxury; fresh water was a rarity in the line. It was delivered, as was the tea, in old petrol cans. It flavoured the food, the tea, everything. It joined the myriad list of foulness in the trenches. Bodies unable to be recovered, bloated and were food for the thousands of rats, latrines were shelled and mixed with the bodies, and the smell of death itself, sweet, sickly, and ever present as was the scent of cordite, smoke and sweat.

Many a night, Julius had sat thinking, *"Did Granddaddy feel this gut tightening fear, had his mouth gone dry as he readied to charge? Did his bowels threaten to shame him as mine have done. Did Granddaddy see his friends faces, distorted with pain, their bodies gruesome and broken, bloody and with pitiful cries escaping on their last breath when he closed his eyes to sleep?"*

If he did, could he tell his children of the horrors, or would he have kept silent, their freedom the gift exchanged for his sanity and silence.

It was summer, 1917. All three men, for that was what they thought of themselves back when they attested in Canada, now knew themselves to have been fanciful glory seeking children then. They knew better now, thanks to the brutal experiences of the last two years.

They had been granted ten days in the rear, to rest, recuperate, delouse, and enjoy a dreamt-of bath. Unless you were first in the queue for the barrel bath, though, it would be filthy from the man in front – or men if you were further down the line.

They delighted at the decision by Woodrow Wilson to finally bring America into the global conflict.

Seasoned fighters now, they recognised the signs: another big push was in the offing. They'd put money on it.

They talked for hours, discussing and considering where it might be that they were heading. Where it might be this time that the earth and mud of France or Belgium would be fertilised by the blood of the brave men of the 10th. They railed at the callousness of the U-boat packs that were indiscriminate in their choice of targets. Though given the sinking of the Lusitania and the Marquette in 1915, they observed that nothing the Germans did now should surprise them. Their determination to win at all and any cost had been apparent very early in this conflict.

It wasn't long before the destination for their next assault was made known, but it was not a destination they had considered. They were heading back to the Somme and the Ypres salient.

Had the 57,000 casualties, over 19,000 of whom were killed, not been enough spent at the Somme?

They joined the long snake of mobilised men, guns, and horses on the line up towards La Bassee, and then up to Merville. They entrained, and hours later detrained in pouring rain in the middle of the night at a place called Zonnebeke; wherever they were headed, it was into hell. Ahead could be seen a sky lit up with shell fire, the air rent with shells exploding, and flames like red and yellow fingers stretched towards the sky. The noise they felt would surely deafen them. And it did.

They were approached by a sergeant from a New Zealand unit, "Are you scruffy mongrels the 10th Canadians?" his accent strong and his attitude relaxed.

Our officer identified us as the "Fighting 10th".

The Kiwi wasn't impressed, "Well head up there, second turn to the left and on for about a mile. That's your spot, mate. They're expecting you. Oh, and they've had it rough and had no leave or rest for months, so get a wriggle on."

Their Captain was not amused but followed his instructions and sure enough after about half an hour and only one wrong turn, they were in the line.

The Kiwis were out of there faster than rats off a ship; two days later Julius would understand their hurry.

The trenches were waterlogged to a depth higher than their puttees and boot tops: more wet and infected feet! The blue clay joined the rainwater and turned a bad situation worse. The bottom of the trench was now a gloopy, viscous consistency and could suck the boots off you, and oft times did.

They were going over the top, their officer informed them in the late afternoon of the following day. This news coming immediately after telling each of the three that they'd been promoted.

"Make sure you've done your paperwork," were his parting words as they left the dugout. He meant last letters home, wills, and so on. It was the military way to recognize that some of them would not be returning.

The three stood shoulder to shoulder at the foot of a ladder, they'd said 'good luck' and all the usual banter; now they were silent. Their intellect told them to turn and walk away, nay, *run* away, and their hearts reached out on prayers for lovers, wives, mothers, but their legs stayed stuck in the foul Flanders mud.

Forty-five minutes later, Julius found himself in a shell hole. It was full of injured or dying men from the 10th. Also sharing this gruesome place were the corpses of those died and buried here in previous engagements.

Unbeknownst to the boys, Julius's aunt Grace was not far from them, she was in a casualty clearing station at Merville. She'd transferred there to be able to nurse her fiancé (though that snippet of information was not common knowledge); Felix Neilson was a Dutchman of Norwegian descent who'd volunteered to drive ambulances and act as a ward orderly after his country had declared itself neutral. He'd been injured when the ambulance he was driving was caught in a shelling in the sidings of a rail junction where he was off loading the injured and dying newly come from the front.

When Nurse Cade-Bell heard this, she immediately requested a transfer from her position on the trains.

She'd arrived at Merville the day the boys had entrained there for Zonnebeke. No-one but nurse Grace Cade-Bell cared for Felix Neilson for the first seventy-two hours after her arrival. At which point two things happened: the doctor declared him through the worst, and Felix opened his eyes.

At first, he believed himself dead, for his angel sat beside his bed, her hand on his, her head dropping as she drifted into a sleep.

When at last she opened her eyes, Felix lay watching her, a smile playing at the edge of his mouth. She was so surprised she let a small scream escape, earning a half-hearted reprimand from a smiling ward sister. His first words to her were, "Will you marry me, please?"

Laughing, crying, she threw her arms around his neck, "You betcha!" was all the reply she managed to formulate in her excitement.

They made plans and sent letters to their families informing them of their engagement and proposed wedding date. The very first Saturday possible after the war.

Julius would not receive this news for almost six months.

The pink shades of dawn crept across the sky above the lines where Julius stood to, beside his two friends and brothers-in -law. The cacophony of whistles, then gunfire and war cries, rent the air and, without conscious thought, their feet took them up and over the parapet. They had barely covered thirty yards when their luck ran out.

First to catch a bullet was Robert. A rifle shot to his shoulder spun him; the second bullet hit him in the back.

Tommy paused, screaming for a medic. The sniper caught him in his crosshairs and the bullet made a perfect hole between Tommy's eyes. He died instantly.

Julius saw the medic arrive beside the two men as he raced forward. The sight of his kinfolk lying dead and or bloodied, drove him to a rage that made him reckless. He was at the German trench in what seemed like a moment. As he leapt down, he saw the startled face of a man who looked terrified and tired. Julius buried his bayonet in the man's chest, screaming as he did so. Soon he was fighting for his life as his enemy's unit turned their attention to this demented madman who was determined to kill them all. Julius faced four men, he did not in his madness consider his back. The soldier shot Julius from behind. The bullet entered just above the kidney area. He went down on his knees; the same soldier used his rifle butt to knock Julius unconscious.

He woke up in a German hospital tent. The doctor spoke excellent English and told Julius that he'd trained in medicine in Edinburgh before the war.

He informed Julius that he would be transferred to Germany and a proper hospital, then to a Prisoner of War camp. It was in a POW camp in woods near Bad Harzburg, where, in November 1918, Julius learned of the cessation of hostilities between Germany and the Allies.

He arrived back in the UK in early 1919. It wasn't until the late summer that he arrived back in Boston.

He was astonished to see Robert with Greta, his parents, Melissa, and his aunt Grace with a blond man who mirrored Robert, with their walking sticks. All waiting for him to disembark from the ship that finally brought him home.

Tommy's body had been privately brought home and reinterred on the Cade-Bell farmstead. The medals they'd pinned on Robert and Julius joined Tommy's and were put with granddaddy Julius's. He vowed on those medals to make sure neither his sons nor their sons, ever searched for glory in conflict again. Never, not ever, not if he could help it.

Julius needed follow-up operations on his physical wounds, but for him, the deepest, most painful wounds were the dreams and nightmares. They came in his sleep: numerous remembered faces, all with hands outstretched, beseeching him for aid. He could give them none then, he could give them none now.

He avoided sleep and took no pleasure in food. The wounds had damaged part of his stomach and it balked at certain food. He never knew which would set it off, so he ate little.

The hospital in Boston seemed uncertain of their next step as Julius was refusing further investigations or surgery.

He was sitting in the hospital gardens when a nurse approached him.

"It's Julius, isn't it? I'm a friend of nurse Cade-Bell, Grace. She asked me to keep an eye on you whilst you are here, I am Ruby, Ruby Anderson, I served with Grace during 1918 in France."

"If I know Grace, she told you to tell me to behave, more like!" They both smiled.

"Well, maybe a little," admitted Ruby.

"The doctors tell me you are giving up."

Ruby knew it was inflammatory language. She wanted to provoke him into defending himself. She had omitted that she had worked at Craiglockhart hospital in Edinburgh prior to joining Grace in France.

Julius surprised her. He ignored the question, she let it pass. *"Time enough,"* she thought.

They began meeting in the gardens daily and as the care he received was improving his general health, they would sometimes take a walk in the gardens.

They were strolling there one balmy summer evening when Julius stopped in his tracks and promptly threw up. There on the ground was the remains of a rabbit or something. It had decomposed and was ripe to the nose.

Julius retched and retched; Ruby held him as he stood bent double voiding his lunch. He then began to tremble. His legs buckled. His eyes glazed. Whatever he saw, it was not the lawns of a Boston hospital.

Ruby pulled him into her arms as he slumped. She cradled him as he yelled orders, screamed warnings and at times gave vent to a fury she'd not have imagined him capable of.

He then began to sob, deep soul wrenching sobs. She sat with him for maybe an hour. He was clearly exhausted and whilst it wasn't a long trek back to the ward, she knew he needed time to bring himself into the present again.

Eventually, Julius lifted his head and, offering up a wry smile, said, "I suppose a date is out of the question now?"

She burst into fits of laughter that then turned to tears and Julius was beginning to feel very awkward.

"I'm so sorry Julius. I didn't mean for you to feel awful. It was just that that was the last thing I expected from your mouth. Then the effect of watching you suffer as you had, well, it just overwhelmed me, I suppose. I'm so sorry."

He smiled, a smile that touched his eyes, "Is that a no, then?"

Ruby looked him in the eye, and held his gaze for a moment or two, then surprised Julius by saying.

"I will walk with you, on one condition: listen, really listen to the doctors tomorrow when they discuss what they think is the way forward. I ask only that you really listen, please."

Julius hadn't expected that, so pondered and rolled it round in his head. "Okay, Nurse Ruby Anderson. It's a deal. And a date."

Julius did listen and, having left his 'poor me' attitude at the door, was encouraged, finally hopeful and in agreement with the surgeons.

Twelve months later, Julius stood at the altar with his best man Robert. Ruby walked like a vision towards him down the isle of the New Cathedral of the Holy Cross on Washington Street in Boston. He thought his heart fit to burst.

His surgery had been successful and his recovery swift.

Rebecca

Julius and Ruby lived in the main house with Solomon and Marguerite, who were now slowing down, worn down by age and hard work.

The couple had only been married a few months when one blowy afternoon there came a knock on the door.

It was Solomon who'd opened the door.

"Hello, I'm looking for the parents of Nurse Cade-Bell. Rebecca Cade-Bell."

"Good afternoon to you, I am Rebecca's brother. Might I ask who you are?" voiced Solomon, wondering at the strange accent.

"Good afternoon, sir. My name is Duncan McRae, formerly a Sergeant in the Royal Scots regiment. I met Rebecca, sorry… Nurse Cade-Bell… in France."

Solomon raised his hand halting further comment by the visitor, "You best come inside, young man."

Marguerite, who had been very close to Rebecca over the years, heard voices and entered the airy parlour. Duncan surveyed the scene, noting photos everywhere of men and women in uniforms of a variety of styles and eras.

Pride of place was held by a folded flag and a selection of medals in a fancy glass case. He began to think that coming here might have been a huge misjudgement.

He watched the face of the woman who'd joined them as Solomon explained the stranger's presence. Grief flooded her face like blood on a white sheet.

Solomon introduced the woman as his wife and Rebecca's sister-in-law, Marguerite.

"Well, son, whilst my wife fixes us some coffee and biscuits, you can tell me why you are here. But first I must tell you that we lost Rebecca at Le Havre. Her body was never recovered."

Solomon watched this young man as he swallowed. The man looked up and held Solomon's gaze as he told his story.

"Sir, Rebecca saved my life, at the cost of her own, I believe. She'd taken me aboard ship. She was meant to take me into Le Havre hospital. I was conscious for some of the events, and I heard her telling a soldier and sailor at the docks that she'd fought to keep me alive from the front line and they 'could bet on her beautiful, black behind, that she sure wasn't going to let me die waiting in line.' Said she was taking me aboard, and they best just stand aside. The sailor escorted us to the front of the queue and then onto the ship. We had just arrived at where a couple of army and navy doctors were working when the first bomb dropped and the world around us exploded. She threw herself over me like a shield and, with me yelling in pain, she forced her life jacket on to me. She acted from instinct, I'm sure. She then used her apron to tie herself to me. That's when the second bomb hit and blew us into the water.

"From there on I was in and out of consciousness. The next that I recall, we were in the water. She was hurt. Her right arm was missing below the elbow. She had to untie the apron to use as a tourniquet. She also had a shard of debris lodged in her left side. She talked to keep me awake, and now I think to comfort herself. She told me all about you all and how beautiful this home you have is. I was drifting in and out. Then I came to, and she wasn't there, hands were hauling me into a boat. That action put me back into oblivion. The next thing I knew, days later, I woke in a nice clean hospital bed on the south coast of England. I was told that whoever had been treating me had probably saved my life. I asked then where Nurse Cade-Bell was.

"I was told that when they found me, I was surrounded by the bodies of soldiers, sailors, and two medics, but there's no record of any nurses being found there.

"Once I was recovered and the war ended, I went in search of her, only to discover she was reported missing, presumed dead. No body was ever recovered. I vowed then to come tell her family of her heroism and sacrifice.

"Now by my reckoning I owe this family, and I was raised to always pay my dues."

Solomon invited Duncan to stay for dinner, explaining, "the other Nurse Cade-Bell, Rebecca's sister, now just Mrs Grace Neilson, her husband Felix, my son Julius, and his wife Ruby and my daughter Greta and her husband Robert, will all be here and will want to meet you."

After dinner, when the table was cleared away, everyone went outside to enjoy the setting sun and now balmy autumn evening.

Duncan was approached by Grace as she'd insisted, he call her.

"Duncan, may I ask you, did you spend much time with my sister?"

"Only on the train up from the front, though that was a journey of, I think, 36-48 hours. I was told by another nurse who was on that train that we left headed through Menen, crossing the border then down by Lille, then on through Arras, Albert, Amiens, Rouen, then north up past Yvetot, then swung south to Le Havre. I was not always conscious, you understand, but every moment of that journey was made tolerable only because of your sister. She could compete with my mother for talkin' the hind legs off a donkey. She kept me alive and as comfortable as was possible. I don't think she slept a wink all the way. She made me talk about my homeland, my family. She told me of yours. About her mother who was married to a hero of the Civil War, and her grandmother who married the man her father died saving. She was so clearly proud of her family and its service and sacrifice to a country that valued her race so little. She was clearly an amazing woman. I am so very sorry."

"Duncan, my sister comes from a female line whose stories you'd hesitate to give credence to, yet they are all true. Rebecca would have hated to have survived and lost you, especially having fought so hard to save you and get you to Le Havre and proper medical attention. So, take her gift to you and use it well. Live your life, live it well, live it to the full, for she certainly did."

"Thank you, Mrs. Neilson."

"Didn't I tell you to call me Grace?" she said smiling softly and resting a hand on his arm, "You are welcome, Duncan."

Solomon had persuaded Duncan to stay for the evening so that all the family might have a chance to get to know the young Scotsman who was here by the grace of God and Rebecca.

The following day, they walked with Duncan up to the family plot and showed him the cemetery.

Later, when Marguerite went to call him for lunch, he was spotted up at the graveyard. Marguerite slowly walked up and softly joined him, not wanting to either startle or disturb his reflections.

He looked up. Fresh wild blooms lay across the cairn of black stone that held Rebecca's name, a grave with no body.

"She was older than I'd have guessed," he said looking up at Marguerite.

"Rebecca was always young at heart; we miss her lively exuberance and zest for life."

"Did she never marry?"

"Nursing was her life. She had offers but I guess none seemed as exciting a prospect to have her give up her vocation."

The next morning, Solomon searched Duncan out and asked him when he planned to return to Scotland and his family.

"I have no-one who waits for me. I've no siblings, and my parents died just before I was demobbed. I got the telegram the day after the armistice. A neighbour's lad home on leave wrote to me to say he saw them just three weeks before, whilst he'd been home on leave. He said they were happy, looking forward to me coming home. Since they were gone, I thought I might see what this land of yours has to offer.

Duncan looked so young to Solomon; he guessed him to be about Robert or Julius's age. He pondered the vagaries of life, that this lad with no-one to mourn his loss had lived and his sister and daughter's husband, with so many to mourn them, were taken.

"Duncan, would you consider working and helping out here? With Tommy and Theo gone, the equine side of our business has been a struggle. The war years were tough, the army wanted anything with four legs. Now, though, whilst Julius and I know a fair bit about the beasts, we are thin spread on a ranch this size. I don't suppose you can ride, son?"

"Yes, sir. I can ride. We had a farm back home, in the lowlands near Edinburgh at the foot o' the Pentland Hills. We had a plough horse and a mare for Mother's trap. I rode the mare all over the hills as a lad. I also helped out on a big fancy estate that our farm bordered. They were oft times short-handed, and I'd get to exercise the temperamental thoroughbred stallions."

"So, what do you say Duncan? Will you give us a hand?"

"I'd be very happy to, sir."

"Solomon will do fine from now on, lad!"

Later that winter, news of the flu epidemic that had been in the papers for months had reached the rural area of Massachusetts. Melissa, Solomon's eldest daughter came out to the farm at her daddy's request as the flu was more deadly in the cities, or so he'd read. Solomon worried for her as a young widow, Tommy having died on the same day that his son Julius and son in law Robert had been injured, and when Julius was taken prisoner.

Melissa had been back in the family home just two days when she took ill. Within the week, Marguerite and Grace had two patients in the house, Solomon and Melissa. Solomon went to bed two days after his daughter but died first. Melissa followed the next day.

Both now lie beside the graves or markers for Khadija, Theo, Alvi's second husband Jacob, who'd passed in 1917, a week after the news arrived of Tommy death, and Robert and Julius's injuries at Passchendaele. The numbers were rising on the hill behind the farmhouse.

In the Heat of the Night

James Cade-Bell was Julius and Ruby's son, the great-grandson of a pioneering black man, Julius Cade, soldier in the American civil war. A man who'd been one of the first ever black soldiers who was a free man and was allowed to fight on the front line in the Union army. His great-great grandmother, Khadija, had been sold on the block in Saint Louis, her line and Julius's was so inspiring that James felt the weight of that debt and was grateful.

As a small boy, listening to family stories of the hows and wherefores that brought them north and to freedom, and the price of the said liberation, paid for in part by his great grand-daddy.

James was barely twenty when his chance to emulate his grandsire, Julius Cade, who was part of the assault at Fort Wagner with the newly formed Black regiment from Massachusetts. And who died in this glorious action saving his step great grand-daddy's life. His granddaddy's name was now one of the revered names in the history of the Black people and the history of America.

James had left his parents' home in Massachusetts, heading for Tuskegee, Macon County, Alabama.

America was in the grip of a great depression, unemployment was rife, nowhere more so than in black communities, where as many as 50% of the black population were without work. Feelings were running high and racial tension was rising as things became so desperate. In the south the lynching of black people in 1932 had declined to just eight; the following year saw it rise to twenty-eight.

James watched as the economy crashed, but initially it did not impact his family's life, due to the family farm and their other business interests.

But soon enough, when he was in his early teens, he began to see the effects on his friends, the employees on the farm, and their neighbours. Farms, businesses, and homes were under threat of foreclosure by the banks. Folk were starving in the poorest areas of the cities, but also in the countryside.

They might live on a farm and were blessed, but his family never stuck their heads in the sand, nor were afraid to show them above the parapets.

His parents organised social aid programmes in their hometown. They shared their crops with their staff and their families, often incurring losses to their own funds. They were always politically aware in his home.

In 1936, James sat with his family and watched the newsreels in the movie theatre. Reels showing Jesse Owens winning Gold after Gold as Hitler shunned the great athletic record-breaking exhibitions of this amazing Black man, which of course proved Hitler's claims of racial superiority to be a nonsense.

James was deeply affected watching this fanatic's attempts to humiliate a great sportsman because he had the temerity to achieve such as a Black man. Along with his family, he was saddened and dismayed when, in 1939, America declined to join their allies in Europe in crushing the dangerous right wing Nazi party. A party of evil thugs, led by Hitler. Hitler who was at that moment invading Poland and the low countries.

He was thrilled though, when in 1938, President Franklin D. Roosevelt announced the expansion of a pilot training programme. Sadly, though, by 1939, it was still not accessible to black men. Then came the breakthrough every black man celebrated. In 1940, in a political move the President authorised the enlistment and training of African American aviators. On January 16th, 1941, it was announced that an all-Black fighter pilot unit would be raised and trained at the Tuskegee Institute in Alabama, an historically black college founded by Booker T. Washington.

James had promised his Mama that he'd do nothing rash, but he desperately wanted to go to Tuskegee to learn more and find out how the unit would be created and what if any qualifications were required. In the first week of April 1941, James was heading south on a journey of more than a thousand miles, headed for Macon County, Alabama, where segregation and racial hatred ran high indeed.

He arrived, found a boarding house, and went off in search of the Institute to learn more.

He had been shocked at the level of hatred and segregation that he'd encountered there in the south.

Later that evening, he sat with some of the other chaps who were thinking to enrol in the pilot programme. They were in a juke joint where some cool tunes were being played by some fine jazz musicians. He was enjoying the relaxed atmosphere but was surprised to see a few white folks in the bar. They were clearly known to many of the patrons, so James paid them no mind.

He got up to get another bottle of coke when a Veronica Lake look-alike eased in at his elbow as he reached the bar. He turned and smiled, moving a little to give her space.

"Hi, I've never been here before, is it always jumping like this?"

She spoke as if she was breathless.

"I've no idea, Miss, I've never been here before either, but I'm loving the sounds."

He smiled as he turned and headed back to his newly found friends and a barrage of light-hearted teasing and winks. A short time later the barman came collecting glasses, as he cleared the detritus from their table he whispered to James,

"You mind yourself with the white folks in here, especially the women. They ain't nothing but trouble and they'll get you hung just by their say so. So go careful boy."

James was shocked but didn't give it much thought. He'd been polite, that's all. However, as they left and he turned heading to his lodgings, this same woman hurried to catch him up.

"May I walk with you? I only live just down the road aways, I'd be obliged of the company." James was torn, he'd been raised to be polite, to protect women and to respect them, but the words of the barman now rang in his ears. Before he could determine his next move, a car full of redneck drunks drew level. They piled out of the Oldsmobile and the loudest yelled at him, "Boy, you going to be sorry for messing with a white woman." The voice oozed hatred.

In seconds he was being thrown over the long bonnet and was absorbing a torrent of blows. It took a moment or two for the shock to pass allowing him the wherewithal to defend himself.

He was strong – and sober – and he fought like a professional, clean, and calm. He caught one of the brutes on the jaw, dislocating it.

The drunk backed away yelling, "I'm gonna' watch you swing afore the sun comes up!"

His two cohorts, though, were still up for the fray. Just then, one of the other lads James had spent the evening with pulled up in a battered old pick-up. The biggest of the two attackers was advancing on James. He was swinging wildly and stumbled when James sidestepped out of the blows range. But the man was still a danger when he got in close. He had rained a few hard swings to James's kidney, and then moved back to take a swing at his face. James moved fast and ducking under the swing brought his own fist up and caught the thug in a perfect blow that sent him sprawling. He went down hard, his head hitting the fire hydrant as he did so.

At the same moment James's friend knocked the last of these animals out with a beautiful upper cut, sending him to the ground unconscious.

Both men looked at James's attacker and both knew him to be dead, his neck was at a very peculiar angle.

The cause of this incident, the woman, had disappeared mid-fracas, but the barman approached as they stood in shock.

"Go, the police will ask me what I know, I'll tell them I believed you were with a group of boys from Montgomery way, up here looking for work. You best go back where you came from by dawn or get enrolled in the Tuskegee pilot programme come morning."

In the heat of the fight, in the heat of the night, James lost his choices.

He'd need to write his Mama and explain why he had signed up to the programme without discussion. But if the whispers were proved right and Roosevelt wanted to join the war, he may yet find redemption for the life he'd taken. Whatever the future held, he was determined to serve and to be a man his family would be proud of.

He fought with the "Redtails" in Malta, earning himself the Purple Heart, presented to Julius and Ruby posthumously. They lie in the box beside others, those of Tommy, Julius, Robert, Rebecca, Grace, Duncan and Julius senior's medal and flag

A cairn with his name on it, sits among the other amazing men and women descended from Grace Koumba and Blaise Ondo, whose bones lie in Gabon.

At the Bus Stop

Sitting at the bus stop, I watched absentmindedly as the bent figure of the lanky pensioner made his way up the incline towards the stop or maybe the shop opposite.

Seeing us in the bus shelter, he visibly straightened, like a soldier having spotted an officer. He lifted his head and smiled shyly at the two of us who were sitting on the horrid sloping plank that passes for seating in a modern bus shelter.

"Good morning, ladies," he said in a soft but confident voice, "how are we this morning?"

In the way that occurs in queues the length and breadth of Britain, we were soon like old friends, especially after the bus due on the half hour failed to arrive at all.

I admit I had drifted off somewhat as I internally debated between macaroni cheese or lasagne for dinner. I looked up in hopeful anticipation, only to be disappointed as the bus rounded the corner.

"Well, this is me," said the lady who worked in the local shop. "Bye," both this lovely gent and I said in unison.

"It's a great place for reflection, the bus stop, don't you think?" Having so obviously been caught out in my drift off,

I had to confess agreement. He laughed, and for just a split second I caught a glimpse of the handsome vigorous young man he'd once been.

"I enjoy trying to guess my fellow travellers, occupations and nationalities. It passes the time and keeps the grey matter in action," he said, laughing.

"Do you ask them? I was wondering if some folk might find the questions impertinent, and the guesses possibly insulting."

"Oh, no! In general, people are as interested in their fellow passengers as I am, and happily join in the game. Would you like to go first or second?" he asked with a lopsided grin.

I considered a moment, then replied, "First, please," entering into the spirit.

"Okay, so what do you think is my nationality?" said the old man.

"Oh, you seem like the quintessential English gentleman, good breeding and well educated. Yes, definitely English," I said with a modicum of confidence.

He smiled, "And now what did I do for a living?" Looking at him, I noted he wore the collar and tie and herringbone sports jacket that was popular in education and commerce. His shoes shone from this morning's careful polishing. He was proud and polite. Not likely that he was a manual worker, he'd had a profession, of that I was convinced. "May I ask a question?"

"No… Observation only," he replied grinning.

"Right, then. I'm going with my gut. I think either a teacher or banker."

He laughed aloud, "Oh, gosh! That elevated me somewhat. So sorry, but you are quite wrong. I'll tell you now, then it's my turn.

"I'm Welsh, but moved to Sussex when I was but a lad. I was a thirty-year Navy man. As for the gentry, nope, a vicar's son. My one claim to any sort of connection to aristocracy was in WW2.

"I was volunteered to go on a secret mission to Norway. We were to smuggle the King and the Prince out and get them to England, out of the clutches of the Gestapo. It was so secret that the records of the mission were only opened to the public last week.

"June 7th. 1940. Seventy-four years ago. I've only just managed to live long enough to enjoy telling the story of what I did in the war and my secret service mission.

"King Hakon and Prince Olav were incredibly grateful and awarded me a medal. They had left Norway very reluctantly; the King said they felt like cowards.

"Ah, here's my bus, cheerio my dear, it's been lovely."

I had been chatting to a genuine hero who was the best part of a hundred years old. I could hear my grandmother's voice saying, "Never judge a book by its cover." Well, it just goes to show, eh?

The Miracle of World War I

It wasn't that I survived World War I that was the miracle. No, it was more *'how'* that was the true miracle.

I had joined up in late 1916, lying about my age. I had just celebrated my fifteenth birthday when I arrived in France. The cruel losses suffered by the British Expeditionary Forces at Mons, Verdun, Ypres, the Somme, and Arras caused the old soldiers at the recruiting offices to turn a blind eye, especially when a well built or muscular farm boy or miner presented themselves. Each would declare themselves eighteen or nineteen to ensure they got to serve overseas. If a lad looked like it was possible that he was old enough, they were attested as soon as the medic gave them a pass.

I was a miner, my father was a miner, and both grandfathers were also miners. It's a job that burns the fat off but builds muscle. I had wiped my mucky hands over my chin and cheeks to help hint at a five o'clock shadow. It didn't fool the Sergeant, but he just winked and stamped my papers. I was in, and off on the adventure of a lifetime.

I may have been a boy that day, but six months later I was a boy no more. With the battles fought and the losses we suffered; I was seen as an old hand. A veteran serving soldier of the Royal Scots.

I pondered once, that the battle honours of this regiment would call for either reduced font sizes on the ceremonial drums and colours, or else they'd need to make those drums significantly bigger. The regiment was in action in most of the biggest battles of the war.

Anyone who was at the third Battle of Ypres will tell you, there are no words to truly describe that hell. The mud, the rain, the cold. The rats, brutality, futility.

The sacrifices, the heroism on those killing fields cannot be imagined. Every one of those words come nowhere close to an idea of the hell that was Passchendaele.

Surprisingly, a couple of my pals and myself made it through and continued to fight at Vimy Ridge, the Marne, and Albert, then pushing the enemy back to the Hindenburg Line, reaching the Selle Canal in October of 1918. It was near the Selle Canal that my miracle occurred, somewhere in the Montay Forest.

We had been chasing units of Jerries from northwest of the Hindenburg Line. They were in retreat and we were set to chase them all the way to Berlin.

It was another cold and wet day, and we were bone tired and heart weary. We had been taking fire from rear-guard snipers and pockets of supporting troops. Some of our chaps had taken charge of surrendering prisoners. They'd emerged from the edge of the wood into the low-lying mist, furiously waving a white flag. One of them, a corporal, an older man, maybe in his forties, was ever watchful of our treatment of these skinny, starving boys in his charge.

He'd made sure they all understood our instructions, to slowly approach leaving their rifles on the ground, as they had, at first, began running towards us yelling *"kameraden."*

Their childish grins almost caused tears from some of us. We fed the poor blighters; some were lads younger looking than I knew myself to be. Children, and should never have been sent to this carnage.

After a few days, we had reached an accord and had exchanged tobacco and chocolate for schnapps and souvenirs. We were now just soldiers, just men doing the best they could under such awful conditions. They never abused our trust, and we were never cruel or unkind to them.

On the third day, we were resting in a half-demolished barn when we came under attack. Some very persistent Germans were determined to make as many of us pay as they could before their inevitable humiliation, surrender and defeat.

As the day wore into evening, things had gone quiet, but we weren't convinced that they had moved on. We put men in the upper story and one right on the roof ridge. We had eyes on three sides, but some small outbuildings backed onto the wood, and they were on the long side of the barn, and it had no view to the back, Only the lookout on roof ridge had a hope of spotting movement there.

They hadn't gone: they'd circled round behind us.

About four a.m., we were suddenly brought from sleep by a shot, followed by the crash of our roof lookout crashing to the floor dead. The patience and eyesight of the sniper had cost us dearly. Jimmy O'Mara was a good chum of mine, and I did not take it well. He was a quiet chap, but with a big heart and Christian values.

It was he who had advocated the standards we used to deal with the prisoners. He was persuasive and needed to be, too. Some of the unit were all for shooting the lot of them.

The Germans had warmed to him too. They noted how he shared all he had. Not once had he asked any military questions, only ever inquiring about their family, children, wives, and the like.

The older German, whose name we learned was Herbert Paul, from Berlin, helped get Jimmy's body into the shelter of the barn and shed tears as we carried the body over and laid him behind the last of the straw bales.

Just then, all hell broke loose as the Jerries charged from behind the outbuildings. For the most part, they were stopped dead in their tracks with our Vickers machinegun. However, unbeknown to us, one of them had used the charge to sneak up into the shadows beside the back wall in our blind spot. We would learn of his presence later.

Dawn came and the morning passed in quiet reflection and anxiety. About mid-morning a spotter plane passed overhead. It was a sight to see, showing the fresh livery of the newly formed RAF on the wings and tail. About an hour after he'd passed, another one was spotted. This time, he approached from ahead of us and the Germans. We were prepared, hopeful of another pass over, and sent up a flare.

The spotter acknowledged it with a roll of his wings. The sharp report of the flare gun caused the Jerries to reply giving the spotter more information as they'd given their position away with their returned fire.

Two hours later we heard the distinct sound of our artillery, and it was getting closer by the minute closing in behind the enemy troops.

The rear-guard German unit was now caught between us and the approaching troops. We had tried sending out a pigeon asking for assistance but had thought it had been unsuccessful as quite some time had passed with no reply.

Later, finally it came. The fawn pigeon alighting on the wooden frame of a horse stall.

The enemy troops chose the better of their options, discounting the option to surrender. They came at us as dusk began to fall, hoping for a breakthrough and escape.

Just before they launched themselves, we'd learned in the message the bird carried: that at eleven a.m. next morning, we had been ordered to cease firing as the war was at an end.

Alfred Von Oberdorff would sign the surrender of Germany, in a forest in the Compiegne region. After four years three months and fourteen days, it was finally over.

I asked Herbert to call out the news to the attacking men, it took a few attempts, but finally as they got closer, they understood. One replied he was radioing his HQ to check. A few minutes later he leapt in the air, threw his rifle down and yelled back. "Englander, we are *Kameraden, Ja?*"

Herbert replied for me in German, saying, "yes, we would settle down for the night and rest till 11 a.m. and we would not fire upon them unless they fired first."

It was agreed the krauts could build a fire and get water from the farm's well. They stacked their rifles like a tipi and sat around a fire and relaxed for the first time in years.

We were all relaxed and excitedly talking of what delights at home we were looking forward to first. A pint, a roast dinner, a cup of tea that didn't taste of petrol -- when all of a sudden, a guttural oath was screamed from a German somewhere.

Herbert was first to see the one man no-one had realised was hiding in our blind spot. Now here he was screaming and firing his pistol. Then Herbert yelled, "runter, get down, runter." He'd seen the stick grenade that fell at my feet. Feet that were frozen to the spot, my brain failing to catch up with my ears and eyes.

Everything then moved in slow motion as my miracle unfolded. My eyes met Herbert's, he smiled, then threw himself onto the grenade. He saved my life and that of the youngest German lad in his care.

The rogue German was felled by bullets from his own countrymen. In their eyes, they were no longer 'comrades in arms,' but men, exhausted human beings, and he now was a murderer. No report of this incident was made by either side.

So, my miracle of survival on the Western Front was thanks to the sacrifice of a heroic German soldier.

"Greater Love hath no man…"

Not Such a Good Idea

Mateo sat in the back seat of the long black limousine. He was reflecting on his ten years' service as a police officer and more lately as an undercover detective with Bogota's police department, in particular his latest mission. He thought maybe it had not been his best idea.

In fact, it was looking convincingly as not a good idea at all.

Two men shared this beautiful armour-plated sedan limo; it was one from the fleet owned by one of Colombia's biggest drug cartels.

He had volunteered to try and infiltrate the gang after their previous undercover agent had stopped communicating over four months ago. The cartels usual act on discovering a traitor in their midst was to display the body somewhere public in his community, to discourage opposition.

It was highly effective; few were willing to put their families in harm's way to end the reign of terror the cartels had in their country.

Cristiano had just dropped off the radar until Mateo had spotted him in the group of heavies used as a personal security for "the Boss". Cristiano had recognised Mateo, too, and imperceptibly shook his head.

Giving a message to Mateo to keep his recognition to himself, it also gave Mateo hope. But could he be mistaken: had the cop turned dirty?

He had kept quiet and again had considered the wisdom of volunteering for this job. The trouble was, Mateo still hated these drug pushing lowlifes. They were the same ones who had drawn his little sister into their web.

She had changed from a beautiful if rebellious teen to a drug-addled whore, controlled by one of the cartel's thugs. She had thought herself in love, oblivious to the warning signs. The flash car, expensive clothes, an apartment in an exclusive part of the city – yet no obvious means of employment.

Within six months, he had her hooked-on heroin and instigated the division between her and her family. No-one in the family set eyes on her again for almost six months. Mateo had been called into the captain's office and listened as his boss gently told him that his sister was in the holding cells downstairs. She had been brought in when they'd raided a well-known cartel owned cat house and drug outlet in the seediest part of the capital.

Mateo visited her in the cells. She looked awful. Skinny, bruised, with track lines in her arms, and very scared. She had also begun to crave her next fix, along with most of the group from the same bust.

Mateo had her taken to an interview room. A doctor was waiting there with Mateo. He examined her and administered a small dose of Methadone. It was enough to stop the shakes, the scratching, nausea, and sweats.

Mateo tried to convince her to turn state's evidence and put these animals away so that he could get her well and home again where she belonged. Valentina refused. Despite two hours with her brother, a shower, and some decent food, she resisted Mateo's pleas. She said she was ruined and that no decent man would want a woman used in a cartel brothel. Even now, there was a part of her loyal to the despot lover.

Finally, Mateo had to return Valentina to the cells. On the way down, he tried one more time to convince her. As the custody officer opened the cell door, she hugged her brother and whispered so only Mateo and maybe the guard could hear,

"I will think about it, *mi hermano*," (my brother).

It was the last words from her mouth he would ever hear.

Two hours later, he took a call at home. Valentina had apparently hung herself with torn-up lengths from her blanket tied to the bars on the window. The others in the holding cell swore they heard and saw nothing, all claiming to have been asleep.

Mateo had asked the duty officer to keep an eye on her, telling him that should his sister ask for him, he was to be called immediately.

The guard had answered with a surly, "If I get time, I will." Mateo wanted to punch him, but instead replied. "Thanks, I'd appreciate it."

Mateo, upon leaving Valentina, had asked a trusted colleague to look into the custody officer. Dirty cops were ten a penny in their force and dirty officers found it very lucrative to be on the payroll of the cartel.

They buried his sister. By the time he left the graveyard he already knew the custody officer was in the pay of Carlos Vargas, one of Columbia's brutal drug lords. The local "Boss".

From his parents' house after the family had fed and thanked the mourners for attending the funeral, Mateo headed to his station. Finding his superior, he requested a transfer to Narcotics. He was determined to help stop another family suffering the fate of his parents. No parent should bury their child.

Six years on, his hunger to bring them down and the work of a dirty cop had brought him here, handcuffed and a prisoner of one of Vargas's henchmen.

The man to whom he was cuffed spoke to Cristiano, the driver, "Take us out of the city, up into the hills and off the beaten track."

"Why all the way up there? Don't we usually display them in their community to keep the bastards scared and cowed?"

"We go where the Boss tells us to go. He wants the piece of crap to disappear. He wants time to get all his family before his body is found, so just drive, and shut the hell up."

"Okay, Ruiz, just curious," replied the man known to Mateo as Cristiano.

They drove for an hour, then the car pulled off the main highway and headed into the hills and the wooded hillside. Once well into the isolated, secluded uplands, Ruiz told the driver to park. Mateo was yanked across the back seat, then dragged out of the car. Ruiz turned to Mateo and removed the cuff on his own wrist and snapped it onto Mateo's right wrist. He told Cristiano to wait by the car.

"Walk," he snarled, pushing his gun barrel into Mateo's back. They were about two hundred yards into the wood when a sound like a *thrumph* caused Mateo to whirl around. He was just in time to see Ruiz fall face-down, a hole in the back of his head. Cristiano stood some way behind them, legs spread, and knees slightly bent, arms outstretched, both hands holding what appeared to be a pistol with a long silencer barrel attached.

"Listen Mateo," began Cristiano, "we need to be quick. You need to put one in my leg with Ruiz's gun and take the tyres on the car out too. Toss our phones, then knock me out and run. I noticed a garage about a mile back down on the highway. Call your family from there and get them out before Vargas has time to move. I am staying. I'm betting this might help me up the slippery pole into Vargas's trusted team. Tell the captain I'll get word to him one way or another within the week. When I come to – "

Mateo interrupted him, "Come to? I'm not shooting a fellow officer or knocking you unconscious."

"Yes, you are, my life will depend on this being a plausible scenario. When I hobble to the garage and call Vargas, I will have given you a chance to save your family. Now get on with it."

"You are mad. Come back with me," said Mateo.

"NO! I want Vargas. Now shoot!" Cristiano grimaced in anticipation of the pain that was to follow.

Mateo put the bullet into the leg of his fellow officer and then hit him with the gun butt. Cristiano fell unconscious. Mateo paused long enough to take out the tyres, then ran.

He arrived at the garage in just under forty minutes Within two hours he was at the airport. His parents were flying to stay with his older sister in Chicago, USA.

"Mateo, come with us," his mother pleaded with her youngest living child.

"No, Mama. I need to finish this."

"I don't think it's a good idea, son," said his father, but accepted Mateo was his own man. They embraced, each wondering, was this the last time they would see each other.

Four days later, Cristiano, as promised, got a message to his captain.

His burning body was displayed crucified one morning on the grass outside the police station. Another dirty cop had sold out to the cartel.

Lady in Red

The room was breathtaking. The coving, cornices, frieze, and mouldings had been painted and gilded by superb craftsmen. Such magnificence was usually only found in these delicate pastel shades in the oldest French castle or chateaux of the Renaissance period. The "Lady in Red" was at perfect ease in such rich and aristocratic fabulousness.

A rich Arab prince whose annual oil revenue outshone most countries' annual expenditure and debt combined had bought the small castle in the Loire Valley to house his European mistress. Few in the world knew his true political affiliations. To the public he presented himself as a forward-thinking liberal Muslim, one who publicly denounced all extremism and declared often that violent attacks by ISIS and the mujahidin jihadists were reprehensible.

In truth he was a supporter and funded almost every mujahidin group in the Arab world. Despite his secret political affiliations, he openly enjoyed the freedoms of the Western world. He had developed a liking for good French wine and long-casked Scottish malt whiskey. His weaknesses also included a British aristocrat mistress, a distant cousin of Her Majesty the Queen.

It had taken Lady Gordon over three years to be seduced by the playboy prince. That was exactly as MI6. had planned.

The prince had doggedly pursued Lady Charlotte Gordon all over London's social scene. This had not escaped the notice of MI5. They in turn flagged this to the chief of the Secret Intelligence Service. (SIS as MI6 was also known).

Charlotte was a very bored, rich socialite who hungered for something more, but had no name for the "more," except maybe purpose.

Charlie, as she liked to be called, leapt at the opportunity that the men from MI6 offered. She would be doing something really important. She was protecting her country and she could bring the arrogant, if rich and attractive, terrorist to justice.

Prince Hassan bin Abdi had one other weak point, one that he was well aware of.

His father was dedicated to pulling their small nation out of the dark ages and was a very moderate Muslim. He advocated the kind of nation that the Turkish government in the 1980's allowed. A country where women could dress as they wished, in the burqa or western fashion wear. They could drive themselves about and go to college and work. Should his father learn of his affiliations and betrayal, he would definitely have forfeited his right to succession – and probably his life too.

Charlie discovered that an evening with a goodly supply of alcohol and her feminine charms could frequently cause the Prince's tongue to loosen. She had also gained access to his phone, computer, and bank accounts. It had taken months of incredibly careful watchfulness. Shockingly, for a man in such a precarious position, with stakes so high, he was oft times indecently careless.

Now, having been his lover for two years, she had provided MI6 with information that her prince was planning to entertain the heads of four major mujahidin groups. A *soirée* was arranged, with minor celebrities and actors invited along with many French socialites of the day.

To all there, it appeared to be an elaborate party to celebrate the birthday of a close friend to the prince.

Charlie had been given her instructions for the sting.

One of the four special guests, Asaf, was well known as a boorish, salacious, sexist, who was often accused of over familiar and lewd behaviour. He would sexually manhandle women he had barely met and who had given no "come on" to the want-to-be playboy.

Thirty minutes after the arrival of these men, she saw Hassan discreetly nod to one of his aides, a familiar sign to

Charlie. He was being told to invite the men to meet the prince in his private office. She made her move.

Slowly she sauntered past the "handy" terrorist. He did not disappoint. His hand caressed her shoulder and quickly swept down her back, groping her bottom shamelessly.

"*Game on*," thought Lady Gordon.

She stopped dead in her tracks, whirled around and sharply slapped Asaf hard across his leering, smug face. The gauntlet had been thrown down.

He made to strike her, but a dashing minor movie star stepped up, pushing Charlie behind him. The blow meant for her instead knocked the actor to the floor. Chaos erupted.

Feigning distress, Charlie ran to the powder room. There she sent the prearranged text code to her handler, then called the local police station.

They had worked with MI6 and were expecting the call. They arrived swiftly, but not so swiftly as to attract suspicion. Hassan was mortified when he learnt she had called the police. She had replied with an innocent countenance, "What else would I do? He struck a British subject and assaulted a titled member of the aristocracy."

Everyone was taken to the police station.

Charlie had previously passed the information they would need to access Hassan's computer, phone, and bank accounts.

MI6 collected the evidence they needed and joined the French police at the station. They had processed many of the guests and sent them home by the time the MI6 agents arrived.

They then jointly interviewed the actor, the slimeball and any who witnessed the incident. Statements were taken.

The End Game began:

A written apology was demanded from the lewd killer by Charlie's rescuer. A handsome cheque accompanied the grudgingly provided missive.

The actor left happy and satisfied. Before he received the cheque, he had to agree to a gagging contract before it would be handed over.

He could not sell his heroic story to the papers nor divulge any details of the incident. It was all under the umbrella of the Official Secrets Act.

The cheque was big enough to gain his scrawl on the page.

Hassan was sitting with an MI6 officer who was spreading photographs and sheets of paper on the table in front of him. The colour drained from his face. It took only a further thirty minutes to turn this aide to the terrorists into a valuable informant.

The following day the newspaper headline reported a fatal crash on the M25 slip road to the airport. A car had lost control and careered over the guard rail, landing on the underpass road.

A lorry driver: (an MI5 agent) parked on the temporarily closed underpass when the car crashed down in front of him, was reported to have sustained only minor injuries when the car had exploded. It said the men were Arabic and had been identified as mujahidin leaders.

No-one from across the world wanted to claim the bodies, so they were vengefully cremated two weeks later.

Lady Gordon would return to the MI6 offices in a month or so for new orders. For the next few weeks, she was going to the family estate in the Highlands.

She had received a lovely letter from her friend and cousin inviting her for a visit to Her country estate nearby.

The buzz on the intercepted communications at MI6, was the jihadists wanted information on the Lady in Red.

Charlie's wish for some excitement could bring more than she bargained for.

The In-Between

The print hung opposite the end of the bed. A glorious highland scene, it was one of the first things she saw as she woke and one of the last before she slept each night. The photo on the nightstand took precedence.

She was called from the oblivion of a deep sleep. Someone, no, not just someone, for she'd know that voice anywhere. And only he called her 'Blue.'

He stood beside the bed. "Come on, sleepy head," he said as he leant over her and covered her mouth with his own. As ever, her heart missed more than one beat. "Get up! Come on, we're going on a trip."

He lifted her out of the bed; she laughed and struggled to be put down. He finally deposited her at the shower door.

"Are you going to wash me, too?" she asked kissing his ear and neck.

"Not this time, wench. Get in there and get a shift on. Breakfast will be ready in ten minutes, and we leave in thirty, so hustle that delightful bustle."

He slapped her playfully across the bottom as she stepped into the hot spray of the shower. He dived out the door, the damp sponge she'd thrown missing him and landing on the floor.

She could hear his laughter as he headed to the kitchen.

She loved the bones of the man. He had ignited her life, opened her darkest dungeons, filled her heart with love and put a song in her soul. She loved him, and he loved her right back.

Heaven lay in his safe embrace.

From their renovated cottage on the edge of a small highland village, it was but a forty-minute drive to one of their favourite spots.

His pipes were in his easy carry pipe carrier, a duffle bag for the *Piob Mhor* (the great highland pipes) and lay alongside a picnic basket in the boot of his dark green Frontera. He had loved the car since first he laid eyes on her. He called her 'Bertha.' He said he felt like the lord of the manor sat high in the front seat.

*   *   *   *   *

He had a great imagination. He told me a story once as we drove round the scenic roads. It was about the telegraph poles and how they uprooted themselves from the verges along the remote highland roads. Then they went dancing in the woods and forests that they so missed, visiting with kith and kin that were still growing there. They would head back to their places just before dawn, their tree souls just needing to re-connect with their own kind.

In no time at all, we were parking up. He grabbed his pipes, passed the basket to me, and took the cooler bag. He looked at me and smiled.

I knew the devilment in that smile. He then turned and headed off up the wide path that would lead up the west side of the loch, and up to the high bank below the hill. That's where we would picnic, in a small dense copse. It was high off the beaten track; he had discovered it on our first ever trip there. He had been trying for an uninterrupted shot of the loch and the island where a crenelated grand house stood. A drawbridge stood to ensure that only invited guests would get a boot on the island. It was our dream home, the dream where you win huge on the lottery.

We loved this place. It was God's country, except at dusk when the Devil releases his wee beasties, the ones called midges.

Anyway, he'd found a small glade on the loch side of the hill. Unseen from the path, and with enough difficulty of access to reasonably ensure privacy.

Over the years since our first visit, our passionate lovemaking on our open and spread kilts had been replaced by a total communion. To just lie in each other's arms in peaceful silence was like glimpsing paradise.

"Come on woman, what's slowing you up? Getting on, are we? Getting old and decrepit?" He was laughing as he stood with his hand outstretched.

"Cheeky sod, it's okay for you. My old bones don't work like they used to." She couldn't keep a convincing scowl on her face.

"That's why you got yourself a toy boy, to haul your rickety ass up hills and do the heavy lifting." He was forever playfully claiming toy boy status for the four-year age difference between us.

"Oh, shut up and help me, you great galoot." He pulled, and in a nano second, I was up, then falling forward into his arms. He was falling backwards taking me with him. We landed on the soft leaf pillowed floor of the copse.

We spent the hours through to noon, and on until early afternoon, in each other's arms, or eating the tasty morsels he'd prepared and packed. The cool box held alcohol free beers and we drank from the bottles. He played for a while as I lay eyes closed listening to the familiar notes of "She Walks Through the Fayre," "The Sands of Kuwait," "Heroes of Kohima," and finally, "Back to my Highland Home," a tune he'd written for me. It was a most perfect day.

As we approached the time in the late afternoon when the midges come calling, we dressed and packed up the detritus of our lunch.

We stood high above the stunning image of the loch, light playing on the surface, reflecting bits of the building, the mountains, and the sky. Magnificent in its glory. He pulled me into his arms, and for what felt like an age he just looked deep into my eyes.

It was the most intimate sensation, it was the most naked I'd ever been, the most seen I'd ever known, and the most loved I'd ever felt.

"I love you, Miss Mercy." He kissed me gently on the lips, and my heart was fit to burst.

We began to head back; we were at the tricky bit where he had hauled me up. As I put my foot down, first my ankle, then my knee gave way. I fell, tumbling down the steep but short distance to the path. I saw it, and tried to avoid it, but the rock loomed. I heard him call my name before the darkness embraced me.

*　*　*　*　*

I was aware of sounds and sensations as my brain clawed its way back to consciousness. The duvet felt warm but heavy, I reached for him. Then the tsunami of pain swamped my soul. Another day waking without him. It's over twenty years now, and it is no less painful, no less isolating. I miss him.

I throw the duvet back and put my feet on the floor and head to the stairs and the kitchen. Tears threaten to escape.

My foot touched the first step but the ankle and then the knee collapsed. I knew this was going to hurt bad!

How wrong I was. I hit the floor, but before my brain had time to catch up with the blow to my head, all was black, and I felt nothing.

"There you are… Are you ok?" he asked as he pulled me into his arms.

"I have been waiting here in the in-between for so long." He continued, "I told Him I would wait here for you before going further."

I looked into the face of my soulmate, "Am I going to wake up in my bed again? I don't think I can bear it anymore."

He smiled, "No, darling. This time, I'm not letting you go. You are mine forever now." He turned, heading us toward the light. "We travel this last journey together."

I sighed as he pulled me ever closer in his arms.

Heaven. I was home at last!

Casualties and Canaries of World War I

Tilly had just left the Millennium Mill factory, now used for the manufacture of munitions. Her shift ending at 6-30 p.m., she filed onto the street with hundreds of other women, all affectionately known as 'Canaries' or 'Canary Girls.' All the women were yellow-skinned, the result of handling the trinitrotoluene, or TNT. As she and her day shift companions filed out, similar numbers were filling in to begin the night shift.

Living only four streets away, Tilly had just taken her coat off and kissed her mother's cheek, about to put the kettle to boil, when the world she knew rocked on its axis and was altered forever. Windows exploded, doors blew in on the wings of hot dust, leaving debris and the detritus that had been her home just moments before. This was swiftly followed by a crunching, rumbling sound as the front of the two up two down terrace collapsed.

As the dust blew around them, her mother began to scramble for the stairs, "Nora and Tommy are up there!" she screamed in terror. But as they reached the place where the stairs used to be and looked up, there was no, 'up there.'

As their ears recovered from the blast, other noises began to filter through. They could hear screams, klaxons, men's voices calling out familiar names. That's when Tilly thought she smelt gas. "Come on, Mam! If the gas main has fractured, there'll be more explosions. Come on!" she cried, pulling her mother's arm.

Finally, after a few minutes, her mother lost all fight. Shock, thought Tilly, pulling her out of the remnants that was once their home.

The warden came running up the street just as they cleared the pile of rubble and hit the opposite side of the road's pavement. He obviously thought we'd been bombed as he yelled, "Come on! To the shelter, ladies!"

Tilly's mother, momentarily stunned by the images before her, now began to scream and turned to try to climb the pile of bricks and masonry.

Mr. Wilkins, the warden, grabbed her arms, "Elsie, listen to me now; if they are under there, they are past our aid, and only God can comfort them. If by some miracle, they are not, then they will turn up at either the shelter or the hospital. Either way, you and Tilly need to be fit to deal with whichever it is, so come on."

It took about twenty minutes or so to reach the shelter; along the way, they had stopped, helping to pull others from the debris of their homes.

As they entered the shelter, two voices yelled in chorus, "Mam!" It was Tommy and Nora. It turned out the wee monkeys had been in James's room, Tilly's older brother killed at the Somme the previous year. Their mother had refused to accept he was dead as no body had been found, and had kept his room, untouched, in readiness for his return. The wee ones had been under his bed looking in what James used to call his 'secrets box.' They wondered at the medals he'd been awarded and imagined his derring-do which won the medals that lay there. Tommy held his brother's tin now, clasped tightly to his chest.

Their mother grabbed them and crushed them to her ample bosom and, looking over their heads through tear filled eyes, said to Tilly, "James saved them. I know they'll always remember him now. How he saved their lives the night the explosion at the munitions factory destroyed the street."

And the Lights Went Out!

Davey was away working on the rigs. The money was better than good, and he loved and excelled in his chosen work. It was exciting and dangerous, but a commercial deep-water diver was all Davey ever wanted to be.

Morag hated the weeks apart; it was lonely being in their dream house alone out on the outskirts of the town. They'd moved to the Bridge of Don shortly after they had been married. The house was back off the Scotstown Road, almost hidden behind a row of oak, rowan, and elder trees. If you didn't notice the missing twelve feet of dry-stone wall as you flew past, you'd never know we were there.

It was a two-story granite house, typical of the manse designs that were dotted all over Scotland. A large double wood door with big lead knocker and globe handles was impressive, as were the long sash windows either side of the door, like sentries at their posts. The hint of blue in the slate roof really was the figurative icing on the cake, and we had loved it at first sight.

They'd renovated every room, lovingly restoring each space to its former glory, even replacing ceiling roses and plaster friezes. The lounge and dining rooms were now elegant yet cosy. The kitchen had a huge scarlet Aga at one end of the long refectory table and a huge old horsehair sofa ran parallel at the other end between the windows, which now opened to the lovely lawned back garden.

Morag had searched the internet for two vintage pulleys. One was in the utility room; the other hung above the Aga and held pots and pans hung on butcher's hooks. Her friends had ooh'd and ah'd in envy when they'd held their housewarming party.

Tonight was one of those awful nights when she hated Davey's absence the most. A night where radiators gurgled, and beams creaked as the thermostat changed and central heating kicked in. The weather had finally changed today; she'd woken to the first frost of the year. She tried to put all unusual noises down to this weather change. However much she tried, though, the sinister sounds filling the house also filled her ears and her heart rate increased with anxiety. She hated being alone on dark windy nights: her imagination always ran amok and sent her pulses racing.

She went upstairs doing the rounds from room to room, closing windows and drawing drapes. The world outside had looked so beautiful mere hours ago. Gold and ochre leaves flew about like a ballet, courtesy of mother nature, and the top of the distant Tyrebagger Hill wore its first white cap of virgin snow. The Kirkhill Forest was a favourite place for them and the view from "The Tappie," an old stone viewing tower was breath taking. Yet this evening as dusk fell, the view looked threatening and sullen from the window.

Morag chastised herself for a feartie cat, and, entering her kitchen, she opened her YouTube page, pulling up her library. Tonight it was a blues, jazz, Motown mix and she opened the freezer to the first strains of Eta James's, "I'd Rather Go Blind."

She began to sway and sing to herself. The music moved Morag to a warm place, calling up the memories of dancing and loving to these sounds with Davey. He was forever pulling her into his arms to dance to these tracks. They were wonderful warm, loving evenings, when her world held brighter colours, more vivid tastes, more evocative music, and intense and heightened emotions. He improved her world just by being in it.

Just as her heart began to calm, there was a clatter from the garden. Whilst her instinct was to panic, her logic said it was like as not their cat. She opened the back door and called for "Major Tom," she heard his miaow, and just as she turned towards the sound, in that split second she saw two figures. She tried to comprehend and to move and managed neither. Her heart was racing, she thought she might have peed herself, when she saw the hand raised, lit by the light of the moon, and the lights went out.

The Explosion that Rocked the Street

Miss Amy was well-known locally. At 85, she still insisted upon continuing to live alone in her small home and was very independent. A number of people visited to keep an eye on her, as she was beginning to fail with memory loss – although she would never have admitted it.

Her daughter lived miles away and relied on locals to keep her informed, as she only journeyed to see her mother at weekends.

It was on a Friday morning in February that Miss Amy, in her kitchen, had the idea of baking a cake for her daughter's visit next day. She gathered the ingredients together and was happily concentrating on what to do next.

She was turning on the gas oven when the telephone rang in the hall. She turned sharply at the sound and tutted at the interruption. By chance, Miss Amy's slipper caught the edge of the door and she fell down clumsily as she'd overbalanced trying to steady herself.

The phone kept ringing, but she couldn't get up unaided, her left hip was excruciatingly painful. She cried out in pain and frustration.

Receiving no answer to her call, the friend became anxious and made a note to call in on her way back from shopping.

Miss Amy lay prostrate on the floor between the kitchen and the hall. She soon became cold and confused. Then she detected the smell of gas. Surely, she had turned the oven on properly. She closed her eyes.

It must have been an hour later that the explosion rocked the street...

*   *   *   *   *

As her head cleared, Miss Amy found herself in a state of disbelief, and not amidst the rubble and ruins of her home as she'd have expected.

Instead, she found herself in a verdant glade, beautiful oak trees grew in a semi-circle meeting the riverbank on each side. The river ran gently and was as clear as any she'd seen. The white-water bubbling over the rocks made her think of gambolling lambs playing on the hills in spring.

As she made to get up, her breath seized in her chest. Her hands were the first her eye lit upon, no longer the gnarled arthritis riddled fingers she'd come to hate. They were creamy and smooth, and not one liver spot in sight. As she examined herself further, she was astonished to see that her body was as it had been when she was about sixteen years old. About the time she'd met her Gabriel; she sighed at the thought of him.

As she thought this, a movement in the treeline pulled her gaze. No! it couldn't be, but it was. Her beautiful, young, handsome Gabriel. The boy who had won her heart, whom she was supposed to marry when she'd reached her majority, on his next leave. The boy whom she had never stopped loving.

The telegram, a week before her 21st in 1943, told of the plane he flew being one of those that had been shot down over Berlin.

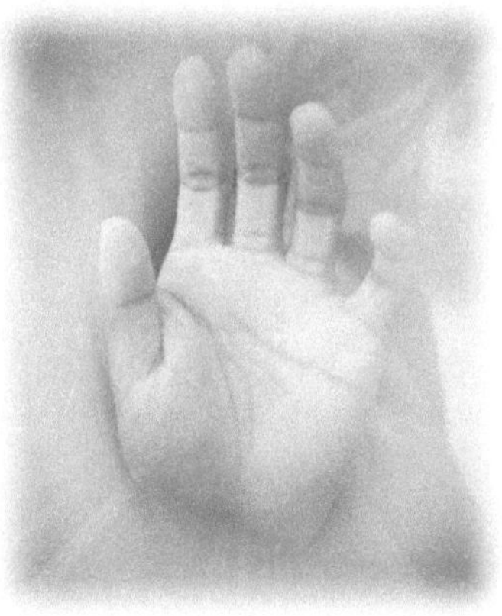

Reaching her, Gabriel took her hands in his. Smiling, he bent and gently kissed her forehead. "At last, darling," he whispered to her, "I've waited ever such a long time for you."

She was flooded with warmth and peace, *"Home at last,"* she thought.

*   *   *   *   *

The firemen found the body of Miss Amy under the collapsed wall in the hall. They all commented how her body was untouched by the explosion, but the most astonishing thing they said, was the beautiful smile she had upon her face.

You Never Can Tell

For the umpteenth time this week, Mary listened to her son and his pals strumming and humming little runs and riffs on their guitars. Sometimes she really wanted the tunes to go on a bit longer, and there were many times when she thought the tunes seemed to have made some headway, when a whole sixteen bars would be heard behind a duet of vocals.

She frequently thought they'd sound better if only her handsome, talented son was singing alone, but she knew that was just her being a biased mother.

She had to admit she didn't always understand the music of today. It seemed wild, and uncontrolled. At least for the most part, that would be how she'd describe it.

She was happy the boys were here though, not on the streets getting into mischief like so many of the local lads. There were a fair few of her neighbours, whose lads were taken in by the "Polis," for a wee chat on a regular basis.

No, her only worry was her son's champagne taste and beer money wages. Ah well, he's a good lad, it'll all come out in the wash no doubt. She pulled the pan of scouse off the flame. Time, she thought, to call him and his mates through for tea.

"Paul, is Pete, George and John staying for a bite or are yous lot off up the cavern again?"

The Hero

That afternoon, having just finished getting the messages in before the shops closed for Hogmanay, she'd put her bags down to retrieve her keys when a small perfect white feather floated down onto the mat at her front door.

She looked around to see where it had come from. A plump little robin tweeted as he soared from the garage roof into the bright afternoon sky and disappeared.

She picked up the soft, perfect feather, musing on the notion of a feather such as this, arriving in such a deliberate way, as well as a wee robin, were seen by some to be a message from a loved one on the other side.

Hours later, as midnight approached, Carla sat gazing into the open fire. She'd considered the idea of Bovril, but her mood denied that comfortable, but unexciting libation. No! She reached for the crystal decanter, a glass of *Uisge Beatha*, (ushki beha), the water of life, a twelve-year-old malt would fit the bill quite nicely.

She needed to remember someone, a man like no other to her, and she wanted to do it properly, with at least a nod to style.

She chose the music carefully. Jim Reeves, Ethna Campbell, Cilla Black, Nat King Cole and others were gathered up.

As the first single dropped in her old suitcase record player, she let her eyes rest on his photograph. The love she felt for this man, her hero, flowed through her, bringing comfort in her loss. The love she'd received from him was the benchmark by which she measured all men. How she missed him. Those twinkling blue eyes, his dry wit, his wisdom. "Happy Hogmanay, Dad," she whispered as she raised her glass in salute to his picture, Slainte.

The bells rang loud and clear as she sipped from her glass.

Another year passed.

Ain't Karma a Bitch

Celia, head bent low, almost whispering the words, said, "Can I have some shopping money, please? We need some sugar and I'm ten pence short."

He looked up from the paper. Ignoring her request, he sneered, "Cocked up again on your bloody calculations? You're so bloody stupid."

In reply she forced herself to say that things had unexpectedly increased in price by twenty pence.

He slowly and deliberately lifted himself out of the armchair and turned to face her. She felt her whole body begin to shake. His hand cupped her cheek, and he moved his thumb and forefinger in a caress down her ear and slowed as they came to her pearl stud earring. Suddenly ripping it off, he tore the lobe in two.

Her involuntary scream startled him, and he let fly with a punch which knocked her out cold. She buckled and ended in a heap in the puddle of her own urine.

Reggie and Elsie lived in the flat next door and could hear every word from Celia and Len's sitting room. Reg looked over to Elsie and said, "That's enough. I've had enough of that despot next door." He dialled 999.

Reg was more than a little surprised at the speed of their response. Within fifteen minutes, they were banging on Len's front door. When he opened the door, two officers pushed straight passed him saying, "We have reason to believe an assault has taken place here." Before Len could stop them, they were in the living room and bending over the inert body of his wife.

The older officer turned yelling, "Call an ambulance, Jim!" as he checked her pulse and put her into the recovery position, checking she was breathing freely and appeared to have no other obvious wounds besides a torn ear and what looked like the beginnings of a black eye. Satisfied he'd done all he could till the ambulance arrived, he stood, turned to Len, and said, "We have reason to believe you are responsible for the assault on your wife, and I'm arresting you on suspicion of causing grievous bodily harm." As he finished reading him his rights, he pushed Len towards the door.

Len, caught off guard, tripped over his own feet, hitting his head on the stone fireplace.

The inquest recorded an accidental death incurred whilst the deceased was attempting an escape from custody.

"Karma," said Jim to his partner as they left the courthouse.

Celia was so grateful to them. The double life insurance pay-out allowed her a very comfortable twenty-five years until her death aged seventy-three. She left each officer half of her estate in her will.

Every good deed, eh?

Counting Tears

Pausing in her task, she sat, her head in her hands. There it was again. She could feel her heart fluttering, racing, and missing beats. She could feel the panic rise in her rock filled chest. The scream building, demanding release from her constricted throat.

All her life had been one long lesson that she had never understood.

Her purpose in life eluded her, she was so inept at everything and of use to neither man nor beast and loved by none.

She was a disappointment as a child. As a mother, she was never quite good enough. And as a wife, she never measured up. Making second place at best, to a bottle of booze, a younger, slimmer, happier version than she had once appeared to be.

The years passed slowly, each year dragging on and on. Occasionally someone would mistake her for someone loveable, but it was never long before she was set aside. She withdrew from the world as much as possible. It was as if she lived in a world of broken glass, every step forward leading to another wound, another slash across her heart.

And she railed at the unfairness and dreamed her dreams, still hoping.

Years later, convinced over time to take a chance. To maybe, at last find value, love, and respect.

Her gut screamed, *"NO, NO, NO!"* but her heart was so desperate to know how it felt to be precious to someone. She let her heart win, sadly, for her husband of barely five years now lives with his secretary, twenty years his junior.

Finally, she understood the life lesson she'd failed to interpret over her long sixty-five years. She really was unworthy, undeserving. She really was unlovable. A waste of good air.

She had cleaned every nook and cranny of her home, laid a rubber sheet under the 1200 thread Egyptian cotton sheet, the oven sparkled like new, and every pane of glass or mirror gleamed.

She feels so very tired, so ready, not a flicker of hope lives now, time to get on with her final task,

One tear, one tablet. 22. One tear, one tablet. 23. One tear……..one tablet. ……..24. one……….. Tear,……….one……….. a long sigh passes her lips…

… and she passes from the world, and no-one notices.

The Highwayman

I was sitting in the comfort of the luxurious coach which belonged to Sir Piers Trevallyan. My stomach felt as if one hundred butterflies had taken up residence since the horses had been suddenly halted.

At twenty, some said I was almost on the shelf. I was an independent woman with no male family left to dictate my course for me.

My beloved father died in Cawnpore, serving with Henry Havelock, in the 78th Highland Reg't of Foot. My mother had died of cholera the year before, in 1856, leaving me an orphan, but a very reasonably well off one.

One spring morning, I'd been shopping with an elderly aunt in one of London's leading fashion houses. As we were leaving through their grand doors, my skirt became caught as the door closed. From a very swanky carriage jumped a dashing figure who knelt to extricate my skirts. He saved my blushes, too, as he positioned his body between the door and the street, effectively blocking the view of my ankles as he disentangled my skirt and petticoat frills from the floor latch of the door.

He had been a frequent caller since then, and it looked like he was setting his cap at my door. Sadly, whilst I was very fond of Piers and really enjoyed his company, I didn't see us as lovers. What I felt was a warm kindredship. I wanted a marriage of fire and passion.

My aunts despaired of me, saying marriages are best built on friendship, respect and honour, and money. Passion, they said, soon fades, but I wanted love, an all-consuming fire.

Which brings me to the moment that my wish was granted.

In Piers' coach on my way to another dinner to celebrate some dull old battle, I was daydreaming as the coach and four raced through the lanes, lined with hedgerows heavy with the dog rose and wild blackberries. Suddenly the coach lurched as the driver sought to stop sharply.

From the side I saw a rider approaching.

The curtains on the windows of the coach had been left open, and in the opening a face appeared.

Well, that's not quite true. His face was masked, his hat and cloak were black, but his eyes, *OH MY*, but they were the most adorable shade of blue. Gorgeous was the word, with long black lashes that framed these large oval sapphire orbs. I blushed as I realised, I was thinking how I'd happily drown in them, given the opportunity.

The rider coughed; his eyes reflected the smile his mask was hiding. He told me, "Step out of the carriage, please." I laughed to myself at the ridiculousness of this highwayman saying *please.*

As I stepped down, he jumped from his glorious example of horse flesh. He picked me up with one arm, pulling me close. My heart was racing so fast I thought I might faint. He looked deep into my eyes, then before I could discern his intent, he kissed me. I was lost forever.

Many reading this will say this was silly. A romantic, childish notion, but I stand firmly behind my own evaluation.

I fell in love in that moment, and I knew he did too.

He threw me up on the horse's neck and leapt up behind me. He leant in close to my ear and whispered, "Well, my beauty, we're both heading into the unknown tonight."

He kicked the great beast and we headed off into our future, whatever it may bring.

Thirty years have passed, and I still can drown in his eyes. Both our children have inherited those sapphire orbs and long dark lashes that captivated me on that desolate country road.

Only I see him in his highwayman's mask nowadays.

The Street Urchin

The street urchin approached the edge of the market square, his eyes flickering over the barrows. The smells of fresh bread and pies made his mouth slaver and tiny rivers of hunger juices filled his mouth with want. His family were never rich, but his father's shoemaking business fed and clothed them well.

That is, it did until the great pestilence came. It claimed thousands, and he prayed to God to be forgiven, but he didn't care about any of them. His parents, though, were a different kettle of fish. Their deaths meant that now he, aged barely twelve summers, was head of the family. His father had elicited his solemn word to take care of his siblings. Jacob, aged eight, and two sisters, Lisette aged seven and Eliza aged five. Luckily, his father had owned the small shop and rooms above, so whilst impoverished, they had a roof over their heads.

He moved from the shadows and, with a brazen wink at the fishwife, nabbed a pie from the stall beside where she stood. He moved on down pilfering whatever he could. Wending his way back up the other side, he noticed the fishwife smile and wave him over. She'd known his parents. Still, the solitude borne out of responsibility made him cautious, and suspicious of everything and everyone. He came to her slow, with a watchful eye.

She laughed as he approached, "Aye ,well, Levi. Mayhap you've reason to distrust the world, but you needn't fear me, lad. Here, these won't go another day, and I'm off home to feed my lot." She handed him a piece of sacking, inside was a large haddock and a dozen or so sprats. Tonight, his family would sleep with full bellies.

Tomorrow of course, well, that's another story.

The Rescue

Stephanie Adams had been a paramedic for over seven years. She'd seen her share of gruesome sights whilst on a shout. She'd seen people at their best and their worst, in the midst of catastrophe and chaos.

Sometimes her job was to ease the passing from this life, and at others to assist the entry into it. All of life's rich tapestry was woven into her daily travail.

She had seen selflessness and selfishness. Generosity and greed. Kindness and cruelty. She'd watched the smile of recognition on a woman's face as her otherwise invisible husband came to hold her hand as she crossed over. She loved her job.

It was her job that had brought her to this moment.

The small plane had tried to land on the motorway to avoid the built-up housing either side of it. With nowhere else halfway flat in the area, it was Hobson's Choice.

At five a.m., this stretch of the A1 was relatively quiet; only a few cars and delivery lorries were regular travellers at this time of the morning.

The pilot had done well. It was down and gradually slowing to a speed comparable with the traffic normally on the road. It looked like they were home free.

Sadly, a husband racing to get his wife, now in active labour, to the hospital, had not seen the plane's descent and landing on the road. He was distracted by her screams of pain and had not seen the events unfolding ahead.

At the last moment, he did. Panicked, he swerved; so had the pilot in a vain attempt to limit the area of impact between the two vehicles.

And it looked for all the world as if all would be well when the lowered flaps caught the top box fitted on the range rover's roof. This caused the car to slew and it went through the barrier. It came to a standstill with one third of the car precariously hanging over the edge.

The difficulties were plain to see when Steph and her colleague arrived. As they approached the car, a policeman informed them the fire brigade was on its way, but it would be twenty to thirty minutes. There had been heavy rainfall these past few days and there was local flooding. This had caused a detour being put in place, adding extra time to the fire engine's journey.

There would normally have been an engine closer, but it was out dealing with a small derailment caused by a landslide, a direct result of the rain. The goods train that had left the tracks had only two men aboard, the driver and fireman. The fireman was trapped and that's where the closer station's engine now was.

The driver of the car would not leave the car whilst his wife was inside, insisting she and the baby take priority. Therein lay the issue.

If she were removed first before the fire engine arrived, the weight distribution would leave the car front heavy, and likely to tip the front of the car over the edge. The weight of his pregnant wife, the baby car seat, and her hospital bag were the critical factor in keeping the car on an even keel.

To complicate things further, by swivelling the woman on the back seat, Steph had managed to examine her. Baby had turned, said the mother to be, she'd felt it just before the pains had begun in earnest. It was breach, and the examination suggested the cord may have gone round baby's neck.

Stephanie was talking to her colleague Mick, "If we don't get her to hospital, and soon, we will probably lose the baby, and possibly the mother too."

"Let's hope they get here fast, then," replied her colleague.

They explained all this to the husband and wife. He was adamant they should get her out, but his wife was almost hysterical at the idea of the car – and he – would tip over the edge and be dashed in the fast-running river below.

Steph had worked with Mick for about five years and she trusted him, He was an excellent paramedic with a soft voice and a calm nature.

She pulled him away from the vehicle and said, "Okay, look. If I climb in the back from the other side and take my bag in with me, you can pull her out and get her to hospital. I can then keep him calm until the fire truck gets here. It can't be long now."

Mick turned to her and hissed, "No, not a chance. I won't let you put your life in danger. You know the rules, Steph."

"Well, now. I'm sorry, but they weren't hard and fast rules last month when you jumped in the river to help the fisherman." She looked askance at him. He knew he'd just lost the argument; He must just accept what she was about to do, then do the best he could to help her.

It was a hairy moment as the weight changed in the car, but as she'd hoped, her weight combined with her pack kept the balance. The woman was eased out onto the stretcher, crying, and pleading to be allowed to stay with her husband. He insisted she go and make sure their baby was delivered safely, telling her he'd be along as soon as the firemen got the car back onto the bridge.

Mick held Steph's gaze, nodded, smiled, then turned the siren and blue light on and took off at a fair lick down the road.

The driver was now drifting in and out of consciousness. In one of his lucid moments, he told Steph of the gash in his leg. She asked the policeman to break a wing mirror off his car and hand it to her. As soon as the chap came to from the smelling salts, Steph asked him to use the mirror to let her see the cut. It wasn't good.

Again, calling the policeman to her side, "Are either you, or your colleague wearing a belt with a buckle?"

The officer whom she had not yet spoken with approached, his hand pulling free his leather belt.

She was trying to talk the man through using the belt as a tourniquet, when the first sounds of the approaching fire truck were heard.

Soon the men were wheeling out the hook from the winch. One chap disappeared from view out the back window about to attach the hook and chain. Just at that moment, the driver slumped forward. The car tipped. Steph threw herself back hard into the seat, but the front kept dipping, and the rear kept rising as they slipped ever nearer the edge, then fell away.

They fell about six to eight feet before suddenly, there was an almighty jolt as the chain took the strain.

Two hours later Steph and Mick popped in to see the beautiful baby.

Her parents had named the infant Angel, "Messenger from God." Her bruised, battered, and exhausted parents were just glad to be alive and so grateful to the two paramedics who came to their rescue.

Ode to a Peony

Peony white, queen of the blossoms

stood all alone, out in plain sight.

Once was surrounded, by peonies blue,

Stood quiet and watched, hidden from light.

Peony white, in a dress white as snow,

Watched as they died, she'd nowhere to go.

A poison had come and swept her small army away,

She didn't now dare, to enter into the fray.

She sheds her gown, white, as you know,

And goes underground, in the earth just below.

She won't be found, proud Peony of white,

not in the dark, cold winter's night.

Watch for her rise in the warmth of the spring,

When she returns, brothers in red, she will bring,

Once more in her land, peonies white will array,

And three Royal colours with pride will display.

The White Peony

Analise sent her poem over the illegal radio waves. She prayed the British would understand the underlying message. Her life would depend on it.

She was French. On the face of it, a collaborator. She had volunteered for the Resistance the day Marshal Petain capitulated and the Vichy Government was formed.

They were the collaborators, the traitors to France, they were cowards. From the very beginning, though, the *Maquis* had wanted to have spies, fifth columnists, in the Vichy administration.

The men once her respected superiors in the government where she worked as a translator and personal secretary filled her with shame. They now kowtowed to the Nazis and had become Hitlerite flunkies. The hatred she bore them she kept well-hidden.

Hidden, that she might better gather information and intelligence to assist the Free French under General De Gaulle and the Allies. The intel she gathered was handed to her guerrilla unit, who were causing havoc for the Nazi war machine in France and Belgium and would soon be assisting the advancing allies in Germany too.

The final days of the war were drawing ever nearer. The Russians were advancing from the East and the British and other allied forces were racing towards Berlin from the west. Their aim: to split the last vestiges of the German army in half. Combined with the ever more erratic and frantic orders of Hitler, destruction should be swift and complete.

Orders from Hitler's bunker were becoming impossible. Sadly, not enough of his high command were willing to disagree with him nor tell him it was futile. It was easier and eminently safer for them to prepare and wait than to challenge their drug addled and disease-ridden leader.

They need only hold out a month or so until the eventual and inevitable surrender. Many, including Jan, had made their secret plans, new identities, passports. And of course, valuables. The gold and jewels they had stripped from the Jews was the fund by which they would re-establish the Reich.

They were set for new lives, a new start. Bolivia, Argentina, and other south American countries were the favourite choices. There they could regroup and rebuild the new Reich, just not under Hitler. More than one of his most brilliant and talented officers had collaborated and attempted to kill the Austrian corporal and effect a coup.

It all failed. Those who were implicated did not live long.

Analise's job was to gather as much intel on Hitler's whereabouts and his orders, no matter how insane or inane they might appear.

She had taken a lover in the early days of the German occupation. She'd been asked to target a staff officer whilst she still lived in Paris and he was there enjoying some leave.

She went with him as he rose in rank and was posted to Berlin. He was in a position with access to the highest echelons of the Hitler war cabinet. *Feldwebel* Jan Hauptman was one of Hitler's staff officers.

He was also so vain and full of his own importance that he never stopped to ask why such a beautiful French woman would betray her blood and abandon her country to be his concubine.

He could not resist bragging to her of his importance, of the inside knowledge he was privy to. For this, she made herself his devoted lover for the duration.

In January of 1945, there was a state of high energy and some frantic activity in the Reich's Chancellery. The Fuhrer had ordered his HQ to be moved into the huge elaborate bunkers built below the chancellery. The Vorbunker and the Fuhrerbunker would be where Adolf planned to micromanage the resurrection and rescue of his failing Third Reich. Everyone knew this to be the fantasy of a man crazed by drugs and disease.

Rumour had it that he was in the last stage of tertiary syphilis. He continued to send out insane orders that would inevitably extend the war and incur needless loss of more allied and German lives.

Jan was lying in the luxurious bath in the rooms allocated to him within the Chancellery. Analise had arrived back from procuring wine and bread, or so he'd assumed. He was wrong, and not for the first time.

Earlier in the day a message had been passed to her by one of the local women who were forced to cook, clean, and do the laundry for the officers and men housed there. She was instructed to meet her contact for urgent new orders.

Analise arrived at the meeting place in time to see two SS men slam her contact against a wall. She stood silent as he was brutally beaten before being thrown in the sedan that would deliver him to very practiced interrogators. He had seen her arrive and with the swiftest of looks drew her eyes to their dead drop. The spot where they'd leave info if they had missed an appointed meet.

She waited till the commotion and small crowd had quietened and dissipated, then headed to the pickup spot. She tipped the planter with her shoe; beneath it lay a half-smoked cigarette. She bent as if to sort her stocking heel and picked the chipped smoke up. A few minutes later as she sat in the park, she opened up the cigarette. Inside was a sliver of paper. It read, "We are moving, and the white peony must be replanted." This was code for a betrayal, she was in danger. She must affect her escape immediately.

She could not just run from here. She had to be smart. She returned to the apartment she shared with Jan. She called out, *"Allo, ma chere?"*

He answered and she found him lying in the bath. He informed her that he would not be at home this evening: they had received information on a local resistance cell. They would be rounding up everyone on the list that the SS interrogators were collating. As soon as they had all the names they could pull from the informer, all would be arrested at the same time. Analise's heart and brain raced.

He passed her a long slender jewellery box. "This is to ease your disappointment at missing the theatre tonight. I know I promised to take you, but I'm afraid duty calls."

Analise opened the box and could not contain the gasp. Lying in a bed of midnight blue velvet lay a white gold and diamond bracelet. The maker: Carl Faberge. Analise had a fleeting thought, *"Someone up there is watching over me."* It gave her hope.

It led her thoughts back to her father, killed in World War One, and her adored brother. He had been killed when the Nazis invaded France in '39.

He had joined his father's regiment only a year before war broke out. Before France was once more just a battlefield, a graveyard in the making. A place where sons of France, Germany, Britain, and her allies would again fight and die. One of those sons was Analise's brother Pierre. He was the reason she had joined the resistance and why no price was too high if it would bring the Nazi regime down.

As soon as Jan left, she gathered anything of value and placed it into her toilet bag. She'd need warm clothes: one decent dress and coat were in a Louis Vuitton holdall; she added the stash of valuables.

She dressed in a warm suit of wool and wore her high fur lined boots with a full-length coat and Cossack style hat that matched.

She had no illusions. These gifts from her *Feldwebel*, she knew they had cost him nothing. He would have selected them from the warehouse, a huge building, full of furs, expensive luggage, Vuitton trunks, and mountains of gold and jewellery.

Jan's expenditure was a few minutes of his time in the selecting. She had no doubt it had cost the owners of these items their life.

She left their apartment and, having loaded two large cans from their petrol stash into the car, disappeared into the chaos of war.

Thereafter, Analise Duval's whereabouts were unknown for three months to either the *Wehrmacht* or the SOE.

Only the British had an inkling of where she may be heading, if indeed she was still alive. They had done all that they could to help save her, should their hunch prove correct. They could only speculate as to the definite meaning hidden in her poem.

Analise drove in the direction she assumed Jan would least expect, towards the approaching Red Army heading towards Lodz. She drove to Poland, praying the Russians would listen before raping or shooting her.

For the moment, with her German ID, she could go wherever she wished. She was stopped by a patrol once near the border. She heard the guards discussing her whilst checking her papers, "It's not her. We are looking for a beautiful woman, not a mouse." Analise did not smile. She did not look up.

She demurely waited to receive back her pass, the one which stated she was a native of Belarus who spoke Russian and was required to assist the SS interrogation officer in Lodz. These were not the details that were on the one Jan procured for her.

She'd taken that to the *Maquis*, and they had created a duplicate, the photo and some details were now altered.

The guards, in truth were too busy chatting to really look at her, past the large horn-rimmed glasses and timid, introvert appearance.

She stayed on the move till early March when she approached a Russian patrol near Krakow.

It took forty-eight hours before the Russians were satisfied; finally, they accepted she was indeed the woman the British had told them to expect. Analise Duval, the White Peony, was safe and surrounded by her Red brothers. Soon she would be going home, where in time, General de Gaulle and the British, would present her the *Legion d'honneur* and the George Cross.

Now lauded a heroine, no longer hated for a traitor, no longer shunned by friends and family, she was free, and so was France.

The Miracle Gift

Living in the quiet village had soothed her tired and broken heart. They'd been together since they were fourteen years old. Engaged at eighteen, married last year in September.

Her eyes misted as she recalled their wonderful wedding day. Their two dearest friends from school as her maid of honour and Steve's best man. Both families blending seamlessly in affection and accord at the reception. The sun had shone and the colours of the flora at the castle they'd chosen to host their wedding threw a display of stunning golds, oranges, and browns, all in their final glory before the dying autumn turned to dark, frigid winter.

She was widowed in late November. An accident, they said. Black ice in the early morning as Steve set out for a meeting in London.

He'd headed out of Keswick where they lived and out through the fells heading south. Descending a steep part of the route, he'd hit a patch of black ice that caused him to lose control. The car left the road. It careered down a steep drop of rocks and trees. It had exploded at some point in the descent.

The crash was discovered on the remote road at about eleven a.m., six hours after he'd left. He'd have reached that spot about an hour and a half after leaving home.

Steve had been dead four and a half hours before anyone knew, and six hours before the police knocked on her door.

How? How could she not have known? She always thought she should have felt something, some gut-wrenching feeling of his leaving her. An omen, something...

Her apparent existence in oblivious emotional distance from the man whom she'd called "her world," left her questioning.

Six months later, she'd moved to the small two bed house on the edge of a village not far from Keswick.

Their home held too many memories and too much pain. So, distracted by it all, the funeral, probate, moving, family, and friends, she only noticed as a passing thought the extra weight she now carried. She didn't care that her joggers were a tad snug.

This morning, she'd decided to take a walk after some weeding. It was such a lovely day, and today she felt Steve's closeness. She decided to pop into the pretty village chapel. She enjoyed its peace and it comforted her sometimes.

She lit a candle and began a prayer she remembered from her girlhood, always coming back to her beseeching the Lord for an understanding, a peace. If she couldn't have him back, then an answer to why He had to take Steve. I want him back was her mantra, all to no avail, of course.

As she stood to leave, a sharp pain stopped her in her tracks. She gasped as it ripped through her and she sat back down heavily.

The postmistress, Mernie Fairgrieve came into the church at that moment, Mernie did the church flowers as well as ran the post office. As Mernie approached, Grace was gripped by yet another searing pain and much to her horror, she wet herself.

Just as she was processing the events, Mernie approached Grace and in a swift assessment of the situation, said, "Well, lass, we best get you home. This baby looks like it's coming now, ready or not."

Grace had just reached the same conclusion and gone into shock.

Mernie got the priest, who got them both into the car and got Grace back to her house. Mernie had called a midwife that lived a couple of miles away and who said she'd meet them at Grace's.

Steve, junior, arrived two hours after they left the chapel. God didn't give her her husband back, but part of him lived on in the miracle of their son. He must have been conceived the night before the crash. A final precious gift from her loving husband.

After the Storm

The beasts lay where their riders had pulled them down, the rags over their faces being shaken off as they struggled to find a solid foothold on the shifting ground.

The men, all straining alongside these incredible ships of the desert, fought to uncover those parts of their bodies and paniers that still were partly pinned beneath the heavy desert sands.

These families were no stranger to the vagaries of the desert. For centuries, this nomadic people had traversed the Sahara. The indigo head covering of the men had gained them the nickname, the "blue men," the sweat of their faces causing the dye to stain their skins.

The Tuareg were a progressive people, their women owned their own camels and tents. Although followers of Islam, they did not require their women to cover their faces, claiming to want to rejoice in their beauty.

This same people evoke ancient, uncivilised, and romantic images.

Their skill as desert travellers covering some of the most inhospitable land in the world was legend. They wander all the lands of the desert, from southern Libya to Mali and Niger in the south and from the Atlantic to the Red sea on the east and west coasts. It is said that the blind of their tribe make the best guides. They apparently used their heightened senses of taste and smell to find tracks and paths hidden by altered vistas of an ever-changing desert.

Shamama was curled beneath her husband's upper body, his torso creating a shield for his woman beneath their blanket. As she rose from the sand, she touched the arm of her husband of fourteen years. Her smile made her big dark eyes crinkle at the edges and made Bouhen ag Chakot's heart skip a beat. Not all marriages in their tribe were a love match. Some learnt to love, some never did, and divorce was a prerogative of the women in this strange and wonderful community.

Shamama and Bouhen were in the small group who fell in love before they were joined. She gloried in caring for him in all the ways of women all over the world. Her footsteps fell lightly when he smiled at her or complimented her on the food she prepared for him. And most especially if she cupped his face in her hands and after kissing his face, saw the fire of hunger light in his eyes. It filled her heart with joy to know that after all these years he still hankered for her. This made her proud and she walked taller.

As they gathered themselves up, preparing to break their fast and take water before their onward journey, a cry went up that at least one of their group had not yet risen from the mounds created by the sandstorm. Redma, wife of Tamat ult Amjer was nowhere to be found.

Tariq ag Salla was called forth, he was blind, but it was he who led them, especially when the landscape had altered. He could taste and smell the route they would need to follow.

They had been to Ghat in the southwest, for a family wedding. The celebrations had continued for seven days and seven nights. Now they were heading to near Surt on the Mediterranean coast where they would spend the summer. They were almost halfway between Sabha and the coast when the storm had risen like an ancient God of old.

Tearing across the dunes at such speed, it had caught them in the open with only enough time to do no more than wet some cloths to cover theirs and the camels faces, creating a rudimentary protection. Like the wagon trains of the American plains, they'd circled the animals and brought them to their knees. The men used their bodies as a shield, placing children and women between the animals and the men of the family.

There had been trouble for a long time between Tamat and Redma. She had finally, after the celebrations in Ghat ended, declared that she was divorcing Brahim, her husband of two years. It was her right to do so in their culture. He had taken it well, but the two now travelled separately. He had therefore not gone to her protection when the storm raged like a whirlwind towards them.

Now, everyone assumed her lost, accepting she had perished beneath the fierce onslaught of sand. By this time, it was also noted she was not the only one to appear to have succumbed to the storm. Ali Ben Abdallah was not accounted for either. Sadly, an infant had suffocated pressed to his mother's breast as she had tried to keep his face covered and free of the sand, inadvertently starving the child of the small amount of oxygen available. Her grief filled wails, carried far and wide on the wind as it passed.

Ali's loss would be sorely felt, although a solitary character keeping himself to himself most of the time. He was, however, always in the midst of gatherings to dig a well, mend or raise a tent. He was good with the animals, too. He was a man always helping to solve the problems and trials of his group, no matter how large or small the difficulty.

With grace and kindness, Ali would apply himself to finding a solution or giving encouragement or support. He was so unassuming as to be almost invisible in the community until need brought him to you. The storm had taken a terrible toll on this tribal group.

It was therefore quite a shock in the wake of the storm to then see a single camel approaching the fires. A man could be seen leading the beast, and a woman was upon its back.

A little confused but very happy were the group to realise it was Ali and Redma.

No-one in the group missed the look that passed between the two, as Ali Ben Abdallah helped Redma alight from the kneeling camel's back. Her arm was tightly bound to her upper body.

The quiet man had seen Redma try to pull her camel down and witnessed the animal's violent resistance. He'd gone to her aid just as the storm was about to hit. Too late to save her from the camels attempt to flee and her fall beneath the stupid beast's hoof. Her arm was broken. He had downed his animal and shielded her with his body.

He had loved her for a long time and was glad to keep her safe. Redma had wanted this man too, but her parents and Tamat's had pledged them to each other as children.

Now she would be free.

The storm was over, as was a marriage, but happiness finds a place in open hearts.

Tamat rode to join with another group of travellers heading northwest, near where his brothers were in Tripoli. His life would be changed, too: a new life rising from the ashes of the storm.

He would head to America, where he hoped he might find love, a love he could never find here. He would find a husband and happiness in the liberal land across the sea.

Later he would write to Redma, to thank her for his freedom.

Candle in the Dark

Lady Cecily Beckett struggled both physically and metaphorically with her present predicament. How could her life have taken such a cruel road? How could it all end like this?

Cecily Alexandra Beckett was born into a titled family in the wilds of sixteenth century Northumberland. Her family's titles were bestowed by King Henry VII in 1501 for services as keepers of the border between the warlike Celts north of the wall and the citizens of Northumberland.

Cecily was promised to the Lord of Alnwick from the time she was barely five summers old. They were married on her fifteenth birthday. Her new husband was in his fortieth year and boring in the young bride's eyes. Her grandfather was but only a few years his senior.

She knew her duty though; it was the same for all females of the day. Marriages were rarely based upon mutual affection, but on politics and advancement of the family. Cecily was just another bargaining chip in her father's ambitious plans.

Five years after her marriage, she had been delivered of three healthy children, two boys and finally a girl. She took great comfort in these wonderful blessings. Her little girl was the apple of her eye. The child promised to be a beauty. This made Cecily sad, for it would increase her value as a pawn in the machinations of men.

Her eldest son Edward had just turned five when her husband informed her that he'd taken into his employ a tutor. He would school Edward, and William, too, when he had reached his fifth year.

The day of the arrival of said tutor dawned, heralding a glorious spring day. It was a day that reminds us what a wonder our world is and how blessed we are to be alive.

Her maid knocked and entered Cecily's solar. She was seated by the window for the light, her needlework on her lap. "The master asks you to join him in the hall, Mistress, and he said to say, 'NOW!'"

Cecily had long since given up rebelling at the *'commands'* her husband issued. Her hopes for his understanding that *'requests'* had far sweeter consequences were dashed time and again. He understood nothing. Cecily resigned herself to a marriage not only devoid of love, but respect too. A marriage where she was merely a chattel, of no more import than an ox or a horse.

It was amidst this atmosphere that the gentleman tutor found himself.

Percival Wingate was the second son of a gentleman farmer and mayor to a small Yorkshire town with no prospects of inheriting the farm, unless a tragedy befell his older sibling. His gentle character made him sorely unsuited to a military career, leaving only two acceptable options: the Church or tutoring. He knew his nature would baulk at a celibate life, so teaching it was!

Surprising everyone but his mother, he proved himself to be an excellent tutor.

Cecily was pleasantly surprised that first day, when her husband introduced the man. He was tall with a slender frame, but muscular none the less. He had long shapely legs and an endearing, warm smile. Grey eyes that spoke of intelligence and kindness gazed out from below a mass of unruly curls. She was instantly captivated. She would later learn she was not alone in that.

Two years passed in an incredibly happy way for the household. Her husband had been away serving his Queen against the Spanish. He had barely returned in the October of 1596 when he was recalled to assist in the Oxford rising which was feared to be the tip of a much wider-spread rebellion about to erupt. It turned out to be a much less serious affair than expected. Terrible harvests had caused such poverty in parts of the country, and the Crown's lack of assistance inspired some brave if naive men to march on London in protest.

They'd hoped to gather large numbers as they headed south. Sadly, it did not transpire. They were caught on Enslow Hill on a cold November 21st. The rising was cruelly crushed.

Her husband had been reluctant to travel home in such inclement weather and gratefully accepted the invitation to spend Christmas with an old friend. Robert Devereux, Earl of Essex.

Essex was the rumoured lover to the "Virgin Queen," just like his father before him. Sadly however, Robert Dudley, Earl of Leicester's son did not have the same character as his father. Robert Devereux was much more reckless and disrespectful of his sovereign's wishes and orders. His royal liaison would end badly for the young soldier.

But for Christmas 1596, he was home from the campaigns in Spain and was enjoying his wife, Frances Walsingham, widow of the poet, Sir Philip Sidney, and some old friends and family.

Lord Beckett sent word with his man to his wife and family, informing them of his intentions to stay with the Devereux's till the weather improved. He dispatched gifts for Christmas in the care of his manservant with orders to hand them out on Christmas morning.

Christmas morning arrived along with a heavy snowfall; excited children were seated at breakfast when the gifts were delivered as instructed. The children were delighted with the thoughtful gifts their father had sent. However, there was no gift for Lady Beckett. Cecily was humiliated and terribly hurt, as it was intentionally done under the gaze of the staff, and worse, her children.

She had not been happy. Her husband made no effort to affect this state and now he treated her as if she were invisible, like the servants.

On New Year's Eve, when the Lord of the manor traditionally threw a party for his tenants and staff, it was Lady Beckett who hosted it.

It was she who handed out the cash gifts. She danced as was expected on this occasion with all the male staff who wished to and were able – including the wonderful Percival Wingate, Esq.

That night changed their lives, their destiny forever altered. That first kiss set them upon another path, another destiny.

They declared their feelings for one another in the first minutes of 1597. The fireworks that exploded above were mirrored in the explosion of passion below. A passion that would lead them to pain and tragedy.

Lord Beckett returned as the buds began to poke their colourful heads out to welcome the arrival of the warm sunshine.

Soon after, he noted that his personal manservant would not meet his eye, and no longer relished in their short chats about the families and staff. He was not the only member of staff to look discomforted in his presence. He was not a warm man, but he had always been good to his staff. Something was amiss and he was dead set upon learning what that was.

After careful watching for a further fortnight, he called upon his old staff sergeant from his regiment. The man was living in a cottage on the estate with his son and daughter. He had saved Beckett's life whilst in Spain. Now too old for service, Beckett employed him to drive his Hansom and his son worked in the gardens. but today, he wanted his old comrade to spy for him.

By September Lord Beckett had his answer, Linus Quinn laid the evidence before his lordship late one evening when the rest of the house had retired.

For two days Cecily had inquired what the din was that appeared to be coming from the cellars. She complained she could hear it right up in her solar. Her husband dismissed her brusquely, informing her it was just improvements and repairs to an exterior wall.

She would soon learn exactly what had been going on.

One night after her enquiry, she retired late, having slipped out to meet Percival.

She had news for him, she was with child.

She had just returned to her bedchamber and climbed into bed when her door burst open, and her husband entered with two men. "Take her down," he commanded. "Unhand me, sir!" she screamed. "What is this? How dare you?" She knew in her gut what it was about. She attempted to bluff her way through, certain in the knowledge that Percival would deny any charges, too.

She was wrong!

Percival had no real inner strength and admitted his guilt upon sight of the red-hot poker.

"You are a whore and an adulteress, and I have no intention of letting your base behaviour and disgrace become common knowledge. My sons will never know the treachery and shame of their mother," spat an enraged Lord Beckett.

She was dragged, gagged, and carried to the cellar below. When she saw the place, she was filled with momentary confusion, quickly replaced by terror as she suddenly made sense of the sight before her. She was filled with panic, wriggling, bucking, kicking, and doing everything to try to break free. Her eyes were wide with fear, like a startled horse.

Edward Beckett gripped her jaw in a vice like grip. Forcing her head round to face him he said, "Why so sad, my dear? I am giving you to him, to spend the rest of your lives together. Is that not your dream?"

He pushed her then into the waiting hands of his men. She was forced against the wall. A wall within a wall, a false wall had been erected, creating a space between of about eighteen inches deep. Shackles hung from the rear wall and it was into these shackles Cecily's hands were forced.

They left her gagged, then made their way out of the cellar. A short while later they returned: a broken and barely conscious Percival Wingate was dragged across the space. He, too, was manacled; his head hung just inches from her own.

He drifted in and out of consciousness for a few minutes as the men began to finish closing up the space wherein they were bound. The last stones were about to be mortared in.

Clearly now, she understood. Edward was going to bury them alive to starve or suffocate. Again, she railed against her bonds and pulled, twisted, and kicked, to no avail.

As the last bit of light was about to disappear, Edward's face appeared in the space, a space directly in front of her face. "Ah, my dear, I recall you do not like the dark, so I shall leave a candle." He smiled his cruel smile and, using a taper, leant forward and lit the small candle on the sconce directly above Cecily's head. She could not see its size, so she would not know when the light was about to die.

The last stone was pushed in place.

Not long after the wall was completed, she heard Percival's breathing change, then stop.

The small candle in the darkness was all that held insanity at bay, but only for a few short hours. She hated that she knew not how low the candle burned.

After a while, rats had found entry to her grave. No doubt fuelled by the smell of death, their tiny feet scurried over her slippers and up her night clothes. Running over her chest and neck, all headed to Percival. They tore his eyes, his tongue, then when she was numb with fear, they started nipping at her ears, her breasts, when one tore out her left eye, she fell into the abyss.

The candle in that darkness, brought neither warmth nor comfort to Lady Cecily Beckett. It just stole the precious air and hastened her release.

Flashback

Whatever, wherever this darkness was, I did not know. Nor how I got here. Light fractured the black. Lightning flashes, the ones that can make you recall the bombing raids in old movies.

In the light I saw a child, alone, sitting on a chair, in a dim, sterile corridor. Like the ones from old civic buildings, like hospitals and schools. It is tiled from floor to a height of around four feet, in a drab, dull green.

Then it comes to me: it's the first children's home. Yet there had been nothing homely about that place.

I close my eyes tight; I really don't want to remember those awful days. I let the darkness claim me again.

Damn! The flashing lights are back, this time they are red, though. Then the image clears and settles. The red light is blinking more than flashing now.

The clouds part, I can see the taillights of the planes in front of me. Maybe twenty-five or thirty of us all in formation. I hear the familiar long ago spoken words, "Bombs away."

Why am I seeing these images, reliving these tiny dramatic plays, fragments from so long-ago moments in my life?

It's not like I'm recalling the good times, these are sad and scary.

Again, I sink into oblivion. It embraces me like a warm, comforting blanket. And I take the comfort in it – as I did in my little bear as an infant.

For only a second or two, I see me sitting on my father's knee, hugging the bear, feeling safe. Then it's gone, and my fear returns, so I let go and let the darkness surround me.

I see a flicker of candles, lots of them. Their light grows but not their flames. I'm in the church, where soon I will be married. I feel the joy, love, and excitement. I see the face of the one I love, smiling. I hear our exchange of sacred vows; we exchange rings. The hand I take is cool, the ring, warm from my hand's grip. I feel the hand that takes mine and slips the ring on my finger. I see the celebrant, serious and reverent. I am so happy.

Then a fierce wind blows the church doors open and the candles are quenched. It's dark again.

I am drawn from the dark by the sound of an infant's cry. A cry that says, "I'm hungry, hurry, feed me before I die." The child won't, of course, die but it is operating from the frontal lobe on instinct, the most primal of all our instincts, to live.

The child need someone to feed it, and it needs to let whomsoever cares for it know, they must provide sustenance. Hence the strident, urgent, panicked cries emitting from the tiny form.

The infant is my daughter, my first born. Even as a grown woman, she would be grumpy when hungry. She lies in my arms as the moonlight dies, the dark clouds extinguishing the light. Darkness creeps across the room in line with the cloud's cover of the moon.

Suddenly, a second before the light dies, my daughter's form fades from my arms. I am alone, bereft, in the dark again.

Now, the light grows slowly. I see the road leading me home.

I'm in my car, it's raining; very, very, windy too. Maybe if I get a move on, I can get home before the worst of this incoming storm hits.

I'm on the long narrow lane leading to the cottage, to home and family. To sanctuary.

There is an almighty crash of thunder, at the same moment a flurry of massive lightning bolts barrage the night sky. I hear a tremendous cracking sound. Then time slows down.

A great oak, just a little ahead on my left is rent in two. The great tree seems to be catapulted from its earthy bed. The tree and I are now locked in a perfect ballet. We come together in awesome symmetry.

Then the darkness claims me again.

I am still in the dark, but capable of conscious thought. "Lord, help me, please," I whisper.

I jump in my skin as a voice almost instantly replies, "I am here. Welcome home, my child."

The light is so brilliant now, and it shimmers with golden stars. My eyes hurt from its beauty, but the darkness is gone forever now.

In the Garden

Julia was determined to best the stubborn root.

She had bought the miners cottage in the small town of Bonnyrigg. It was perfect for her. Not a mansion, just two bedrooms, sitting room, kitchen, and bathroom. None of the rooms were overly large, but it was easily enough for her and any visitors she might have.

Julia had been working in London, for the Imperial War Museum, transcribing old documents and records onto a digital platform. It had been a fascinating, engrossing task, and Julia had loved it. She especially had enjoyed being part of the "Lives of World War I" project.

A plethora of amazing stories had been uncovered and donated. Thousands of families had loaded photos, records and her favourite items, letters. Families: lovers, friends, siblings, and neighbours all had been avid writers to their boys away fighting in the years between 1914 and 1919. Letters of survival, death, heroism, love, and of course, loss. Some had elicited a tear or two. It was to be her swansong at the Imperial War Museum, although she didn't know it at the time.

She had been approached by the curator of the National Archives of Scotland at a conference almost a year ago.

Lauder Hunter-Forrest wanted Julia to join her team in Edinburgh. The Scotland's People website and archive was a unique tool for Scots researching their family tree. It had grown and expanded over the years, and they were now looking for a new department head to take the site through its next few decades. The current head of the site was retiring the following year and Lauder had wanted Julia to step into the breach.

She had been very flattered at the offer but hadn't wanted to leave the IWM at the time she'd been approached. It never ceases to amaze how swiftly life can change, in just the blink of an eye.

Franklin, her other half, was an American, and whilst they'd never discussed it in too much detail, it was loosely accepted that they'd stay in the UK after they married. They had never set a date, nor was there a ring to show it officially; they'd just been too busy to bother. They'd agreed it was not urgent that they tie the knot as it was enough that they were happy. It would happen when the time was right. At least that had been Julia's understanding.

Just two months after she'd been approached by Ms. Hunter-Forrest, Julia had come home late one evening to find Franklin and his belongings were gone.

A note had been left by the coffee machine; in just a few lines her life was turned upside down.

He'd left, his flight back to the states had taken off as she'd had her three-p.m. meeting in Oxford. She'd gone to collect some memorabilia from the granddaughter of a WW I Voluntary Aid Detachment nurse, a VAD. This heroic nurse's letters, medals, and uniform were all perfectly preserved and were being donated to the museum.

Franklin had known she was going and would be late home because of it. "The yellow-bellied coward," she growled, as she threw the note in the bin.

Two weeks later she was in Edinburgh for another meeting with Ms. Hunter-Forrest and the head curator of the National Archives of Scotland.

The flat in London was hers: she'd sold it for a small fortune.

The miner's cottage in Bonnyrigg was just eight miles southeast of Edinburgh city centre, her office was at the east end of Princes Street, in the General Registry building. Her office window looked out at the beautiful castle and gardens. She would have a short commute to and from work, bang in the centre of one of the most beautiful cities in the world, yet she would be living almost in what could only be described as countryside. Perfect!

She loved the wee house. Decorators, and builders were now done and she'd used an eclectic mix of furniture and accessories to create an intimate and cosy home.

She delighted in opening her front door, where from the end of her hallway, bathed in natural light from the newly installed skylight, Frida Kahlo's "Frida in Green" canvas, welcomed her home.

She loved her new job and her beautiful new home. If only this blasted root would play nice and come out, she'd be able to plant the eight-foot-tall magnolia sapling.

She had to abandon her task as the light slowly faded and the need to prepare some dinner combined to determine the end of work for the day. She would begin again in the morning.

By nine the next morning Julia was in her jeans and t-shirt, kneeling by the offending piece of flora. She'd gotten her small hacksaw out and was sawing through the largest of the roots when the sound of metal on metal screeched from the twisted roots. She let out an expletive worthy of a navvy, and was both startled and embarrassed when she heard her neighbour cough and chuckle, then ask, "Are you okay over there, Julia?"

"Oh, Bill," she said standing to face her lovely neighbour over the privet hedge. "Gosh Bill, I am so sorry, my temper and mouth got the better of my good breeding there for a sec."

Bill laughed aloud and replied, "After years in the pit, there's naught you can say, hen, that I've not said or heard afore. Now tell me what caused your momentary slip of the tongue."

"This blasted bush," she said kicking it with the toe of her boot.

"Now then, seems to me you could do with a hand. Away in and get the kettle on. I'll be round in about ten minutes with help," said Bill.

"Bill, you are a darling, but really I'll manage. I don't want to put you out."

"Don't be daft. Now do as you're told and let an old man retrieve his old 'knight in shining armour' outfit."

He went out the back door chuckling, leaving Julia with a relieved smile on her face.

Almost to the second, Bill chapped on her front door; he wasn't alone.

Another man stood behind Bill. He was younger than her neighbour, but still no spring chicken. In his hand he held a root grinder.

"Go on through," she said ushering them to the back door.

Bill and Tommy were all masked up and plugged in when Julia remembered the hacksaw. She knelt and, raising the branches and some fallen foliage, reached to draw the saw blade back, exposing the metal she had hit.

Using her trowel, she dug out an old tea caddy. It was rusty, but still held traces of a beautiful blue and some gold writing.

"Well, I'm damned," said Bill, "we had one of them. The wife was given it by her mother when we got wed. Her Mother had bought it she said in nineteen thirty-six, for the coronation of the old King."

As Julia wiped it off with her pinny, she heard a clunk as she tipped it. "There's something inside. Shall we go into the kitchen to open it? I can clean it off properly, and you two can use your manly strength to get the lid off."

She winked as she turned to lead these kind retirees into her kitchen.

Bill poured the tea whilst Julia washed the years of dirt and grime off the tin. It really was quite lovely, about six or seven inches tall and cylindrical. It looked to have a picture on it of a Victorian type shop front with shoppers in the fashion of the time. A gold laurel sat below the name 'Jackson of Picadilly', also in gold.

Bill smiled and reaching to Julia said, "Okay, hen. Give it here. Let's see what treasures it holds."

She handed the tin to Bill and after ten or fifteen minutes and much grunting and groaning, the lid finally revealed its long-buried contents.

Bill tipped the contents onto an old tea towel Julia had laid on her table. It was one she'd used for decorating and ruined, so had saved it as a rag, perfect for this job.

All three sat in shock to see what precious pieces had fallen into the cloth. None could quite get their head around why someone would have buried this in their garden. One thing was certain, it had been put there after nineteen thirty-nine.

There, having been wrapped in wax paper, they'd found a small brass tin. It was from 1916. Inside they found some papers relating to the tin.

Tommy said, "I've one of these. It was my granddad's. Princess Mary sent them to all the frontline troops for Christmas that year."

"She did," said Julia, "it had tobacco or cigarettes inside, and a wee card wishing them Happy Christmas." In another piece of waxed paper, they found two lots of medals. The oldest were marked 'Cap't Lawrence Monaghan.' There was the 1914/15 Star, the British War Medal, and the Victory Medal, known affectionately as Pip, Squeak and Wilf. And, causing Julia to exclaim, "goodness," there lay a Military

Cross. A very brave man had been awarded this group of medals.

The second set had the standard campaign medals for WW II, and it also had the George Cross, the citation with it said it had been awarded to a Private L.R. Monaghan.

Julia grabbed her phone, and on the Commonwealth War Graves Commission's website, typed in the information on the WW I medal rim. Name, rank, and service number. A list of a dozen names came up, but only one was the correct regiment and service number. Lawrence Monaghan had been killed at Passchendaele on November 11th in 1917.

The Imperial War Museum showed records for the George Cross in the name of L.R. Monaghan. Having served in the army and suffered a Blighty wound, he'd volunteered with the ARP, and became a warden. He received the George Cross after his actions following a V2 rocket attack.

A house had taken a direct hit and collapsed, bringing two either side down with it. This hero ex-soldier had rescued three children from one of the houses, then went back to get the mother, who'd refused help till her children were out and safe.

The frame and roof collapsed as he endeavoured to free her. They were both killed.

Julia used her new employer's site, "Scotland's People" and Ancestry.co.uk to search for any records of the two men.

It took her about two months of researching after work. She visited the small church in Bonnyrigg and went to the war memorial there too. In the church records, she discovered records relating to both men. There were two birth records, and one marriage recorded. Both men had been christened there, and the older of the two married in that pretty church in September 1913.

His service records showed he joined up in the September of the following year, just weeks after war was declared.

He had one leave between 1914 and his death in November 1917. He left his wife and eldest son, Lawrence Robert at home when he returned to the front in the late November of 1916.

As France was being drenched in the blood of her allies at Passchendaele, Captain Baird's wife was drenching the linen of her marital bed, with the blood of a new life.

Captain Lawrence had enjoyed his wife and his eldest son Lawrie only once in that late autumn of 1916 leave. His youngest son, Ian Hendry Monaghan, was born in the July of 1917.

As soon as Julia had garnered as much information as she could, on any family members associated with these men, she posted on most of the social media sites, Facebook, Twitter, and Instagram, giving only the names, rank, and regiment of the two men, and asked if anyone knew these men's names, or relatives of theirs.

A week later, when Bill had asked if there had been any news from her tweets etc., she had aired her deep disappointment at the lack of any responses at all.

She took another look over all the records and realised she'd missed one of the census records; the 1921 records had just been released. Her search through them yielded a result. They had lived for a brief time in a village called Rosewell. Isabella Monaghan had lived in Park Neuk cottage with her sons, Lawrie and Ian, in her parents' home in Rosewell. At least they were there on the night of the census, despite their normal home being in Bonnyrigg.

She posted again, adding the latest information on the grandparents and Isabella's siblings.

Next day she'd received two messages on Facebook: The first, a woman who claimed to be the great, great, great niece of the soldier, and the second thought he was possibly the great, great grandson of the valiant Captain.

The woman was contacted first, but it turned out to be a wild goose chase caused by an error on an ancestry tree three generations earlier. It was one of the dangers of blindly copying tree information from other member's trees.

The second was a joyous revelation. Archie Lawrence Forrest-Monaghan was indeed the descendant of both the heroes. And he knew why the medals had been discarded.

Lawrie Robert Forrest-Monaghan, the oldest son of Captain Lawrence Forrest-Monaghan, had been killed in the second war; his mother had received both sets of medals within twenty-five years. She hated the sight of them. Lawrie's brother came back from World War II but was a broken man by the time he returned from the Burma railway camps.

For Isabella, there was no glory nor pride to be found in her grief. So, she always said, she put them where no-one would be inspired to rush off again to be fodder for a gun.

Archie Forrest-Monaghan was invited to tea. Bill and Tommy would join Julia and the young man who was possibly the rightful owner of these medals. Bill would be taking notes for Julia to check, to ensure no other tree errors had been made. In truth, Julia was grateful for the support, and you can never be too careful.

Captain Monaghan's descendant was only a few years Julia's senior.

She was grateful to Bill and Tommy for their input that afternoon. Archie was not only easy on the eye, he was also intelligent, funny, and so immensely proud of his antecedent.

Julia got the caddy from the Welsh dresser. When Archie opened it, his demeanour changed. The pride, awe and sorrow were written all over his face.

She gave Archie the medals that day, and her heart soon after.

He swears he gave his heart in exchange for a tea caddy.

The Ticking Clock

Sorcha focused on the ticking clock.

Ever since her very first time. It was like yesterday, her eighteenth birthday, and she was filled with equal measures of terror and excitement.

Mikhail's face, his fingers stroking her back, as she lay naked under a large soft fur, and the reassuring tick of the old grandfather clock, they had all helped keep her panic at bay, as she lay beside him and waited...

She let her mind drift back to the summer of her eighteenth year. In the May her mother had taken her to the mountains for some girl time. Her four aunts and three cousins all came too; she had looked forward to it. Usually, the boys, her father and her uncle were included on the trips to the family's chalet. How good would it be without the boys constant teasing?

Her cousins were Alana, Didi and Coco. The four were as close as any sisters could ever have been. Occasionally they appeared to be psychic, finishing each other's sentences or knowing when the phone rang, which of them it was on the line.

The second night, her mother, aunts, and her cousins, who were all approaching eighteen, gathered in the huge comfortable lounge of this luxurious mountain retreat. It was owned by the family collectively.

Her first thought after her mother finished speaking was that this was a new game, or a joke, but no-one was laughing, especially not the girls, who sat together holding hands on the sectional sofa. They were all struggling with the implications of all her mother and aunts had divulged.

All four railed and ranted at their respective parent and bombarded them with questions, each listened very carefully to all they were told.

Finally, emotionally exhausted, the girls retired to the large room they had shared since they were tiny.

Over the years, they'd played, talked out problems, shared secrets and eased each other's worries in the large comfy room overlooking the woods.

Tonight, there was but an ominous silence, broken occasionally by a sob. The ticking of the clock in the hall, gave no comfort that night. It only represented the passage of time and the death of innocence.

Sorcha suddenly had another question and flew to her mother's room. Hours later, she returned to her own bed, if not exactly happy with the new answers, she was at least less distraught.

They returned home two days later. The mothers had had much to show and share with the girls, and in some cases, they were still a little in shock. The girls were now aware and getting, at least in their head, prepared for their future. The mothers, satisfied they'd managed it well enough; all were now more accepting and relaxed at what the future would bring.

Their upcoming birthdays were looked upon as absolutely wonderful days in the life of the Vadim family.

Immigrants to America in the 1890's, they'd worked hard and now had a very lucrative business in import and exports, focusing on wines, tapestries, and furniture from the place where the Vadim family origins began. They carried their old traditions to the new country.

Then in June in the year of her majority, Sorcha met Mikhail, and fell in love.

He came to stay with her Aunt Katya and Uncle Boris for the summer. He was the son of one of the elders of the town where her great, great, grandparents had been born, and whose father was a partner in the family business.

She'd heard he and his parents were coming, and as was the custom, all the families would attend a dinner to welcome him.

Her uncle opened the door and ushered them in, making introductions as he went. Sorcha barely said 'hi' to the two oldies, before she shot passed him blowing a kiss at her Mother, and headed for Alana's room where she knew she'd find her other cousins, too.

As she bounded around the corner, she ran headlong into what felt a lot like a wall.

Looking up, she was all at once aware of a clash of emotions: anxiety, excitement, attraction and, overriding them all, was a strange sense of belonging.

The attraction bit was confusing, though, as it felt more like addiction mixed with homecoming. He was ripped and obviously no stranger to the gym. His long black hair was in a topknot man bun. His cheekbones were high and sculpted as if with a knife and he had long thick lashes framing beautiful warm brown eyes, the same ones that were laughing at her.

He introduced himself very formally. It should have felt pompous or pretentious; instead, with that divine accent, it was drop dead gorgeous, like the owner.

As she looked into his face, she spotted over his shoulder three faces peering round the door just behind him. All were grinning like Cheshire cats and wiggling their eyebrows. Finally, she managed to mumble, "Hi. Well, I'll see you downstairs. I need to go see the others."

She hurried towards the door where mere moments ago her cousins had been, and from where giggling could still be discerned.

"I shall await you without a breath. Until then!" He bowed and headed to the stairs.

Coco and Didi were on one of the beds holding their stomachs with tears rolling down their faces, Alana sat on the floor in much the same condition.

"*WHAT?*" Sorcha was livid but was not sure why. She just threw pillows and cushions at her cousins who still could not contain their glee.

She sat down trying to understand what had just happened with Mikhail and let the ticking of the clock calm her. She sometimes wondered why each family house had an identical clock and how the ticking seemed to calm her when she was anxious or afraid.

Over dinner, Mikhail was entertaining the four girls with stories of his life at home and of his closest friends, Drago, Gregor, and Tito, who all sounded like good fun guys.

All the girls agreed it was unfortunate they had not travelled with him. At which point, Mikhail's face took on a puzzled expression and Sorcha didn't miss the looks exchanged between her uncle and Mikhail. Curious, she thought. It was barely noticeable, but her uncle shook his head at the boy.

Whatever it was about, Mikhail was not pleased.

The rest of the evening went on to be a pleasant time of easy laughter and casual chatter.

Mikhail asked Sorcha if she enjoyed swimming or hillwalking. She was surprised and delighted that he, too, enjoyed the wide-open spaces. They later agreed to meet and take a trip out to Glacier Park to do some serious hill walking on the following Saturday. It was one of Sorcha's favourite places and a beautiful piece of country. Montana had an abundance of awesome rugged and stunning spots.

She loved the lush green valleys and the great pine trees that stood so tall it made your neck ache looking up to their lofty canopy. They found an easy peace in each other's company and over the summer they fell head over heels in love.

*　　*　　*　　*　　*

That sounds terribly romantic and idyllic. It does not reflect what they felt, especially Sorcha. Everything her mother told her to expect was manifesting itself, except it was one hundred percent more powerful than anything she'd imagined. Her need to touch him was overwhelming and she found herself grieving when they were apart.

"If this was love," she said to Didi one day, "then they can keep it," adding, "it feels more like addiction." She hated and loved that she physically craved his scent, touch, and the sound of his voice – though she hated the sense of dependency it invoked.

About four months into their relationship, Sorcha had organised another trip, this time into the Rockies. She also invited her cousins and half a dozen or so of their friends from school. All was fun and going very well until they stopped to swim in the lake.

Leo, one of their school friends and one of the school Jocks, suddenly picked Sorcha up and ran hell for leather, towards the water, then very unceremoniously dumped Sorcha in the freezing waves.

Everyone was watching and laughing so loud they didn't at first notice Mikhail as he tore down the path and grabbed Leo by the scruff of his neck, then turned him into a sledgehammer of a punch.

Leo went down like a pack of cards and there was a moment's silence before everyone was yelling variations of, "What the hell's the matter with you?"

Sorcha was standing knee deep in the water, staring at Mikhail.

Across his shoulder was the most beautiful tribal tattoo she'd ever seen. She was so stunned she failed to notice the gasps as she passed the rest of the group all gathered around Leo. She was spellbound at this growing artwork.

Mikhail became aware of the speculative looks. When Sorcha reached him, he walked around her, and sure enough, across her shoulder was the same markings in negative.

He pulled his shirt from his rucksack and covered her. She would have sworn she heard him growl at the others and hiss, "*Femeia mea*," (my woman) though she would not learn its meaning for some time.

That evening, Sorcha and Mikhail were summoned to her uncle's home again; her parents, too, had been called in.

Her uncle wasted no time on pleasantries. "I assume we are all aware of the momentous happenings today between these two young ones."

Mikhail smiled across at her. She was missing something. He'd decked her friend for no reason, behaved like a caveman, and all but dragged her home like a wayward dog.

Suddenly she heard her name, breaking her momentary sojourn from reality, and focused on what her uncle was saying:

"They need to marry before November when we all gather in the old country for the festival. Mikhail would be driven to distraction with so many single males there. There would be intense attention on Sorcha as a single girl. The men would all be searching for a life mate, and testosterone levels will be high – "

Her uncle went to continue but Sorcha interrupted.

"Wait, wait… Who must marry whom?"

Her father replied, "You and Mikhail of course. Your markings are the sign of the mating bond, Each a mirror image of the other. This bond declares a love that will last forever. He will love you, offer his life for your protection, and die if required to keep you safe."

"Well, that's all fine and dandy, but I do not want to marry. I'm too young. Can't we just go on as we are till, well, until I'm older and finished college?" Sorcha offered.

"No, *Nici o fato*, (my daughter) in two weeks your markings will be almost complete. By then, you must be married. The power of your bond will demand your union."

Sorcha's mother spoke, "Let me take Sorcha to the city this weekend. We can buy her wedding dress and I can have this time to make her understand all that is happening."

Her uncle looked hard at Sorcha and gently said, "Go with your mother, but understand we do not say this MUST happen without great love for you both. In time, you will understand. We are to blame for your confusion. We were so busy protecting you young ones, we forgot to teach you who and what you will be."

"Sorcha," it was Mikhail, "know this, *Inema mea*, (my heart) all but the date of our marriage will be on your terms. Your happiness is my responsibility from this day, and I swear I will not fail you."

For some strange reason, she believed his every word, and was comforted by them.

Sorcha and her mother, Elena, spent many hours talking and discussing the ways of their people and the secrecy they surrounded themselves in. Sorcha got it; this was all just freakin' out there. It had hit her life like an atomic bomb, and she was struggling with it.

However, she also found she dreamed of Mikhail and physically ached to be near him. By Sunday morning, having found the "knock out dress," she pleaded to be taken back to be with Mikhail. It hurt so much to be away from him; she now began to understand why.

Her markings had developed and were now almost fully down her spine. A beautiful T shape in ancient tribal art, and she loved it and couldn't wait to see Mikhail's.

Their wedding was an ancient traditional ritual, a priest from home had travelled with so many relatives that the customs officer jokingly asked, "Is this an invasion"?

The venue was no great surprise to the bride and groom, who by this time, didn't care where, so long as it was soon.

Their day dawned with clear blue skies and light winds. They'd travelled the night before to the family-owned summer house in the foothills of the Rockies, to find staff had been busy, having had rooms prepared and the tables and chairs laid out on the lawn by the lake. They had decorated the whole place with garlands and flowers for the wedding. Potted plants and gazebos in pastel colours were decorated and crockery all carried the vivid patterns Sorcha recognised from her visits to the old country.

The cousins were excited as Mikhail's friends had arrived and were all getting on famously – which was a blessing as they were all bridesmaids or groomsmen.

The girls swooned and ooh'd, and ah'd over Sorcha's bridal gown, and the dresses she'd chosen for them.

All of theirs were a dark blood red. Lace over satin shifts, with one shoulder sporting only a string strap under an inch-wide strip of lace and nothing over the other shoulder, accentuating the beautiful line of their shoulders and neck. The bodices were snugly fitted with a line of sparkling

Swarovski gems below the bustline of the simple shift that fell in folds to the floor.

Sorcha's was winter white and covered her back and shoulders and had a mandarin collar that circled her throat. Below that was a V-shape cut away that plunged between her breasts and almost reached her navel. The design hid, as modesty demanded, every bit of her almost complete markings.

She felt very sexy and grown up. Her hair was hanging in loose waves and curls and she wore only a circlet of wildflowers in her hair. She was a vision of beauty, purity, and youth.

As she walked down the aisle towards him, Mikhail thought his heart would burst. His knees threatened to buckle, and he was stifling the urge to howl out loud from joy. He was so full and overwhelmed by the intensity of his emotions. He knew he'd never hesitate to give his life for hers. He loved her with his whole heart. He also felt such passion for her, his inner beast was prowling, at least that was the only way he could describe it.

After the ceremony, her mother whispered, "Sorcha, it is time. The sun is going down. Do not be afraid. This is a wonderful thing and what you have will evolve into something so much more than the love you feel, or could ever imagine."

Mikhail was by her side, "Come, *Inima mea*," (my heart). He led her to the large chalet, given over to the couple for their wedding night. The master suite was at the top of the stairs next to where the grandfather clock stood. The room was beautiful and the canopy above the bed was covered in Jasmine flowers and fairy lights. Crisp white sheets and the finest furs covered the bed. A table had been laid with wine and finger food, and a fire was burning in the huge fireplace.

Mikhail took her in his arms and softly kissed the top of her head.

"We can wait. There's no rush. We have our whole lives ahead of us. When you are ready, my love. I will try to be a patient husband, but do not doubt that the very scent of you drives me to distraction," he laughed.

She looked up into his dark smouldering eyes and knew she was ready, at least for one part of tonight's rituals.

Hours later, lying in his arms, she whispered, "Miki I'm ready."

He sat up and took her hands in his, "*Lubirea mea* (my love), are you certain?"

"Yes, my love, I'm ready." It took less than two minutes; they'd spread the furs on the floor before the fire, and after the sacred rites were done, they lay naked in each other's arms. She thought the teeth would have hurt more but it seemed like the most natural thing in the world.

Now, she felt so alive, and the ticking of the clock on the landing seemed so much louder tonight, yet still her heart slowed into the rhythm of its tick, tock, tick, tock.

The moon had just made its appearance from behind the clouds when suddenly she felt it. Her mother had said she'd feel it first in her hands and feet, but it happened so fast she barely had time to say, "Miki," before it was done, she could smell him so strongly, she opened her eyes, the transformation was astonishing.

Before her was a large black and grey wolf. She was startled at its size but the eyes... they'd not changed: her Mikhail stood before her. She thought, "Am I such a beautiful animal as he?" In her head, she heard his voice say, "Such a beautiful wife in all your forms. And yes, my love, we can read the other's thoughts."

She laughed and headed for the stairs. "I want to see if I'm as fast as you. Could I escape you in this guise?"

They spent the whole night running, playing, feeding, and never seemed to tire. As dawn approached, they came home. As they lay on the skins and returned to their human form, she heard Mikhail gasp, "You are so beautiful. Your markings have finished. They are amazing," he pulled her into his arms and they slept.

When they returned to Lone Pine, her cousins were full of questions, about the ritual, her wedding night, and wanted to see her back. They, too, gasped in wonder at the intricate design. Sorcha sat back watching her cousins, who were her best friends, and hoped they'd find the kind of love she shared with Mikhail.

Three years later she is again lying on the furs in the master suite near Columbia Falls, Mikhail is holding her, and the midwife is kneeling, watching her. The pains were coming hard and fast now.

Sorcha focused on the ticking clock and felt at peace with the world as she delivered their precious son.

She must remember, finally, to ask why they all had the clocks: where did that tradition come from?

The Telephone Call

Jenny heard the phone ring, groggy from the depth of her slumber. She squinted at the clock: 3:47 a.m. No call after 11 p.m. and before 8 a.m. was ever going to be good. She so did not want to answer. In fact, she decided, she would indeed refuse to pick it up. After what seemed an eternity, whoever was on the other end rang off.

Jeffrey had been her childhood sweetheart. Now, they were engaged and had plans to save hard and marry on the anniversary of Jeff's proposal. It had been set for April 18th, 1942, but Hitler and his cronies had put paid to that.

Now the wedding was indefinitely postponed.

Her dress, made from parachute silk, hung in its long canvas suit carrier in her bedroom. A large grey hat box sat atop the wardrobe that held her dress. Inside were the veil and head dress, the garter and the box containing her grandmother's pearls. Her mother and her Nana had enjoyed wonderful, happy marriages, and both had worn those pearls on their wedding day.

Her bottom drawer was chock-a-block. There were quality cotton sheets and pillow slips which her mother had patiently embroidered with hyacinth for constancy and chrysanthemum for fidelity.

The table linen had dainty daffodils. They were for appreciation or forgiveness. Her mother knew that her daughter was not an instinctive cook and foresaw some teething disasters in her daughter's kitchen of the future.

That Jeff should appreciate her efforts and forgive her failings was her maternal hope in each tiny stitch.

Her going away outfit was carefully folded in a suitcase Jenny had bought especially for the honeymoon.

The same case held new lacy undergarments and a very racy black lace negligee set, like one she'd seen on a star of the silver screen. That was what her Jeff would see her in on their wedding night.

As soon as war was declared, she knew her lovely Jeffrey would be in the line to volunteer, it was just who he was.

Duty, responsibility, honour, all the qualities she so loved about him, how she'd hated them in those awful weeks. Weeks where she'd begged, cried, and begged some more. All to no avail.

Eventually she realised, she loved the whole of him and must accept him whole or not at all, including, and especially those, characteristics.

Those same traits that were now to put him in harm's way: he wanted to be a pilot.

A chap he knew, a friend, had a small plane. It was bought cheap from an auction when a company that had made parts for the Royal Flying Corps since the beginning of the Great War, closed up shop. The company had continued after the RFC amalgamated with the Royal Naval Air Service in 1918 but sadly failed in the depression. It had been used to deliver parts all over Europe to the newly formed, RAF.

Danny had picked it up cheap when the company was auctioned off.

He and Jeff flew together frequently, and Jeff was hooked.

Jeffrey was born in 1920, a baby born in the shadow of the war to end all wars. Now, not quite twenty-five years later, here he was, taking up the torch, thrown in the poem by John McRae, *In Flanders Fields*.

Both Jenny and Jeffrey had family who'd served and lived through that awful four years, three months, and thirteen days, days filled first with pride, parades, and bravado, to be soon followed by news reels, casualty lists and grief. Jenny knew what the wake of war looked like.

Many of her friends grew up never knowing their fathers except through a photo and stories. Others never knew the man who'd been at their conception. Only the broken wrecks or angry men who had returned from hell.

Men who had the name and look of their father, but who, thereafter, held but a faint resemblance.

Jeff had been sent north after his training ended, then he was posted to far flung, exotic named places, and now he was in Europe, at least she thought he was.

In late spring 1945, a chum from his unit, home on leave, had brought her news and a letter. Apparently, Jeff was now to be this man Jack's squadron leader when the man's leave was over.

His letter hinted they were to be part of the final push, hounding the Jerries all the way to Berlin. He also said it was truly almost over, that Jeff could really be home in time for Christmas.

Jack would never know that his news, meant to reassure her, had sent her anxiety levels through the roof.

Jenny was now so afraid her lovely fiancé would be snatched from her in these last desperate days of the war.

So, at 3:47 a.m. that night in August 1945, she believed her worst fears had been realised. She didn't want to hear the faceless voice of some officer, or padre, telling her of his regret, how brave Jeffrey had been, or of his sorrow, or any of their damned platitudes.

She refused to move into another day without him in it. She concluded if she ignored the calls and never heard the words, then it wasn't true.

The phone rang again at 5:45 and 9:15. By twelve when there'd been no further calls. She anticipated they'd send one of those awful telegrams.

She determined that she would refuse to answer the door. If that lad from the village, the one who delivered those terrible, sparse, and devastating telegrams leant his bike outside her cottage, she would not answer his knock.

At 13:30 hrs, he did just that. And she did not answer.

He posted the thing through the letter box.

"No, No, No, I will not let it be true," she wailed and threw the diabolic thing on the fire.

By 4p.m. the house had been cleaned from top to bottom. The rabbit that her gamekeeper neighbour had brought round yesterday was gently cooking with a piece of ham fat and vegetables from her garden in the range's large oven. It was a favourite of Jeffrey's. The potatoes would go on soon, fluffy white mash and rabbit stew, perfect. It would bring memories of other times when she'd cooked his favourite meal. Times when peace had reigned.

She'd gone to freshen up and, raising her face from the hand basin. she caught her reflection in the mirror. The eyes challenged her, challenged her behaviour. *"What are you doing? He is dead. You have to face this,"* they seemed to whisper.

Resolve dissolved and the tears tore through the dam of disbelief, and she sobbed, slumped on the cold bathroom flagstones.

A little later, she'd almost cried herself out when she heard her back door open, Caroline from next door often popped round about then for a natter and a cuppa, and usually came with a fish or, like yesterday, a rabbit from her gamekeeper husband.

She sluiced her face quickly then patted it dry, then hurried down the stairs.

She walked into the kitchen saying, "Hello, Caroline. Shall I -- " Before she could finish the sentence, she was struck dumb, for it was not Caroline.

There in her kitchen, large as life, stood her Jeff. Thinner, gaunt, tired, and smiling, was her man, in the flesh, alive.

After much hugging and kissing and crying, he said, "I tried ringing you, before I took off in Germany, when I landed, and again at the train station.

"When I couldn't get you on the last call, I sent you a telegram, didn't you get it? Where were you?"

212

More tears were shed as she explained what she'd thought in response to that call in the early hours.

Through the telling of it all, he held her, her beautiful husband to be. He was home, comforting and protecting her, just as he promised he would when he proposed.

What a Revelation

Cat hadn't been home for three years. Her father's sudden marriage to her stepmother when she was but eight years old had precipitated her being delivered up to a boarding school, one of the best in the country. Nevertheless, it was a banishment borne out of her stepmother's disdain for Catriona- Rae.

Over the interceding years she had returned to her father's home on high days and holidays only – until the Christmas when she was twelve.

Her stepmother had redecorated throughout her home. Only her father's study was left untouched by her hand.

Her father had also given his den a "do over." He'd added Tudor style panelling and lots of glass-fronted bookshelves. This was the one and only time she had entered what her biological mother used to jokingly call "the inner sanctum."

It had always been off limits, even to his precious daughter.

Cat's home no longer looked like her home, and she felt like an intruder.

She'd watched, too, as her father changed over those years. Gone was the fun loving, laughing man she'd adored as a little girl. No longer did they go punting in the summer on the river that flowed past the bottom of the garden.

Even his beloved easel had been banished to the shed.

She'd asked him once when she was home on an Easter break if he'd like to get it out. They'd go together to a favourite spot on the river to try and capture the onset of spring: ducklings, daffodils, and wonderful scudding clouds.

Her stepmother answered before her father had had the chance. "No, darling, your father has to be careful now. He's not as young as he used to be, you know. And he'll get filthy on the riverbank."

She saw her father deflate in front of her very eyes. She knew then that she, stepmother Arabella, ruled this roost.

Cat refused to go home during holidays at every chance she got. Her Dad occasionally insisted; those were the rare occasions that she did return. She hated to see him beaten like that. It was as if all the life had been sucked out of him. She rarely saw him smile and never, did she hear his laughter or see the twinkle in his eyes anymore.

Three years ago, the sixteen-year-old Cat was in history class. It was the last week of the term before she was due to go home for the Christmas break. The principal entered the class and called her out.

Catriona followed Miss O'Leary to her private parlour. By the time they arrived at the door, she was trembling, it had to be serious to be invited to her private rooms.

"Catriona, I'm afraid I have some very sad news for you. Your stepmother just telephoned to tell us that your father passed away. I know it has been expected, but nonetheless this is a sad day for you, dear."

Catriona was nonplussed, "What do you mean 'expected,' Miss O'Leary?"

"Well, dear. We have known this was coming since last June when your father was diagnosed with stage 4 cancer."

Something in my face must have alerted Miss O'Leary and she said, "You *did* know he'd been given the news that his condition was terminal, did you not?" Miss O'Leary looked askance at the girl.

"No, Miss, I didn't! I hate that woman!" she cried out in pain; "she has stolen all those hours we could have had together; I will never set foot inside that house again whilst she's in it."

As it happened, this suited Arabella too, for if she'd disliked Cat before, she positively hated her after the will was read.

Her father had found some gumption in those last months. He'd found and paid for a small bungalow that he left for Arabella along with half his savings and current account balances.

The house Cat had been born and raised in, her mother's home, was left to her with all her parents' jewellery and any and all capital and investments he'd owned, especially any he'd inherited from his wife.

After consultations with her father's solicitor, she instructed him to inform Arabella that she may stay in the house until Catriona's studies finished, two years hence. If she were prudent, she would have a tidy nest egg put by if she rented the bungalow out in the meantime.

Catriona did this in memory of her father. It should serve Arabella well in the years to follow.

Those two years soon flew by in a way you least expect in the wake of such a loss, but life does go on, in spite of us.

Cat had been cut off from her father for so long before he died that it impacted little on her day-to-day life, though she did miss him terribly at times.

She threw herself into life at university. She was in the first teams for both the rowing and the debating society. In combination with the awesome social life students enjoy, and her part time job in the local bar, she really had little time to mope anyhow.

Then, in what seemed like no time at all, her courses were finished, the results were in, two firsts, great grades across the board. It was time to go home.

Mr. Bruce had written to say he'd received notice from Arabella that she had left the house and had enclosed the keys. A visit to the property by himself confirmed it was empty and ready for her arrival home.

Catriona arrived home in the second week in June. The sun was shining, the house and gardens looked so wonderful, and the knowledge that the she-devil was not inside let her experience a warm glow of peace that settled on her as she opened the front door to her childhood home.

In a moment of wistful thought, she mused it was maybe the spirits of her parents there to welcome her home at last.

She'd accepted an offer of employment with an editing company and could work from home for the most part. With that in mind, Catriona had determined to re-do the whole house but especially her father's den. She'd contracted a builder and decorator, and chosen a palette of pale greys, off white, sage green, and lavender throughout the house. Mr. Murphy assured her it would be done in 10 days. She was determined to wipe any trace of Arabella from her home.

They were fair whizzing through the work.

This morning they'd begun the "inner sanctum."

Later, at about 2 p.m., Mr. Murphy knocked on the kitchen door where Catriona was amending some work before dispatching it off to head office. She wasn't really very enthusiastic when he said, "Miss, you need to come see this before I carry on with the room."

Somewhat begrudgingly, she followed him through the beautiful, light, and welcoming hall.

"It's on the wall behind the door," he said stepping aside and not following her in. His two sidekicks were by the front door, looking very sheepish.

Cat entered the room. Upon turning around and closing the door, she had a clear view of the wall where her father's desk had been.

All the panels had been removed. The revelation was the most glorious painting, obviously done by her father, of her beautiful mother, when she was about twenty-five years old.

Apart from the obvious fact that the painter adored his muse, and her father had perfectly caught the look that divulged the love the subject held for her artist, the astonishing fact was that that her mother wore only a fabulous smile and a gossamer scarf strategically draped to protect her modesty. Catriona was amazed and delighted in equal measure. The painting had to have been done at the time of the panelling. She chuckled now as she recalled Arabella's complaints that her father had insisted on doing it himself and it taking him so long, when a decorator could have done it in half the time.

The sly old fox: the knowledge of its existence, must have sustained him till the end, of what had come to be such an unhappy time for her darling father.

"Mr. Murphy, this will stay. Can you adapt the colours and design to accommodate and best compliment this, please?" she asked with a laugh.

"That'll be no problem at all, and it'll just be me that'll finish this room. The lads will not see its inside again.

Two months later Catriona-Rae sat in her captain's chair swivelling on the wheels surveying her new office. She was so incredibly happy with the results and not just in here. The whole house was now marked with only her stamp, and only her mother's image and her father's talent now touched the fabric of her family home.

The Archaeological Find.

Bridie had been out since first light. Since the arrest of her father by the British soldiers, it had fallen on her to gather the peat to keep a fire burning in their little cottage. She was on open land, or common land as the British called it. It belonged to no English Lord, but to the people of Ireland.

The cottage was just two rooms and a hut out back for the lavvy. Cooking was done over the fire. It wasn't fancy like the big house: no grand chandeliers or thick Persian carpets. But to Bridie it was heaven when the stew pot was simmering o'er the fire, the candles lit, casting a golden glow. With her sister sat on her mammy's lap on the rocking chair, Bridie would be sat at her feet. Oh, then, then she was so happy.

There her mother recited the stories of the heroes of Ireland's past, or from the Bible.

She could not have been happier, nor more blessed, except on the rare occasion when her Mammy sang the old songs in the Gaelic tongue. Oh, that was heaven indeed to young Bridie.

That wintery morning Bridie was struggling. She'd taken a chill and now shivered despite the heat on her face. She was almost done when her small peat spade hit something solid.

She cursed, then felt the shame, the shame she'd have felt had her Mammy or Dada heard her profanity, or worse, Father Daniel.

She knelt and using her blue tinted fingers that were stiff from the cold, she cleared away the dirt around the object.

It took a few minutes, but each handful of earth removed, increased her excitement until at last, it was free.

She'd never seen anything like it except once on a painting in the big house.

An ancient ancestor of the original owner of the fort-like house. Some ancient Celtic Queen. The object was shaped like a sort of horseshoe, but not so open at the back end. Where the nail holes would be on the horseshoe were glistening stones of red, white, and emerald, like the grasses on the heath in summertime. The stone's colours were against a background of a gold tinted red, like the setting sun, or the fancy letters in the Bible at home.

She wrapped it up and picked up the two heavy pails of peat and headed for home. When she showed her mother, she gasped, then she sent Bridie for a jug of water from the pump. Her mother then warmed it over the fire and using only her fingers, she slowly and carefully washed the thing until it gleamed and sparkled in the firelight.

A little later when the haar had cleared revealing a bright sunny morning, they took the piece outside, and there its true glorious colours sprang to life. Each piece of the coloured stones had flashes and prisms of colours in every hue Bridie's eyes had ever beheld. The base of this object showed it was not a single colour, for it looked like three strands had been braided, two in a soft, rich gold and one of an almost white silver. The silver created a beautiful accent through the plait. It was magical and wonderous.

Her mother said, "Tomorrow we go to my brother's home. I've a mind to see your Uncle Mick. You mind that you say nothing of this to anyone." Bridie nodded, she felt, rather than understood the need for secrecy.

Next morning, as her mother had arranged, they met farmer O'Mara with his cart at the crossroads. He was heading to Cork to the market. He often allowed Mercy O'Donoghue and her children to climb on the back of the cart and they'd travel to Cork. He'd set up his stall and Mercy would visit her brother and get her supplies at the days end when the prices were lower. Today was to be no different. They'd leave Jimmy O'Mara at the market cross and meet him back there at four for their lift home.

They made their way through the market square and out onto the main road. Michael O'Donoghue's face broke into a wide smile at the sight of his younger sister and her girls.

"Mercy, ah sure, but aren't you a sight for sore eyes, so you are. What are you doing here so unexpected like. Is everything alright?"

Mercy embraced her brother, who pulled her into a bearhug that lifted her feet off the floor. She laughed and said, "Aye, it's grand to see you too, Mick. I've need of your advice is all. But it can wait till you break for a bite and a rest. I'll away through and see Maggie and the bairns. I'm parched, and I'll lay odds Maggie's kettle is boiling as we speak."

"Aye. Away through. I'll be done in a bit, but it's grand to see you!"

When Michael sat down and had finished his cheese, soda bread and a mug of ale, Mercy explained the reason for their visit. From her chatelaine, she unhooked a soft drawstring bag; this she opened and from it drew the piece that Bridie had found.

The intake of breath from both Michael and his wife was audible and they looked on in wonder.

Michael recovered first. "Where did this come from?" His voice was quiet and unusually serious.

"I didn't steal it, if that's what's niggling your mind. For shame on you, to not know me better than to even think that, Michael Shamus O'Donoghue!" Mercy was hurt at the thought.

"Now, lass, I never said that, now did I?" he smiled, "but, I need to know exactly where you got this. It's important and will influence what we do next. This Torque will change your life, and where you found it will determine whether for the good or otherwise. Now tell me."

Bridie spoke then and recounted the morning's peat collection and the details of the find on the common land on the top of the slope above where they lived at the bottom of Keyser's Hill.

Michael O'Donoghue was grinning from ear to ear, "Are you certain it was up on Keyser's Hill?"

"It was, Uncle Mick, about halfway across the common above the Lee."

"Ah, Sweet Jesus, Mercy, if I'm right about what I think this is, you'll be a rich woman, so you will, and no mistake."

"What do you mean, Mick?" said Maggie.

"If I'm right, this is a Viking highborn woman's torque. The stones are rubies, emeralds and diamonds and it's gold and silver they are set in. And it's Irish gold of that I'm certain. The strands are braided gold and silver, two gold to one silver."

It took Michael three months to travel to Copenhagen in Denmark. He had written to the curator of the museum in the Danish capital before setting out.

When he arrived, word had been left that not only was his meeting for two days hence with the curator, but also attending would be some important Danish government officials. They were extremely interested in his letter's content.

He found the men in a state of high spirits and excitement, which after he'd shown them the piece and recounted where it had been discovered, they were almost euphoric. This was an especially important find for the Viking people.

Michael was so excited when he left their offices, he wished he had Mercy and his wife there to speak to. It was astonishing to think that the name of his family would be remembered in perpetuity in the museum, as the finder of this ancient piece of royal jewellery. *Life can be surprising, can it not?*" he thought as he almost danced his way back to his lodgings.

He wrote a letter and sent it post-haste to Mercy. The wait was agonising, not only for him, but the men of Viking blood too.

Finally, the day came when Mercy and Bridie disembarked in Copenhagen. The following day, a second meeting had been arranged with the same men and his sister and his niece.

When they left, the Danes had explained that they'd checked the legality of ownership through their solicitors and in a hypothetical consultation with the British. It was indeed Bridie and Mercy's property. Mercy left with a banker's draft for £2,500 to be drawn in the Bank in Cork.

When the sale had been finalised, the Danes announced their purchase and the wondrous archaeological find. They sent images to London museums offering to allow an exhibition of the piece at a date to be determined if it was of interest. The British government did try to challenge the sale.

However, the documented hypothetical dialogue and the maps confirming the find site was on common ground and not the crown's, settled the matter swiftly.

Mercy applied to the jail to purchase her husband's freedom by paying the fine for his grazing of sheep on Crown land. Bridie had been wrong, heaven was the addition to the cottage, a bedroom just for her and a feather bed to boot.

Uncle Michael invested the gift of £500 from Bridie, for as her Mammy and Dada said, "Sure it was her that dug it up, it's hers". She had her father deposit £1,000 in the bank in an account in her name and gave the other £1000 to her Mammy and Dada. It was a rare find indeed.

Well, I Never Expected That!

Jeanette lay languishing in front of the log fire, a large glass of pinot grigio on the side table alongside a giant bar of her favourite chocolate. They were testament to her total lack of self- discipline. She'd intended this to be a sort of pre-Christmas detox.

A week in this country cottage on the edge of the Devon -Cornwall border would be picture postcard perfect. It was a place where time stopped, with log fires, grandfather clocks, roll top baths, wooden beams, and four-poster beds, just like in a fairy tale.

However, she was aware of the perfection being tainted a little, the niggling thought at the back of her mind, Geordie hadn't batted an eyelid when she said she was going away alone for a week. For some reason yet to be identified, she'd felt disappointed.

It was her first night there and, after a microwaved lasagne and more pinot, she'd spent a good hour basking by candlelight in the roll-top bath, reclining until only her head cleared the water and mass of bubbles. She'd primped and pampered herself before donning her pj's and warm fluffy dressing gown and socks.

Suddenly, there was a loud knock on the door. "Who is it?" she said through the door. "It's me, love, let me in its bitter out here."

She hastily opened the door. "What are you doing here?" she asked.

"All week, it's been driving me crazy knowing I wouldn't be seeing you for seven whole days. After I waved you off this morning, I decided I needed to follow you."

He knelt beside his rucksack. Pulling something out, he turned and looked up at her. "Marry me, Nettie, please. I never want to spend even one day apart ever again.

"I realised as I pondered a week without you, I want us to be married, I'd have been here sooner, but drove over a nail or something that ruptured the tyre, took an age to sort out. Will you marry me, please, Nettie?"

She squealed as she nodded grinning and all at once laughing and crying.

The Grail

The tiny ray of refracted light stole in through the slender crack in the masonry of the alcove which held the piece of glorious goldwork crafted in the mists of time. As the sun rose in the sky outside, this sliver of sunlight lit upon the ancient altar and illuminated the most famous artifact the world has ever sought.

Alistair had been speechless when he'd gone to the National Records Office of Scotland in Edinburgh. He'd been excited as he ascended the steps up behind the statue of Wellington on his horse. As a child, he'd always referred to it as his Papa's statue. It reminded him of a photo which hung in his Nana's home: a black and white image of a soldier sat high on his huge grey mount, arrayed in full uniform, sword drawn and resting on his shoulder.

In Rhodri's childish mind, they were one and the same horse and rider. Speaking in a voice reserved for the library or chapel, he announced his arrival for the meeting set up for eleven a.m. with a research professor in the genealogy department.

"Ah, Alistair, I presume?" Most people referred to him as Rhodri, although Alistair was his first name. Since his early childhood, his parents had always only used his middle name. For the purposes of investigating his family tree, he had to avail the expert genealogist of his full name as it appeared on his birth certificate.

"Yes, Professor. Alistair Rhodri Sinclair. Please call me Rhodri. It's awfully good of you to see me, and for all your help online."

Rene Gilchrist guided Rhodri through the security and down the hall to a comfortable sitting room come office.

"My dear boy, I have some wonderful news for you. The point in your paternal tree where you hit a dead end was due to a remarkably simple error made earlier in your research. On the timeline around two hundred years ago."

"You mean my hard -won information going back to the Ninth Century was a waste of time?"

Rene smiled at Rhodri, "It really was an easy mistake to make. One doesn't expect a regular 'John Doe' to be the son of 'Sir John Doe,' unless, of course, you're researching in a time or country in conflict and upheaval, as was Scotland in the Eleventh Century.

Your ancestor, Sir Francois Saint Clair, married Eleanor Doig of Perthshire. They had a son whom they named John Saint Clair. He sided with William Wallace and Andrew de Moravia, when Edward the First, known as the "Hammer of the Scots" interfered in Scottish affairs. That began a time of terrible upheaval and civil conflict.

Their son, John, fought with Bruce at Bannockburn. Sadly, for the Saint Clair family, in 1603, when finally the unrest culminated in the Union of the Crown and the subsequent subjugation of Scotland's people, they were on the wrong side.

Many lairds, barons, knights, and princes lost their titles and land and some their heads too. And here... Sir John Saint Clair became plain old John Sinclair. Therein lies the point of your error."

Rhodri listened intently to Rene, who was bringing his ancestors to life.

Rene leant back in the comfy wing backed chair and continued, "I have followed the new correct line back to the year 40 B.C. and the really exciting news: that your line leads to the Merovingian Line."

"Isn't that the fantasy bloodline, from the "Da Vinci Code?" Rhodri asked laughing.

"That's the line yes, but it's no fantasy. Mary Magdalene and Christ had a child, sent or taken as an infant to France for her protection. This bloodline flows from her to you in a direct line. You are descended from Christ himself."

"What? You are kidding me, surely?"

"I most certainly am not, and what's more, there's a research thread online. Someone is searching for descendants of Francois Saint Clair, searching for you!"

Rhodri left having arranged a further meeting with Rene for a month hence. He wanted time to go through the dozens of boxes in his parent's home. It had been the sudden loss of both parents in a freak car accident two years ago that had propelled him into researching his tree. He hadn't realised how little he knew of his family until his parents were no longer there to ask. His paternal grandparents had passed before he was born, and his mother's parents were dead by his twelfth birthday. He was an only child, as was his father. There were no aunts or uncles to go to for any help with his tree, either.

Two weeks later, Rhodri was in the attic of the old baronial hall that was his childhood home, bought by his great grandfather with money made on the stock exchange in the early part of the century. Alistair was sat in a rickety old rocking chair, going through a trunk. As he threw the last thick volume of "A History of the Templar Knights" back into it, he heard a distinct click. Investigating further, he discovered a secret partition in the back of the trunk.

The panel fell forward, revealing a tome of some very dry, old looking papers, and an envelope, apparently addressed to him!

He sat back in astonishment as he examined the envelope. It was addressed to him alright, but not in the hand of either of his parents. His curiosity was piqued, so he carefully opened it. If he was intrigued at the find, it was mild by comparison to his emotions upon reading the cryptic and undated text on the page.

Salutations, Alistair,

You who reads this now is of my blood. We may never have met, but powers higher than you and I will guide your hand to find this. Just as they guided your parents to call you by the name you carry. Only a man named so will have been endowed with the character to do what must be done and who will have the intellect and the funds to foil your enemies and keep your heirloom safe from those with evil hearts.

God go with you, my boy.

With affection,

Your ancestor,

Sir Alistair Henry Saint-Claire.

Rhodri almost fell off the chair. He also almost laughed aloud. But, he had, if he was honest with himself, to admit his first response to the news was one of, *"at last, my purpose is revealed."* And after acknowledging that, he almost laughed again. *"How strange all this is,"* he mused.

Just then, his mobile rang, an unknown number. "Hello?"

"Good afternoon. Mr. Alistair Sinclair, please?"

For reasons too unclear, Rhodri went on his guard. "Who may I ask is calling?"

"Of course, *excusez moi*, my name is Michele Dupont, a distant relative of Mr. Sinclair, is he available?"

"May I inform him of the nature of your call, *Monsieur* Dupont?"

"Just tell him it will be beneficial to us both if we might meet."

Rhodri replied, "Mr. Sinclair is not at home at the present, but I will be happy to give him your message upon his return. He will call, I'm sure."

There was a click, and the line went back to the dial tone.

How strange and rude, he thought. He also thought it an odd coincidence that on the very day he gets a letter warning him to beware of evil hearted people, he is suddenly contacted by a previously unheard-of relative!

He headed for the kitchen, setting the percolator on for some much-needed caffeine. He sat at the large refectory table and re-read the letter then returned to the attic and brought down the rest of the papers. As they spread onto the table in the kitchen, he spotted a fresh-looking envelope he'd missed previously.

Inspecting the writing, he realised this letter was penned by his father's hand. He opened it, hungry to find a way of feeling the connection he always found between him and the father he sorely missed. It began in the same familiar address his father had always lovingly used:

Dearest Boy,

How sad I am knowing that if you are reading this, they have succeeded and our demise was in all probability an assassination, albeit appearing to be an accident, just as it was with my father. I pray that they have left you your mother, but I am not optimistic now that I know they have discovered us and our whereabouts. As I write this, I know they draw close. The need to keep you safe was your mother and I's life's work. It was the reason we only ever used your middle name, Rhodri. I implore you not to ever use your given first name. It will draw attention to you and put your life in the gravest of danger.

I don't have long to write this as we are leaving for the Czech Republic tomorrow, where I assume my post in the Embassy in Moravia. I doubt they'll think we'd return to the source of our bloodline. However, it is obvious I must leave things to help prepare you if the worst occurs. It will be hard, dear boy, for you to grasp what I will share with you. Just as it was for me when my father was killed. I learnt of our inheritance in a letter, too.

Well, here goes: We are direct descendants from Christ and Mary Magdalene. I have left your inheritance hidden in the troue de pretre. You must guard it with your life.

Father to son this task has passed since the death of Our Lord. The power of the Goblet is phenomenal, but mankind is not yet ready. Evil rules too much of the world.

Until the Father is ready, we must keep it safe and hidden.

Our love for you is eternal son, God keep you.

Your loving father.

The letter continued, but in a change of handwriting:

PS, My darling son, I beseech you to take care of yourself and the family you will eventually have. Family, love, and children, it's all that is important to make you happy. We miss you.

Your loving mother.

xx

A stray tear fell from his nose, the first since the funeral. It opened a floodgate and for the longest time he just sat and cried and let the pain wash over him. To lose both parents is traumatic enough as an accident, but to believe it was murder was too hard to bear.

Later, as darkness fell and shadows crept across the kitchen through the French doors that led to the large established garden, he was brought to the moment by the lights coming on, flooding the lovely garden that was his father's pride and joy with soft light. He went to the cloakroom and splashed his face with cold water. Lifting his head, he looked at himself in the mirror. Eyes red and tired looked back, an older version of the face he'd shaved that morning.

Going back to the pile of papers, there was a small envelope he'd yet to open. It bore no name or title. Opening it, he removed two photographs. One an old sepia print and the second an obviously much more modern snap, going by the quality of the image. Both, the same object. The colours of the goblet in the recent image were stunning, bronze, black and gold, if he had to guess. The old sepia image, though less impressive as a photo, was so very much more of a treasure from the scrawled words on the back: The "Grail," taken by Alistair Saint-Claire, 1830. In the family *troue de pretre*, the priest hole.

He was shocked and dropped the photo. In the same moment that he bent to retrieve it, the French door glass shattered and the plaster wall opposite the doors exploded from the impact of a projectile. Over the noise of the glass breaking and plaster crumbling, he heard what he recognised as a rifle shot. In that instant, he understood, on a fundamental level his life had changed forever.

The Hooker

She sipped her champagne, smiling at her newest client. Yes, she was a 'working girl,' but an extremely high end one. Her Battery Park view from the condominium window, was courtesy of her oldest client, an A-lister in the movie scene. The Morgan sports car in the garage had been a gift from her English Duke. She wanted for nothing in the material world.

Her earnings were disguised behind a classy boutique on Rodeo Drive out in Beverley Hills, California. It was opened as a favour to her Italian stallion.

He came in from Chicago to spend a weekend with her every couple of months. He managed the stocking of the shop and kept the books, too. On paper she made enough to cover the money in her bank accounts.

Another of her clients was a real cutie, an accountant and they had a deal. All her personal IRS files were never late and always perfectly filed in exchange for the regular dinner and a movie night with all the frills, no charges.

Life wasn't perfect, but it was perfectly acceptable.

So, when Tony from Chicago arrived unexpectedly and asked could they meet, she was a bit put out. She was meant to be meeting "Mr. Movie man" for dinner.

He didn't call so often these days as age was catching up on him, which made her loathe to cancel.

However, she said, "OK, but not till tomorrow as I'm busy." She was therefore livid when ten minutes later the doorbell rang, and Tony stood there bold as brass. This guy really took the biscuit: he carried an overnight bag and was not taking no for an answer. He said it was really important that he was off the grid for the next day or so.

She was not impressed. Tony was an alpha male and only tolerable in short visits. Usually, he had his own hotel room. They'd meet for dinner, then return to his suite and she'd leave in the wee small hours, meeting him again maybe for lunch or dinner next day – then he'd be gone.

His demanded presence in her apartment, where no-one stayed over, was pushing her irritation to the nth degree.

Just as she was coming out of the kitchen, she heard him on the phone. Judging from what was said, it was obvious he was hiding here, and some heavy hitters were looking for him. He'd effectively put her in the cross hairs.

When challenged, he said he had a hernia and needed to see his doctor here in New York; it was booked for the next day. She called her sweet accountant friend and asked, "Were my accounts all in order"?

"What's up? You sound anxious," he said, and she was moved by the genuine concern in his voice.

She explained that her silent partner in the shop had just dropped in unannounced and was here for a consult with his doctor the following day. She said he was showing signs of real anxiety and just wanted to be sure all was up to date re the shop just in case he asked.

Tony left the next day, stating he would see the quack then go straight to JFK for a flight to Italy, "I am going home for a rest. I need some space," he explained unnecessarily. He seemed in a real flap. He was sweating and had been fidgeting through his bagel and coffee breakfast. She was beginning to get anxious herself: if someone was after him, she wanted him gone from her home ASAP.

Later, after he'd left, she called the movie mogul and arranged to meet that night. Whilst they were having pre-dinner drinks at the bar in Le Cirque on 151 East 58th Street, the background radio programme broke for a news bulletin.

She almost choked on the martini she was enjoying, when the news announcer said, "Today, Mafia member Tony Luciano, had died on the street outside the doctor's office he'd just attended on Park Ave. It would appear he had a massive stroke. A doctor said he'd just advised Mr. Luciano to be admitted to the hospital. He believed him to have had a problem with his heart, and not a hernia as the

Chicago hospital had previously thought." He went on to say, "Mr. Luciano had refused and had taken a call and appeared agitated as he left."

She enjoyed brunch next day in the Russian Tea rooms with her accountant, Rick. He handed her an envelope and said, "Courtesy of Tony's partners in Chicago."

Tony had apparently been playing fast and loose with two of his partner's wives. His little heart problem had been diagnosed correctly, but the doctors he saw in Chicago were *"family"* and had been instructed to misinform him and to send him to New York to see a top specialist.

The rest was simple. He couldn't be allowed to get away with such disrespect to Don Vito Martellini.

Hernia symptoms can be easily confused with heart issues: All they had to do was just create the right atmosphere conducive to straining his heart to the limit. The whisper from one of the wives that her husband suspected him was enough to send him running. He did the rest himself.

Inside the envelope was a fortune, and the deeds to the shop too.

Pulling her into an embrace, Rick said. "I will be doing the books as well as your accounts too now." We settled for the first of many early nights.

Hidden Treasures

I had just acquired the house, a bungalow. I knew it needed a lot of work to modernise it, but I loved the feel of it. It had stood empty and unloved for many years and time had not been kind to it, though the structure proved to be sound.

It was the litter, the pigeon poo, rat droppings and the dreadful decoration that needed to be dealt with. I had inherited it when my aunt had finally passed, having been in a home for over ten years suffering the rages of Alzheimer's.

My girlfriend was horrified when she saw it, crying out, "Why on earth would you keep this horror?"

Like many people would, she had looked little further than the current state of the property. I persuaded her to help with the clean-up and we soon had the bungalow reduced to an empty but tolerably clean shell.

Now the real work could begin.

A number of floorboards needed replacing, some of the walls needed re-plastering. The electrics, plumbing and the kitchen needed a complete makeover. The old coke boiler would have to come out, too, and be replaced by a modern eco-friendly option.

I took a torch to look in the loft to check on the cold-water tank. In addition to a plastic tank, there was an old, galvanised metal one. It had been left up there probably because it must have been put in when the bungalow was built as the loft hatch was far too small for it to go through. I made a note to enlarge the trap door of the loft and to fit a light as I stepped carefully across the joists to the metal tank.

Peering in, my curiosity was piqued by the hint of an interesting box, partially hidden by old Hessian sacking, like the one potatoes were sold from in the fifties & sixties greengrocers. Lifting the corner, I disturbed a wee mouse who scurried away into the eaves. Recovering my composure, I reached down and lifted the box out. It weighed more than I expected; now my curiosity was seriously engaged.

Pulling an old sea trunk up, I sat down below the only light. I then lifted the lid on the beautifully carved and mother of pearl inlaid box.

What met my eyes caused my heart to skip a beat or two. Some of the most beautiful pieces of marquisate and diamond jewellery I'd ever seen lay nestled in a scarlet nest of shot silk and organza. Evidence of a timorous beastie's attention showed in the scattered holes throughout the ancient material.

Two weeks later, I was armed with letters written from Vienna by my grandfather and father, to my aunt in London in April of 1938 – one month after Hitler put the SS in charge of Jewish Affairs in Austria.

In them my grandfather said he would be travelling to England as soon as possible but wanted the enclosed family items to come to his son or grandson, should anything happen. And happen it did.

They'd been caught up in a public meeting as they tried to reach the main station. There were indiscriminate shootings by the SS troops; both were killed because they were there.

My aunt had volunteered to bring me to England for schooling in 1933 when things began to change and had become very threatening for non-Aryans in Germany and Austria. Why my aunt hadn't given these treasures to me, I do not know.

The news we received from home told us that her parents, siblings, and grandparents, all her extended family had disappeared. Maybe it was just too much for my aunt to deal with and accept, or maybe it was just too painful to contemplate back then.

And, of course, by the time I was 21, she was in the firm grip of Alzheimer's disease. She probably didn't recall them any longer. I'll never know.

At last, here it was, the inheritance. Twenty stunning pieces, and some loose diamonds too.

At Sotheby's, provenance papers, private letters and these beautiful pieces made an interesting and valuable item according to the assessors.

Just a week later, with a cheque for more than one million pounds in my pocket, I sat in a corner of Berkley Square Gardens. I needed a place of peace to assimilate this new situation.

I was already reasonably well off as a university lecturer and published writer. What did I need with all this money?

I took out my pen. On the blank envelope that Sotheby's had secreted the cheque into, I wrote the address Google gave for the Offices of International Human Rights, because even today there are people who think like Hitler. I signed the cheque tore it from my cheque book and popped it in the envelope. I'd sent the majority to them. There were people in the world today, still suffering fates similar to my family.

Now off to get the paint and order the new boiler. I whistled as I dropped the envelope into the post box.

Desert Island Discs.

I remember a time in my childhood, the summer of 1962: I was on the steps outside my Nana's home. I was allowed to play on the stairs whilst she sat by the open window above my head listening to 3-way Family Favourites. I was stopped in my play as Petula Clarke's voice carried on the warm summer breeze. This was the first cognitive realisation of my deep and abiding love of music, music of all kinds.

I had been reared with my grandmother's gramophone playing. She sang me all of her favourites, Jeanette Macdonald, and Nelson Eddie's "I'll Be Calling You," Doris Day, the "Black Hills of Dakota." Titles like "They Cut Down the Old Pine Tree "and "Streets of Laredo" were as familiar as any nursery rhyme. I still have bits of them in my head now, more than sixty years later.

My mind now jumps forward a year. My father bought our first portable record player just so he could play, over and over again, Jim Reeves's golden tones singing, "Distant Drums." It still evokes a lump in my throat today. Dad's second purchase was his all-time favourite from the sixties, Cilla Black's hit, "Anyone Who Had a Heart."

As I broke my heart on learning we were leaving Scotland and home, the Righteous Brothers raced through the charts with "Unchained Melody," It was years later I learnt that in 1955, national treasure and British DJ Jimmy Young had had a hit with it. I loved that song. I still do, and it now holds other different, poignant memories too.

My teenage years were blessed with a plethora of wonderful music. Moments like picture postcards are burnt into my hard drive. Scott McKenzie's "San Francisco" as I shopped with my mother one sunny Saturday afternoon. Elvis was a family favourite, but there were too many to choose between them. I left school in 1969 to The Move's, "Night of Fear", "Revolution" by the Beatles and "Honky Tonk Woman" by the Stones, blaring daily from my bedroom from tapes made so carefully from the top twenty countdown on the radio, recorded on a Sunday evening.

Then in 1972, I met my eldest son's father, a soldier serving in Ireland. The strains of Ben E. King's, "Spanish Harlem" and Smokie's "Lay Back in the Arms of Someone You Love" played at our wedding reception. However, at home, it was Joan Baez's folk songs of freedom and love and Luke Kelly's gravelly vocals on the Dubliner tracks that played long and loud.

When he returned to duty in Northern Ireland in seventy-four, "Billy Don't Be a Hero" was at number one.

And in 1975, when my eldest son was born, "Oh Boy" by Mud played daily in the ward throughout my fourteen-day confinement. And in seventy-nine when his father left us, "Baker Street" accompanied my tears as I held my son, who understood nought of the import of the moment.

As I look back over the span of my years, tracks call to catch my attention, like eager children. Meatloaf, "Paradise by the Dashboard Light," "Ballad of the Green Beret" by Staff Sergeant Barry Saddler, and Judith Durham's haunting tones as she offers up "The Carnival is Over." All of them recall, as vividly as any smell or picture, moments of true emotional connections. In these my late middle years, I find myself welling up to Casta Diva by Vincenzo Bellini in the Gautier advert. Then, Megan Trainer and Charlie Puth remind me with their "Marvin Gaye," of his great song, "Let's Get it On," Megan's song, "All About the Bass, Hozier's "Take me to Church", or James Bay's "Hold Back the River" blend and mix with all my own collection which is in the hundreds, and jostle for the title of "My Desert Island Disc."

So, I assert that this needs to be expanded to allow for so much interesting music. I don't want to never again hear Disturbed singing the old Simon and Garfunkel song, "The Sound of Silence," I cried the first time I heard it on the radio. Nor can I discount "These Arms of Mine" by Solomon

Burke or Eta James singing, "At Last," any more than I could refuse Sam Cooke's "A Change is Gonna Come."

So, if I'm to be castaway on a desert island, I'm taking a solar powered phone that has my YouTube loaded and signal for global radio. If not, kill me now, for music really is the food of life, and for me, it must play on.

Chance, Choice, or a Memory?
A Philosophical Question

Eilish settled back in her armchair, her granddaughter on the floor at her knee. They were discussing the course that Mercy was taking in psychology,

"But Nana, it all seems so very deep and profound and I'm not sure I'll get it."

"Oh, child, the boundaries of learning are endless surprises and discoveries. You'll see. When I was doing my diploma degree in person-centred psychology, I discovered how to accept my faith, despite having baulked at a fundamental point from an early age.

"I remember being thrown out of my Catechism lesson because I asked how could there be three in one – "

"Always getting into trouble, were you, Nana?" interrupted Eilish, chuckling.

"But on the Counselling & Psychotherapy course, I did find a way to believe.

"I learnt about transactional analysis and how we humans work from three basic ego states, the adult, parent, and child. Like a lightbulb, my brain lit up with the understanding of "the Father, Son and Holy Ghost" being a possibility after all. Come to think about it, that course taught me an awful lot."

"Tell me, Nana. It might help me, too."

"Ok, but remember what I've always said, 'comparisons don't work, I'm not you, and you're not me.'"

And this is what she told Mercy.

"I was in my second year, and we covered three modules that really had a very intense effect upon me. The first was as I said about the ego states. You should read some of the books on T.A. You'll see it's a fascinating theory. Another module was about how the microcosm reflected the macrocosm. We looked at the phenomenon of how, in times of war, civilian murder numbers increase drastically. Now that at first seemed shocking, until I considered that the government and religious leaders were advocating the taking of life in the defence of the realm and how we had 'God on our side.'

"It was now ok with the ruling influence of the era to take a life; permission has been given by all we have feared retribution from previously.

"Is that not astonishing, Mercy? Amidst all the global loss of life, we here at home were committing more murders than in peace time!

"We also looked at how we as humans can now clone ourselves due to the discoveries in DNA. All that we are is in one wee drop of the stuff. I learnt in that module that science has yet to definitively pinpoint where memory is stored.

"In that afternoons learning I discovered something that I believe utterly and have absolutely no proof to substantiate it apart from what I tell you here.

"We are leaving my college time for a moment to explain some background.

"Around that time, I had begun investigating my family tree. It had started after my mother's death: there would soon be no-one left to ask about her middle name, "Merville" and how she came to be called Mernie to all her side of the family. Turned out, it was to remember her uncle Gabriel, killed in World War I. From what I could gather, they believed it was the name of the place where he'd died. As I researched this young man, I found myself truly grieving for a man I never knew, never met, and barely had heard of.

"By the time I'd discovered all I could about him, I'd put flesh to other members of my family lost in the Great War and the same haunting loss gripped me for these men, too. A great uncle and a great grandfather, both young, both much loved and desperately missed.

"Also, I had taken a trip to Scotland and wanted to go to Glencoe, a place that every time I spoke of, I always misspoke, saying I wanted to "go back" there. I had previously never been. On that trip, I bought books on the clans that I'm a part of, and there it was: I am a descendant of those MacDonalds massacred in the Glen. I stood in the glen, my heart aching as it did the day my grandmother died, I felt the loss like it was mine.

"Ok, now back to Memory stuff," Nana Eilish continued.

"We were told science didn't know exactly where memory was stored. We were also told, 'all that we are is in that DNA droplet.' Within that afternoon I put it to my tutor that all the instances of *déjà vu* and past lives can be explained here.

"I was asked to elaborate on my theory.

"I was full of excitement, I can tell you, that my tutor thought I might have something to say worth listening to. I was shaking with trepidation. What if I made an ass of myself?

"Well, this is what I said:

"Wherever our memories are stored they are in that droplet of DNA, according to the macro/microcosm ideal. If that is so, all my DNA contains a dilution of the DNA of all my ancestors. Maybe these *déjà vu* instances or past life experiences are just the memories of our ancestors that are the most powerful of their memories. Their pain of losing two husbands within a ten-year span. A mother's loss of a much-loved son, or to witness the massacre of your family, friends, and neighbours. To feel a soldier's fear or heroic motivation.

"I told how I had been attracted to the tales of the Indian Mutiny and how some of the men on my mother's side had taken part in the siege of Cawnpore and the relief of Lucknow. The stories my paternal grandmother told of the clearances, and our Irish ancestors dragged in their nighties into the streets in the snow by the Tans. My choices for reading included all of these areas in history, and how I'd found we were from O'Donoghues of Cork and Kerry, strong early IRA recruitment areas. My father and my grandad loved books, art and drawing; my mother was a seamstress. I love crafting, poetry, and writing.

"So, I ask you this: is it chance, choice, or memories in my DNA that drew me to these many and varied subjects and made me who I am today?

"Will my memories manifest themselves in my descendants? I hope not; some of the most powerful will make for the stuff of nightmares.

"But my DNA carries the memories of the strongest emotions of my antecedents, grief, love, fear and courage, anger, and sorrow"

"Nana that is *big*," said my beautiful granddaughter, who looks so much like me as a girl. Mercy looked thoughtful, then said, "I'm more excited than scared now, Nana. Thank you. You have also given me much to think about."

Eilish kissed the top of her head. Seeing her grow had been such a privilege.

The Visit

Elise Bucholtz sat in the back row, almost in the corner of the room. She was a shy, retiring child with a head of pale blonde wavy hair and bright, intelligent blue eyes. Her father was Prussian and was away serving with the army. He always said Elise was a *mini mutti*, a miniature of her mother. And in that, he said, they had been blessed.

Elise was seven years old and had been attending her Protestant School for almost two years now. The year was 1942, and many of her school friends had lost a father, brother, uncle, or grandfather to the war.

Her father was immensely proud of his heritage, and had joined the Prussian Infantry Regiment Number 6, affectionately called the Potsdam Giants. He had been allowed home only twice since she was four. The last visit had been just a month ago. Elise was anxious and had been since that visit. Her father looked tired, and he and her *Mutti* had spent much of his visit talking in whispers; she had heard her *Mutti* crying more than once. Things felt unsafe now in her little world.

It had been a very scary day. Just after lunch, the war came to Köln where they now lived. The teachers had run to the windows and witnessed a host of what at first looked like a swarm of angry bees but were soon identified as a great squadron of aircraft. Terrifying plumes of grey, white, and black smoke erupted on the other side of the city. Each time another rose, it was clear they were coming closer and closer. The children began to cry.

The teachers told them to stand, to get into pairs and follow the teachers to the *Stadtbahn*. They were there, for what had felt like eternity to the frightened children but was in fact just two hours. Finally, the principal had declared it safe to return to the school.

They had not been back in class long when the headmaster entered with her Pastor. Her name was called out and she was ushered out of the room. The Pastor told Elise that her *Mutti* had had an accident and she was to stay at the church orphanage until her father arrived. He would be arriving the following day.

The Pastor, *Herr* Schwartz said she was to stay at the orphanage only for tonight, it would be a wonderful adventure.

She cried. She'd never been away from home before, and she was to sleep in a room full of children she didn't know.

She cried all that night. She cried for her mother. There had been no stories before bedtime, no lullaby sung to send her to sleep. Some of the other children were rough and had pushed her around; one horrid boy had pulled her pigtails.

They were woken by a bell; the Matron of the home was in a flap. "Quickly children! We must dress swiftly. We have an unexpected visit from a very important man." Still rubbing sleep from their eyes, the children shuffled into the dining hall, they were told to sit.

Behind the long refectory table where the staff usually sat, stood a man in the black uniform of the *Waffen SS*. These soldiers were feared by everyone. Even Elise of only seven summers knew they were men to be very wary around.

He had sheaves of paper with lists of names on each page. Many of the children in the hall were told to go and line up in the corridor and to wait there until everyone else had been dismissed and sent to their classes.

Elise held her breath. She didn't know if it was good or bad to have your name called out, but she sensed the fear from everyone, even the teachers.

Her name was not called out; she was still afraid and began to softly weep for her *Mutti*. She was in a line with those whose name had not been called; they were then led out of the hall. One line on the right, one to the left. They were told to wait in line in the corridor for a teacher who would come for them in a moment.

The children all stood, each line eyeing the other, but avoiding eye contact. They knew instinctively that one of these lines of children were somehow in trouble. They'd seen lines in the streets before. Some crying, some bored by the bureaucracy of the checking of papers.

Just then, the hall door opened, and a teacher called her name. She was taken to the big table where the man with the lightning bolts on his collar stood watching her. *Frau* Meyer, one of the teachers, was telling the SS man that she was sure she'd heard one of the washer women say that *Frau* Buckholtz was a Jewess.

Elise knew this was not good. She'd witnessed the women being beaten in the street by the men and boys in brown shirts. The ones who called these poor women dirty Jews as they hit or spat at the women doing nothing more than going about their daily tasks.

Now she was very frightened and her bladder failed her. She stood, shamed, and crying.

The officer squatted down to her level and was about to speak when the hall door flew open. And there in all his finery was her soldier father. A Prussian elite troop Captain.

Frau Meyer was aghast and spluttered, "But of course it's just gossip, I'm sure."

The SS Captain and her father saluted and said, *"Heil Hitler,"* as was expected.

"And you are?" said the SS man.

"Captain Buckholtz, Prussian Infantry Regiment Number 6. And you are… who? And what can you possibly want with my daughter?"

"I am Captain Müller, and it seems that Frau Meyer has made a mistake, I'm sure. However, I must ask that you bring your wife here, please, with her papers."

"I only wish that I could, but it will not be possible, Captain Müller. I am here on compassionate leave to collect my daughter to take her to my sister and parents in Bremen. Our home was obliterated in the bombing yesterday. My wife was orphaned in the First World War and raised by my cousin in Berlin. That's how we met," he pulled his wallet out, "this was my wife."

The soldier stared at the photo. The woman had almost white, blonde hair, and vivid blue eyes, Nordic would be a perfect description.

Hans Buckholtz picked up his daughter and said, "If you'll excuse me, I have an internment to arrange, my wife was at home when the raid occurred." He hoped the man would understand his allusion to his wife's death; he did not want his precious daughter to learn of her loss this way. Not here with these weak, vindictive people around her. His wife would never have forgiven him.

The SS man understood, he straightened, clicked his heels, and saluted, "Apologies Captain, and condolences."

Hans left, and later that night he carried his daughter to the car. They drove all night till he crossed the border. Breathing a huge sigh of relief, he handed his new passport to the hotelier in Basel. Tomorrow he'd drive to Fribourg, to his sister in law's summer home, and to freedom. He would keep his promise to his wife and go to America after the war.

They had talked of all the possible eventualities that her ethnicity might incur; Their homeland had changed so fast since the new regime came to power in '33.

Their plan was to head to Switzerland if they were separated, and after the war ended, they would go to America.

He was heartbroken by all that was happening in his beloved homeland, but he could look away no more from the evil that had permeated so insidiously across Germany and half of the world, all emanating from one evil little corporal.

First Love

Like most little girls, first my heart belonged to Daddy, my loving, laughing, hero. But what this story is about is the first time I gave my heart to someone outside of the family. That scamp was Duncan Brodie. He was my first experience of that overpowering obsessive need to see and be near to another human. My first taste of the sweetness that inspires selflessness and the wish to see the other happy. He was also my first experience of heartbreak.

We met at my grandmother's home. I was playing in the communal "back green." My judgement was never as good as on the day I first set eyes on this boy. He was a kind soul, a brave explorer, and a loyal heart. He was perfect to me.

We don't often get the chance to catch up with our first love, and I was no different, though I did try. I reached out on a social media forum to try and reconnect with old friends. It was seen by his older brother; it was he who contacted me.

I was deeply saddened to learn the object of my childhood crush had died. He was so young, leaving a wife and family.

I'm not ashamed to say I cried thinking that his twinkling eyes had closed forever.

He was about six or seven and I was a precocious four- or five-year-old tomboy when I first laid eyes on his lovely face. A shock of wild curly hair, the darkest, most intense eyes I have ever seen. And a wide, full-lipped mouth that seemed set in a permanent grin.

We spent long summer hours and days re-creating battles between Custer and Sitting Bull. Or the Red Baron to my brave British fighter pilot. Our imagination took us to darkest Africa and the Zulu wars, the wild plains of North America and the blood curdling gunfights of the Yukon gold rush.

We also emulated the sports heroes of our history.

I have clear recollections of a black eye delivered by the shot at goal by one of the "Hibee" frontline. I was sadly the horrid Heart of Midlothian goalie, who not only let in the goal, but cried from the sting of that heavy leather ball. The goal tally for Hibernian was never as high as that summer day.

I would have followed him to the ends of the earth. I did stick to him like a lovesick puppy. All through long summer holidays, Easter breaks and any weekend I spent, and there were many, at my adored Nana's home.

The back green was a world full of wonder for us. We built camps that alternated between a Wild West fort, Wallace's castle, or an Indian Tipi. We'd rework it to suit our game. I adored my ever brave and dashing hero with the innocence and absolutism that can only be found in the hearts of the young and unsophisticated.

At the tender age of about nine or so, he taught me another lesson, that all things pass and are fleeting. One beautiful summers day, we were recreating the race between Harry Abrahams and Eric Liddell. Childhood takes no heed of facts; our runners were hurdlers. We were to race from one side of the green to the fence separating it from the next stairs area, leap the fence like it was a hurdle, run to the far side then back again. There was another child there, of whom I have no recall, only that he held and dropped the hanky to start the race.

Duncan took off like a whippet, with me not too shabbily at his heels. Over the fence we went like sleek young thoroughbreds. When we hit the far fence and set for the return, there was less than an arm's length between us. I knew I had still plenty to give and as we approached the fence, I was confident I could take him. I drew level, one great leap, and disaster struck.

I'd jumped too soon and landed too close to the fence. The spindle post caught the loose leg of my shorts, I landed face down in the grass. I was at first only filled with rage at my error, this fast turned to horror as I espied said shorts still attached to said fence post.

They'd been torn asunder, and I was in my knickers in front of the boy I adored. And he, at first anxious to know I was unhurt, then dissolved into uncontrolled gleeful laughter. He sat with tears rolling down his face in the grip of a fit of giggles at my indelicate attire and expense.

My humiliation was complete.

I ran and never looked back. And for the longest time I avoided him when I visited – and if I did come face to face, I was cold and distant. More than once, I saw hurt in those lovely eyes of his, but my shame and embarrassment were total.

Years, like summers, passed and my parents moved us to England and we didn't visit home for a year or two. Finally, when we did, I learnt he'd joined up. I never saw him again.

I heard he'd married an English lassie and lived in England on the south coast somewhere.

It was ever in my childish heart that I wished I'd had the courage to apologise to him for the hurt I caused. I'd rejected a dear and good friend and my first love.

They say you never really die so long as someone lives and remembers you. Well, until the day I die, he is not dead, for I remember him with great affection every time I think of my Nana's house in Marionville Rd, Edinburgh.

In memory of Duncan Brodie. R.I.P

On My Terms

Friday the 13th dawned in the same way as every day did in Greenacres Retirement Facility. However, today was no ordinary day for Frances Goldie, 'Frankie' to her friends. Today she had the upper hand at last.

Miss Higginbottom, the "Matron," was in for a shock. Today, the glorious revolution!

Frankie had been in Greenacres for three and a half long years. She was subjected to slips of girls barely out of school insisting they wash her, without thought for her modesty or dignity. Words she doubted they even knew, far less understood.

"Health and safety, dear," they spouted, in their patronising tones. No more a luxurious soak for a couple of hours in a regularly topped up tub, surrounded with flickering candles and a large glass of bubbly in hand.

"No! No more bubbly, Not with those pills, dear," the officious besom of a matron dictated. "Can't have you lying in there for hours. We simply do not have the staff and you most definitely cannot be left unattended."

She spoke as if Frankie were a toddler, "We'd be sued for every penny if you should have a fall," she said in her overbearing and authoritarian tone. Miss Lucinda

Higginbottom, "Matron," was the monkey on Frankie's back. It was she who had made Frankie's life intolerable.

Frankie would not be turned into one of those drooling shells that sat around the walls of the lounge. Never! She just could not bear it. She would not.

That woman had all but hijacked the plans for Frankie's 80th birthday party. She'd vetoed and changed orders for food and drink without asking, then had the cheek to cancel the amateur operatic singer that had been booked. "My friend's son sings better, and he could use the money to help with his book requirements at college," Matron Higginbottom rationalized.

Poor Frankie was furious. He'd been at Christmas and was second rate on a good day. The harpy had lauded it over all the plans, you'd have thought it was her party.

Frankie had at least managed to keep the guests to just her children, grandchildren and two dear friends of over thirty years, who also had reached the lofty heights of feisty octogenarians.

The balance of power was changed two months previously, unbeknownst to the harridan.

Frankie had been taken by one of the flippity-gibbets who called themselves "carers," to the local hospital to get the results of some routine tests. Little Miss Know-It-All wheeled her into the consultant's office. She bristled with her own self-importance and flashed her brightest smile at the handsome man with the stethoscope round his neck.

As the young girl started to sit down, Frankie interjected, "Thank you, dear. You can wait outside. This is private and I really don't need you to hold my hand." Her tone was sweet but firm.

"No, no, Mrs. Goldie. I should stay, just in case."

"Actually, Miss," said the handsome consultant registrar, "if Mrs. Goldie doesn't want you here, then here you will most certainly not be." Pouting and huffing, the wannabe celebrity carer left them in peace.

Mr. Daniel Ellington, the consultant, entered almost as if in a synchronised ballet as Rhianna left.

Frankie's anxiety increased instantly. She'd never seen her consultant so serious; his greetings were always jovial.

"Mrs. Goldie, there's no sugar coating these results, I am so sorry, but you are dying." He let the words hang in the space between them as she absorbed first the words, and then the implications. She let out a long slow sigh.

"Well, we are all dying, Mr. Ellington, and I've had a damned good life until recently, which makes accepting this news so very much easier. I can think of no regrets nor things left unsaid, at least not to any loved ones. So, tell me, do I have enough time to seduce this handsome registrar of yours?"

Both men laughed aloud at this audacious comment from such a vivacious and courageous woman. Mr. Ellington looked directly at Frankie, who held his gaze with deep blue eyes that just about held a tear from falling. She said, "I am no sissy, tell me truly the bald facts, please."

Mr. Ellington nodded. He'd met others like Frankie who met life and death head on and who had made their peace with death long before he ever saw them.

Now here she was, her party over, such a lovely time, despite Lucinda Higginbottom. The grandchildren played happily together, her children were animated and full of, "do you remember" stories of their childhood and teen year escapades. It was a lovely coming together of family.

Her two oldest and dearest friends had delighted in the sharing of those memories, many of which they'd been a part of.

One of those two friends whispered in her ear as she was leaving, "You cannot fool me, Frankie. We've been pals for over fifty years. I know you are up to something. I'll be back in the morning. You can spill the beans then."

They had promised all those years ago to have no secrets and never had; they'd shared it all. Such friends are God's blessings, and Frances Goldie believed she had truly been blessed. She'd enjoyed long and fruitful friendships with four women in her life and two were still by her side. She kissed her friend's cheek and hugged her as tight as she dared. Smiling she said, "Okay, hen, see you soon."

Her friend cocked her head questioningly at Frankie, squeezed her hand, then left. She never saw the crossed fingers nor saw the tear fall.

Frances wanted the world to know how these homes were run, stripping coherent adults of their will and rights. She'd written a long letter to the local paper and registered a copy along with the changed will.

The gardener had witnessed it and her son had taken it into the solicitors last week. She'd received a copy of the updated will, excluding the bequest previously set out to the home. Lucinda would not be happy with either of Frankie's actions.

Frankie giggled, and thought aloud, "I'd love to be a fly on the wall when the proverbial hits the fan."

When Rhianna came around with the drugs trolley, she carefully counted out Frankie's tablets and asked her colleague to counter-sign as was required in the dispensing of restricted drugs like morphine.

Frankie took a long swallow of water and palmed the two pills into her hankie, *"Not yet, but soon,"* she thought to herself as she showed the girl her tongue, as if she were a four-year-old that couldn't be trusted.

She readied herself for bed and sat and penned a letter to her children. She explained the diagnosis and the prognosis of what would not be a dignified death. The idea of that awful passing, here with Lucinda deciding what was and wasn't good for her, Frankie knew would be a living hell, and definitely not a death she intended to have.

Since the day the lovely Mr. Ellington had given her the news and all it meant, she'd saved every tablet and had even hammed it up to the locum GP when he visited to get the highest dose possible. Now she had quite a stash. She wasn't accepting the death that was on offer. Nope, she had lived on her own terms, and so would she die.

The letter to her children said all this and sent her everlasting love. She begged their understanding and forgiveness.

Frankie popped the last of the purloined morphine in her mouth and washed it down with the last dregs from what had been a half bottle of exceptionally fine brandy.

"Poor Louise," she thought. She'd broken her word, "No secrets," they'd said all those years ago. "Oh, well..." she sighed, closing her eyes.

278

The Love Poem

Sixteen-year-old Caroline sat in class. English Literature was her favourite, not least because Geordie sat three rows in front. She sat transfixed by the way his hair curled over his collar. How often had she dreamt of running her fingers through those delicious curls. Only every week in this class, where happiness was just being able to watch him.

She was suddenly aware the lecturer was speaking to her. He asked, "Caroline, have you attempted the love poem required for this module on the greatest love poems of the twentieth century?"

She had never considered that anyone but Mr. Carstairs, the tutor, might read it. Never in a million years would she have expected having to read it aloud to the entire class. It was just too embarrassing, especially if Geordie's eyes would be staring directly at her.

She'd spent hours trying to capture Geordie's looks, personality, and his eyes, all in some literary masterpiece. When she'd done the best she could with it, she thought it neither inspired nor rhymed to her satisfaction.

"Yes, sir, I have," she softly admitted.

"Come on then. Let's hear it.

"What?" Caroline was mortified. She would die of embarrassment. He'd know it was about him. Her face and neck reached a new shade of puce ambitiously aiming for scarlet.

"Hurry up, girl," said Mr. Carstairs impatiently.

She stood. Oh, Lord, her mouth was drying up, and every drop of moisture disappearing from there was pouring into her palms. She gulped and focused on the picture behind the lecturer's head.

Five minutes later, after class had been dismissed, she was hurrying out of the lecture hall when Geordie tapped her on the shoulder. Oh, how she wanted the ground to open up and swallow her whole.

He smiled shyly and handed her a note, winked, and turned back into the hall. Not a word was said.

Waiting until he was out of sight, she opened the sheet of paper. She read:

My Daydream

I feel her eyes, resting soft upon my back,

Oh, for the traits, my personality lacks.

Confidence, to tell to you, my muse.

How everything, I'd gladly lose,

For just one chance to show,

That maybe love could grow.

So, now I put my heart out on the line,

To win this beauty's love divine.

Meet me please, tonight at eight,

By the church's kissing gate,

Geordie Boy

For her this would always be the greatest love poem.

The Milestone

Lucius Caeso had been a Legionary since his fourteenth year, when the time had come for him to enter into military service. Such was the lot for the second sons of poor farmers or dishonoured statesmen.

An unguarded word, a dissenting argument in the forum and a powerful man with the ear of the emperor and all could be forfeit. Such was the fate of Lucius's father, a good and honest nobleman.

Lucius went with his closest friend, Gaius Appius, when their summons arrived by the same runner. The culture shock of Rome was eye opening.

The poor were left to die in the streets from hunger. Children were taken for servants to Rome's statesmen or just rich Romans for no other reason than the child was amusing or pretty.

Lucius was disgusted at the gatherings he was forced to attend as scribe to his officer, Titus Manius. And the food wasted afterwards, when all the great and the good had gorged themselves on all the pleasures of the flesh was fed to the pigs. Knowing that the poor of Rome were dying yards from these aristocratic doors, it made him ashamed to be a soldier of Rome.

Gaius often had cause to calm his friend, preventing him giving vent to his ire within earshot of others or his superiors.

They'd been in Rome for almost two years now. Their bodies had become accustomed to the rigours of forced marches at double time and the one-on-one gladiatorial training. They were as fit as any soldier in the empire's service.

Both were on notice that they were soon to be posted to a garrison and had been given some leave.

They were headed to the hot baths one humid afternoon, when they witnessed a man pulling a lovely, but obviously noticeably young and frightened girl into an alley that led to the fields beyond.

Lucius neither paused nor thought, just acted, and went to the rescue of the child.

He came up behind the man swiftly and as he grabbed the man's shoulder with one hand, he landed an effective rabbit punch to his kidney with the other. As the man tried to turn, he was met with a flurry of fists bringing the fury of Lucius's disgust upon himself.

Gaius pulled Lucius off the man, fearing his friend might kill this toga-wearing brute. As the man fell, he landed in a somewhat undignified heap on his back, allowing both young soldiers a view of this beast's face.

There, sprawled among the dung, was Titus Manius. In that moment, the lives of Lucius and Gaius changed forever.

They were arrested, of course, and brought before the *prefectus castrorum*. The camp prefect was a good and fair man, and he did not like Titus. He knew, however, that Titus had influential friends who had secured him his position as a *principales*. (low ranking officer.) And he also knew he could not allow the attack by these two good soldiers to go unpunished.

He did all he could. In the end, he banished them to ten years' service in what all Roman soldiers considered the rear end of the world. They were sent to *Provincia Britannia*.

Wild warlike people, cold and wet weather, and for ten years. Grateful for their lives but miserable. Lucius begged for mercy for his friend, stating his involvement was only to protect the man. However, the girl had run away as soon as Titus loosed his grip on her, so there was no independent evidence to support their claims.

Titus enjoyed seeing Lucius's distress for his friend.

Two years after the pair arrived in Britannia, Lucius found himself on the wall north of *Eboracum* (York). He had shown himself an excellent negotiator with the Brigantes and Parisi tribes. Often, he was sent to sit at the table below the Eagle standard, in disputes between the tribes and Rome or indeed between themselves.

The Romans allowed the tribal leaders to stay in place which meant, in return for their allegiance, Rome became a client-kingdom and gave the tribes a powerful ally against non-friendly tribes.

It was during one of these tribunals that Lucius first met Eithne. She was an ethereal pale skinned Celtic beauty with a head of wild titian locks that flowed to her waist, and the greenest eyes he'd ever seen.

He spoke with her concerning the theft of her family's cattle. This was unusual to a Roman, but within the Celtic tribes, women were not discriminated against. They did in fact fight alongside the men in many cases. Her father had taken a fall and her brother had to take on the chores of their farm alone; Eithne had been sent in her father's stead.

Lucius was struck not only with her beauty but her intelligence and was delighted when she agreed to accompany him to a nearby settlement of Parisi.

He had a notion of where her cattle might be found.

The journey proved both pleasant and highly informative through the varied conversations they shared on the back of two hardy northern ponies on route to the Parisi hamlet.

Lucius learnt much about Brigantes culture and found an unfamiliar perspective now and also a not too paltry measure of respect for these indigenous people.

When they reached the settlement Eithne instantly spied the corral that held half a dozen cows. Most villages had been built with a stake palisade surrounding the main dwellings on the site, with a ditch dug below to deter assaults from rival tribes.

The corral was built with the outside palisade as one of its boundaries.

Eithne had leant over and without fuss or drama told Lucius of the cows and drew his attention to one in particular with a piece of coloured calico attached with a cord round the animal's neck. She cautiously lifted her outer skirt, showing a shift below of the same material, minus a strip. She explained quietly and efficiently that the cow had gotten tangled in a copse, where thick barbed plants had sorely scratched her cow. She said she'd chewed some rosemary to ensure the gashes did not become poisonous and had used her underskirt strip to keep the poultice in place.

Lucius was impressed: these were remedies the Romans also used. She was an unusual woman and an herbalist, too!

Lucius began by approaching the head of the group. He could see as they sat down together that the old man was anxious. Lucius had barely sat and been offered mead when a younger man burst in, demanding to know what a Brigantine and a Roman wanted with his village.

The elder, blustering, tried to quell the fire in the words from this interloper, but inadvertently gave the game away by spluttering in panic, "I've told them nothing!"

The younger man turned to run, but Lucius had already blocked his exit whilst the man had confronted the elder. The tip of Lucius's *gladius* now rested neatly between the man's chest muscles, his death but a breath away.

At this point, wishing no blood to be spilled nor to bring trouble to these people from the Roman garrison, Eithne interjected, showing wisdom and diplomacy, and mercy too if these men had the wit to see it.

"Sire," she said, "it would appear you have found my father's cattle: they can be identified if you require more than my word. I'm certain my father would want me to recompense you for their care and feed." She then produced some coins that would have been a reasonable amount for such an action.

The old man saw his way out and said, "Indeed, maid, I sent boys out to see if anyone was searching. The lazy dogs likely lie in some grassy glade with their sweethearts."

The elder continued, "This young man here found the cows two days ago and, after waiting through that first night by the river with them, he returned here with them in tow. He thought his prayers to the saints were being answered and he'd have a dowry and so find a way to marry his lass. 'Tis the disappointment that clouds his judgement today. I beg your indulgence, sire.

"Thank your father for his generosity, but I will take no payment. It's as it should be between neighbours and allies, no?" the Elder said gently.

Violence and a broken peace were thus avoided by the swift thinking of this young woman.

That was the day Lucius fell in love and the day Eithne gave her heart to a soldier of Rome. They shared their first kiss at the *miliarium* just outside her village. It showed the distance to *Eboracum* and it became their meeting place. All through the winter and early spring of that first year, nothing could cast a shadow on their relationship.

In the month approaching *Latha Bealltainn*, (May Day) Lucas was summoned to his superior's tent. This usually meant he had another tribunal to attend and another issue to resolve. Not so this time.

Lucius was told that his officer was being replaced. He was recalled to Rome, his reward for keeping the peace along the wall. His replacement was due to arrive in time for the festivities that celebrated the arrival of spring.

"Do we know who it is, sire" asked Lucius.

"Indeed, we do. Titus Manius will be my replacement."

"By all the Gods, what dark fortune is this?"

"You know the man? A friend, mayhap"?

Lucius paused, "No, sire. Quite the opposite, in fact."

"We shall appeal to the Gods that soldiering has changed the man," commented his superior before dismissing Lucius.

The days passed slowly, then Eithne came to see him in a state of distress and agitation. "Eithne, what causes you such sorrow and discomfort?" Lucius asked.

"My father has promised me to the leader of another tribe of Brigantes further north, but who is a relation of my mothers. I cannot marry anyone but you. My heart would break, and I learned just before my father told me this, that I carry our child. Lucius, what can we do?"

Lucius drew her into his arms, he knew exactly what they were going to do; he had made plans to ensure Eithne would be his bride. Not one *denarius* had he squandered since he met his Eithne. It was no fortune by Roman measure, but here it was more than enough within this land he had come to love and whose people he now respected.

"In two days, the festival begins. Security will be lax. My superior is also being replaced and he leaves the day before. There will be much arranging and confusion."

Lucius continued, "Meet me at the *Eboracum miliarium* at dusk the day prior to the day the festival begins. We shall leave here and make a life for a time over the water in Hibernia. There are Brigantes people there where we will be lost to Romans eyes."

"Will I ever see my family again?" she said, wiping her tears.

"I pray it will be so." He held her fast to him, appealing to the gods of both their hearts to protect them.

The following day as the men ended work for the evening meal, word arrived that a cohort of soldiers approached. Their new commander had come early!

Lucius tried to avoid being seen and hoped that Titus was unaware of his position at this garrison. Sadly, the gods had turned their face from Lucius. A *munifex*, the lowest ranked soldier, came; ignoring Lucius's position, the soldier spoke as if Lucius were his equal.

"My commander demands your presence in his tent, so get your helmet and bring your seals. Now!' He spoke rudely. Lucius now was certain Titus was aware he was here, and this ignorant summoning was to provoke him. He resisted.

"Ah, at last, Lucius Caeso! Are you so arrogant as to not come to present yourself to your new commander? Did you think I was unaware of your whereabouts? I have followed your movements ever since that apology of a *prefectus* leniently sent you here. He also blighted my rise up the ranks, ensuring I got the worst postings until finally I was sent here. And all because of you. Now I can make your life as miserable as he made mine! Now get out! You will pay dearly," Titus cried out laughing.

Lucius kept his head down until it was time to meet Eithne. He rolled his uniform up, stowing it with the small number of personal possessions he owned, and donned his off-duty garb.

He waited till supper was being served and the majority of men were in the food hall, then, casually walked out the gate and headed to the *miliarium*.

He thought he had left the garrison unseen but he was mistaken. Eithne and Lucius's liaisons were not as secret as he'd believed and Titus was a master at eliciting information and secrets.

Lucius saw Ethne at the marker. She sat with her back against it. Her head was bent and he thought her lost in thought as she neither moved nor looked up as he softly called her name. He was maybe ten *pec* (feet) from her when he saw it: her dress was drenched in blood.

He ran and gathered her into his lap. That was when he saw the back of her skirts were also bloodied. Her death had come from a knife across her pale slender throat. Lucius was trying to stifle the scream rising from his soul when he saw three riders emerge from the trees behind the marker.

Titus sat high on the lead horse, his face bearing a satisfied grin. Two of his junior soldiers were his escort.

"Ah at last, Lucius Caeso. Your Brigantine whore fought me well, begged me to spare her as she carried the child of one of my men. Her innocence was amusing and increased my pleasure and that of my men no end. Knowing I cost you more than just your heathen whore is just divine."

Titus laughed as Lucius gently lay Eithne's body on the grass. He never saw Lucius's *gladius* until it was under his nose, embedded in his chest. The two soldiers, though shocked, were trained and experienced and eventually overwhelmed Lucius.

As darkness fell, Gaius, who had heard what had occurred, went to the milestone to *Eboracum* and buried both his dear friend and his beloved Eithne.

Titus lived barely a month, when a small Brigantes band caught him out hunting with only a six-man escort.

All were killed, but Titus took two days to die. Eithne's brother made sure there was no honourable death for his sister's killer.

Missing

Johnny was one of those teenagers who loved to go exploring on occasion. There was so much to investigate and experience beyond his home.

His mother, at her wits' end most times, relied on his good sense and caring personality.

To ensure she did not worry unduly whilst he was off on one of his escapades, he would leave a text message on her iPhone to say where he was, or what was happening.

Now seventeen, he was keen to experience "real life" as he called it. His Saturday job had given him extra cash to buy tickets to events, where he might meet one of his favourite stars of television or music.

He wanted to be part of the action and was drawn to such venues.

At a recent concert, he'd met a couple of lads. They were older than him, but they seemed to like him, and he was thrilled to have made some new friends.

Johnny was delighted that these guys were giving him the time of day. Obviously more sophisticated and men of the world, he thought. They'd said their names were Larry and Colin. They spoke of political rallies and policies the government should be ashamed of. Johnny stayed quiet, as firstly, he didn't agree with some of their views, but secondly, a lot was a bit over his head, and he really didn't want to seem gauche – especially as they'd asked if he wanted to join them at a music recording studio. The group had sold a limited amount of tickets to fans who wanted to see how the recording of a record happened. Johnny was wild with excitement.

Separated into groups, the small crowd finally were allowed in. Johnny's group were ushered into a recording booth that overlooked a small auditorium where a small dais was set up with microphones and a drum kit. The guy in charge said the chart-topping group would be on in five, and to just chill till then.

Colin and Larry had detached themselves from the group slightly. Johnny thought this a tad rude as they'd said he could tag along with them, even offering to let him stay at their crib if he wanted. He was just heading over to where they were when the glass partition separating them from the auditorium shattered and he saw Larry lob a small projectile at the stage where the group had arrived. Suddenly an explosion ripped through the whole place.

Hours later, lying in the hospital where he'd finally allowed the paramedic to bring him, he was shocked at the strength of the fingers he was more used to seeing in the sink but that now gripped his hand so tightly that it hurt.

She was shaking as she explained what the police had told her, that the two lads he'd been chatting with had been arrested but were also injured. One seriously.

His mother, ashen-faced and trembling asked, "Johnny, is it true what they are saying, that you wouldn't leave till everyone was out, even though you were hurt?"

"No biggie, Mum. There were people hurt really bad and something just kicked in and I had to help get them. It taught me something about myself, Mum. Much as I love music and always will, I am going to be a fireman. They were awesome today. What do you think, Mum?"

"I think you are determined to turn me grey," she said laughing. She then reached for him and wrapped her arms around her beautiful son, saying, "I think it'd be a fine way to live son, I am so proud of you."

Right is Right

"It had been having a good day," Aisha thought to herself. They'd avoided the thugs who attacked, robbed and worse, the weaker, more vulnerable ones. She didn't trust their guides, even though they'd brought them thus far.

They'd continually demanded more and more above the original price, until almost every dollar they had so fiercely clung to was almost gone. She knew freedom was never free.

Escaping the war and its awful violence, the poverty and disease of the war zones that once she'd called home, had cost them everything. Some, at the hands of their guides, had paid with their lives.

Aisha had seen her home destroyed. Her younger brother and baby sister had died alongside their mother in the refugee camp after those first attacks on the towns, and villages, including theirs.

Her oldest brother and father had died in the fighting when the ISIS troops attacked the ancient city of Damascus. She'd wondered, if the Christ that Christians talked about had he been real, and if so, what would he make of the once glorious city. It was now a mass of rubble, destruction, and bodies.

Only her other brother, Shahriar and herself had escaped the bloody wrath that was ISIS.

They had what they stood in. Luckily for them, they'd been on their way to a family wedding, not only wearing most of their own jewellery, but were also carrying a substantial gift of gold items for the bride and groom as was the custom. They never actually got as far as seeing the two lovebirds; the attack came as they alighted the car to walk to the hotel wedding venue.

The car had saved their lives that day and the gold would finally save them today. For now, they were only hours from London and a cousin who promised work and a home – and safety.

The channel was the final obstacle. They would arrive penniless if the guides had their way, demanding more for the final part, the entry into the UK.

She hated that it had to be illegally, her father had been a judge back home in Syria, and both her parents and teachers had demanded truthfulness and integrity in all she and her siblings did. But now they had no choice, Naseem was their only living family. Where else could they go?

Her brother was not yet 18 and she only 14; they needed a guardian. All other avenues took years. They had to get to their cousin.

They sat cramped, cold, and hungry on the beach, a beach where once men had died in heroic fighting. Sword Beach was to the left, the lights of Ouistreham were behind and to the right. She felt the chill of their ghosts and shame at her stealing a freedom they'd died for. Her father's love of history and the films of World War II had taught her so much as she'd sat beside her adored Baba.

They were to be put ashore somewhere between Brighton and Eastbourne on the southeast coast. From there, a van would take them into London. In a few short hours, she'd be safe again, would be able to sleep again, to bathe and be a teenager again. She felt old. It was true, Shahriar was older, but since the day they buried her father and oldest brother, he had been just a pale shadow of the boy he'd once been.

He believed he should have been in the other car with the men, the one that had been stopped at the crossroads as they tried to escape the oncoming attack. He had raged at his father for telling him to go with his mother, his little sister, her friend Gülten and her mother.

"I am not a child," he hissed to his father.

"No, indeed you are not," his father had said, "which is why I need you to go with them, to protect them." Gülten's mother had seen the truck's arrival.

As they approached, she'd put her foot down and sped through the intersection, just beating the first truck. Her father and brother, in the other car with friends, had not been so lucky. Making Sayan and Gülten stop, they got out and doubled back via a couple of alleyways to come out beside the junction. They got there just in time to see the anger of the soldiers of ISIS, their cruel and tortuous murder of all in the vicinity, even the small son of the bread seller whose stand was on the street corner. They were assaulted with machetes, pistol butts and finally shot as they lay in unbearable agony. Shahriar had been unreachable ever since.

They had waited, then when the soldiers had moved on in search of new targets, brought their father's car up beside the bodies, loaded their father and brother into the car and drove out intending to meet up with Gülten and her mother if possible in Aleppo. At the next town, they buried the dead and momentarily allowed grief to flow.

The only good news was that the dogs who'd killed her father, and who'd searched all the cars in the street, had failed to find the floor safe her father had had installed on a whim. He'd seen it in an American movie. His whim might save their lives. And now, after weeks of cramped airless lorries, freezing storerooms, no clean clothes, or hot food, they were in sight of safety. She'd let nothing stop them now, nothing, Aisha whispered to herself.

The guides called them and hurried them down the beach. There, waiting in the shallows, was a small fishing vessel. They had to wade out and climb up a short rope ladder. The sea was freezing and the boat was bobbing about, but finally all managed to scramble aboard. They were told to get below into a small cabin, all seven of them; again, they were crammed in like tiny fish.

Aisha had studied for two years in a prestigious girl's school near Oxford and had been home for the summer vacation when the troubles came to the family. From the age of seven, her father had sent them all to a private tutor to learn English. It was now as easy to think, listen and speak it as her native Arabic.

Her stomach was raging against the motion of the boat. Out in the open water of the channel, the sea was choppy. She could see huge tankers ahead and a ferry on her left. She prayed for their safety: they were running in darkness, all their lights doused, their vessel black against the night, invisible, or so they thought.

Their guides finally pulled up onto the beach, if that was what it was, Aisha had never seen a shoreline of pebbles before. They'd just begun to climb out when the boat was lit up in a spotlight fit for one of the rock stars that her brother loved.

A stern voice called out to them, "This is Her Majesty's Coast Guard. You will not be harmed. Sit down with your hands on your head."

Instead of following instructions, one of the guides reached below the seat and pulled out a Kalashnikov. In one fluid motion, he began to spray the beach in front of them, at the same time yelling to the wheelman, "Get us off the beach!" Suddenly a large arc of lights came on arranged higher on the beach. This was no accidental capture. They'd been waiting.

As the boat went into reverse, Shahriar was screaming and charging the first gunman, but he hadn't seen the older man pull a pistol from his coat. He raised his arm and was aiming at Shahriar's back. Aisha was galvanised into action; she could not lose another brother. She threw herself forward, knocking the pistol sideways. Raffi, the older man, swore and swung his fist at her, but she was pulling Shah down, and the blow missed its target.

As she ducked, she could see a line of officers on the beach and realised Marcel, the other guide, was about to

304

open fire on them, she knew she was about to end all hope of safety and getting to her cousin, but "right was right."

Aisha jumped, grabbing the barrel of the weapon, Marcel screamed at her and pulled the gun to try and shake her off. She clung to the barrel even as he put his finger on the trigger again. She heard Shah call her name among other voices screaming orders and the guide, cursing trying to escape. Then the pain of the bullet erupted, and a blessed darkness swallowed her.

She regained consciousness in a clean hospital bed. The pleasure of its cleanliness and warmth were her first coherent thoughts. As she focused, her eyes fell on her brother asleep in an armchair. Two policemen guarded the door to the room.

She recovered quickly, and they were sent to a detention centre, until three months later they attended court to give evidence against Marcel and Raffi.

The others who they had travelled with all still had family back home. They had none, only each other. There was nothing ISIS could use to ensure their silence, and so they accepted the deal offered and gave their evidence. In return they'd been offered immunity and visas for both to enter the country as asylum seekers.

Some of the police and Coast Guardsmen had given evidence that both she and her brother had behaved with integrity and bravery and had, by putting themselves in harm's way, saved some of their lives that night. Their visa was granted.

That was five years ago, Aisha now is working towards becoming a solicitor and Shahriar is studying to be a doctor; he wants to go and work in the camps.

The Resolution

The resolution, when it came to her, was so simple. She was shocked it had taken so long to reach.

She and Abraham had been married for over twenty years. The marriage, whilst not physically forced upon them, had been declared and tenaciously demanded by both families. Neither had much hope of escaping the plans laid down by both sets of parents. Garfield Adams and Lindsay Campbell had been partners since just after the Great War.

In 1921, they had, after returning from the blood-stained fields of France, began their import business in partnership with two largish vineyards they'd encountered in the Compiegne and Bergerac areas of France.

They had been in the same unit and on two separate occasions when they'd been out of the line, they'd been bivouacked in one of the many vineyard barns. The winemaker was friendly but struggling.

After an evening where a couple of bottles from the wine maker's diminished cellars had been shared, Garfield and Lindsay had come to an arrangement with the man, for after the end of the war. A hasty contract had been drawn up and signed by the three parties.

They were moved on next day, neither party exactly hopeful that their idea would bloom. It would depend upon so many variables. The outcome of the war, the survival of the two soldiers, and the men who would try to save their homes and livelihood's, the men whose names were written on the papers each held a copy of.

As it was, they came across another vineyard before hostilities finally ended, they made the same deal with the second vintner.

Come spring, 1921, they travelled back to the vineyards and were delighted to find their partners had survived and were in the process of getting their vines and grapes planted and processed. The agreements would stand.

By 1925, they were making good money importing and distributing the much-missed wines.

In 1928, Garfield married a timid parson's daughter, who kept a beautiful house and said nothing to intimate to her husband that she was painfully aware of his voracious philandering. Nor did she ever speak of his cruel and terrifying rages. It was not something that Emily Adams, nee Standen, wanted anyone to know about.

The following year, Lindsay, too, married. His wife though, was no shrinking violet or church mouse. She was unafraid to speak her mind. She was a gregarious and vivacious woman, one who knew how to manage her husband as many beautiful women often can. Rebecca Ogden knew how to use her feminine charms. As Mrs. Campbell, she wielded them carefully.

In 1946, both men had worked again rebuilding their business in the wake of yet another war.

Their children, Garfield's son, Abraham, now eighteen and Lindsay's daughter, Charlotte, who was approaching her seventeenth birthday, would inherit the business from their fathers. Neither father liked the idea of an outsider getting any control of their hard-won successful business. They came up with the plan after a casual remark by a guest at a dinner party who commented, "What a lovely couple Charlotte and Abraham made," as they swirled round the dance floor together. And so began the pressure on the young couple who, up until that point, had harboured only lukewarm feeling towards each other at best.

Lindsay and Rebecca informed Charlotte that her engagement would be announced at the Christmas ball, and the two would wed in the April the following spring. Charlotte begged, pleaded, railed, and raged to no avail. Neither parent would brook any argument.

Abraham was incandescent with rage and declared he would have none of it. He acquiesced finally, but only when Garfield spat that if he did not marry Charlotte, that he would be disinherited. The seed of disaster was planted in that moment and bloomed into a full-blown and vicious resentment. Charlotte, he vowed, might become his wife, but he would not be faithful, just like his father.

He did not consider however, that Charlotte was not like his mother. She was an independent thinker, with a bright intelligent mind. She was also beautiful; this he'd not been oblivious to, but her outspokenness and obvious disinterest in him, did nothing to endear him at all. He was, after all, a rich and successful, influential, and vain man. One that was not outwardly unattractive to members of the fairer sex. Plenty had shown him since he was in his teens that they would welcome his advances. And advance he had.

The wedding went ahead, and they had two children who were the apple of their mother's eye.

Abraham did not visit his wife's bed after the birth of their second child.

Charlotte was grateful for that, and she was happy in her role as a mother and doted on her two children. Bertram was her first born. Affectionately known as Bertie, he was a mischievous and daring boy. One who beguiled and terrified his mother in equal measure. His twinkling blue eyes and wide loving smile always diminished her anger, and he filled her heart with love and pride. Elizabeth was born two years later. Charlotte could not have been happier, given the circumstances. Beth was happiest with either a cat in her lap, or a paint brush in her hand. She was a sweet and gentle girl who became a talented artist, and locally her work was very much admired.

The years passed and whilst Charlotte was content as she enjoyed the years of motherhood, she still hungered for someone to love her as a woman. She was only in her forties. There could be as many years before her as behind, and the thought of them spent as a glorified housekeeper for Abraham filled her soul with sadness and dread. She was no wife to him in the truest nor broader sense of the word.

Then one wet winter evening Abraham returned early and in high spirits. After the family had dined, he asked Charlotte to join him in his study. He wasted no time in small talk, he just declared that Beth was to become betrothed to a merchant acquaintance of his. Charlotte knew the man he spoke of. He was the same sort of age as herself, not that that would have been as much of an issue for her had he been a kind and considerate man.

The man Abraham proposed to tie his daughter to, Stanley Carruthers, was a corpulent, loud, garrulous bully of a man who was always in his cups. Her husband declared it an excellent business match. The man was also an importer from France, but not wine; he dealt in cheese. The two businesses would merge when their two children inherited.

Charlotte was horrified and wasted neither time nor gentleness in expressing her dissent. She would not, could not, sanction a marriage that would be as bereft of human compassion or love as hers had been.

That's when Abraham made his fatal mistake.

He slapped her hard, the back of his hand crashing across her cheek. He spat at her, "Woman, you will obey me."

Charlotte vowed she'd find a way to spare her daughter. Until then, she would make a pretence of acceptance.

The following week, she asked Abraham to take them to their small home in France near one of the vineyards. It was to be a last family holiday before the announcement.

That she had finally been graceful in acceptance of the situation had put him in a generous mood, and he agreed they would go. Sadly, Bertie was in India with his regiment by then and would not be able to join them, just as Charlotte had anticipated.

Abraham's fondness for doxies and drink was only outshone by his love of horses. He often rode early, before anyone in the house stirred. He declared he loved the solitude and peace of the early hours.

Their small summer home was near where Abraham and Lindsay had been billeted in 1918. They kept horses there. A local farmer cared for them, and his son exercised them daily. Her husband was looking forward to some fine riding as the dawn broke in the Dordogne.

Charlotte kept up the public appearance of a dutiful wife. She deferred to her husband when the temporary staff were attending to their needs or when they were out visiting her husband's acquaintances, and always when Beth was in their company.

On the third evening of their stay, as she and Beth made to take their leave to retire, Abraham said he might be late or absent completely for breakfast in the morning. He had planned his first ride and would be gone before first light with no idea how long he'd be.

Charlotte opened the small valise. She'd carried it herself as they returned from a shopping trip the day before. Inside were a set of breeches, a wool shirt, a cap, a warm winter coat and leather boots. Bertie was of a similar height and build as Charlotte, she'd gift them to him when they returned to England.

She sat in the lee of the small section of the dry-stone wall that had no shrubs or trees in front nor behind it. It sat at the rear of the small paddock behind the stables. Abraham never dismounted and opened the gate, he relished the gallop and flight over the span of stone, it heralded his release. To gallop wherever his fancy took him, to him, this was freedom!

She was cold, stiff, and chasing thoughts around her head. So many "what if's," her nerve and resolve were beginning to wane when she saw the lantern light from within the stables, then saw it extinguished.

The faintest light as night died and dawn broke allowed Charlotte to see him leave the yard and begin his race towards the wall.

She watched from behind the hedgerow to the right of the visible area of wall as he drew ever closer. Then she just concentrated on the sound and vibration of the galloping hoofbeats.

Startled, wide eyed and nostrils flaring, the beast skidded from full gallop to a dead stop. The look of astonishment on Abraham's face, seeing her rise from behind the wall as he simultaneously catapulted from the saddle at breakneck speed, was priceless.

"Whatever is it, Angelique?"

Her bedroom door opened and the girl from the village who'd been engaged to help said, "Madame, you must come. There has been an "accident terrible!"

Abraham's horse had returned to the stables, He was found by the stone wall. His neck was broken, and he had some serious contusions to his temple and skull. He'd obviously been thrown and sailed over the wall. It was unclear if the broken neck or the fractured skull occurred first, either of which would have caused his demise.

Bertram passed the daily running of the business to his mother, but after one of his visits home, he saw that it was in fact Beth who was the driving force behind the success they had enjoyed since he'd inherited the company.

He made a progressive decision and made Beth a full partner in their family business.

Two years later, Charlotte accompanied Bertie to a regimental dinner and there lost her heart to Colonel Andrew Carnegie. With no effort at all, he fell under her spell. He was so smitten that he approached Bertie for permission to ask for his mother's hand a meagre six weeks later.

Charlotte never did give Bertie the contents of the valise, she threw it from the train as they'd travelled home with Abraham's body for burial in the family plot.

Charlotte and Beth were free.

The Anniversary

Mernie sat in the graveyard, the sun warm on her shoulders as she let her mind go hither and thither, allowing it to stop where it may. It occurred to her that the passing of time speeds up and slows down and inspires a quasi-schizophrenic state.

Her thoughts expanded; either it accelerates as we get older because we are now so aware of how little time we have, or, as in daily life, things we do not like or wish to do, like the dental appointment or the trip to the hospital for breast screening, increase their passing speed. Those anxiously approaching dates, seem to race through the days on our calendars.

The date with the man of our dreams a week Friday, though, seems to take an eternity to pass. Just as the Christmases of our childhood, or the anticipated annual holiday to sunnier climes dragged the days out on the calendar.

Whatever the cause, it felt but a day or so ago that she'd stood here at this grave for the first time. She remembered thinking then, had it really, already, been ten days since she'd arrived moments too late at the hospital.

The day she'd broken her vow. They'd made the vow to each other in the heady, glory days, of their passionate love affair. That the other's face would be the first to be seen each morning and the last to be seen before they slept, up to and including the final sleep.

She'd failed him.

She'd taken the anticipated call, flown from the house to drive to the hospital to be with him as he left this world. She flew through the first part of the journey and had a moments indecision at the roundabout that offered up two options. The main artery road that led directly to the hospital, or the side roads, which were usually only faster in peak times.

The main road should be thin on traffic at this time she thought as she went to pull out. Just then a large postal van came out of the turning on her right, she gave way then pulled out behind it.

He entered the artery road, then sat on the centre line all the way.

She prayed for a place and space to overtake, but it wasn't to be.

Cursing the driver as she drew into the carpark, she abandoned her car with no ticket in the parking lot and raced as best her arthritic legs would allow. She barrelled through corridors and ward doors like the devil himself was on her coattails.

As she put her hand on the door handle to his room, she tried to gulp in some desperately needed oxygen. Her heart was ready to burst, and she could barely see.

She opened the door trying to put a smile on her face for him.

He lay, hands on his chest, eyes closed. She knew, and unbidden, a scream rose in her chest and escaped like a demon possessed.

"Nooooh! Oh, God no! Oh, love… oh, my love! I'm so, so sorry…"

She laid her head on his chest and, holding his hand, she wept like her heart would break – and it did.

Why, she considered a little later, was it that the two men she'd loved most in the world, her father, and her soulmate, had gone without waiting to say goodbye? The days leading to the funeral went by in a blur of tears, pain and "doing."

And now, here we are, already another twelve months have passed, was it seven years, it felt like twenty and at the same time, only last week.

Seven long years since she'd felt his arms, heard his voice, husky in her ear, or enjoyed the sound of his laughter, or tasted his kisses.

The pain said it was only last week.

This anniversary was not the only one in this time anomaly. Deaths of friends, parents, grandparents were similar.

At this stage of life, she felt time had changed the rules and goalposts, she was just waiting for her time. And time now dragged, oh so slowly.

A New Arrival

Hal had always been unorthodox in his approach to business and life. It was why he and his father had argued so much. His father's health having now failed meant he felt the mantle of running the family business settle uneasily upon his shoulders.

The books were showing that they were barely breaking even. Upon further investigation, it seemed this trend coincided with his father's appointing of a manager three years prior.

The last locking of horns had been five years ago, which had precipitated Hal's trip to the U.S. and Canada. Initially meant as a month-long trip, it had drawn out until last month, when his mother had called and, using her power of attorney, appointed Hal to take over the company immediately.

He acted swiftly and sent a friend in as a prospective big hitting client. He asked him to get a feel for the staff and atmosphere. The report from his private investigator chum was much worse than he'd expected.

Morale was virtually non-existent in all departments. Dictatorial management had alienated the workforce. There was neither pride nor loyalty on show at all.

On February 28th, dressed in jeans, polo shirt and cashmere sweater, Hal arrived and clocked in as the new assistant manager. His resume' was any company's dream application. He'd been in the top five in his graduate year, all excellent marks with merits across the board and glowing references from two of the U.S.'s best companies. He was also not too proud as to snub the somewhat low pay offer.

*　　*　　*　　*　　*

Mr. Daniels, the manager, gave me the 'what's where' tour, then showed me to my office, small but functional, then left me to it.

Sally, the junior secretary for the admin office popped her head round the door and asked, "Would you like a tea or coffee?,"

I smiled; she didn't. "Thanks, but I can see to myself, I'm sure you have enough to do without wet nursing the new arrival." She looked shocked,

"Is something wrong?" I asked.

"Well, it's pretty much all I do except taking and collecting the lunch orders."

Sally and I had a good old chinwag over lunch that day and I discovered much about the people and the running of things here.

I mentioned to Mr. Daniels that I might use Sally as my PA as she had some free time,

"Indeed, you will not," he replied coldly.

"My secretaries, Jenny and Lynn, do all the managers' admin work. That way I can keep my eye on things."

I ventured then to ask, "Then can I advertise for a part time PA to deal with my diary, making appointments and scheduling trips to the clients and suppliers?"

"Very well, I will email the salary allowance and it will be a three-month trial contract only. Understood?" I nodded that I did indeed.

I interviewed about a dozen women. One was acceptable; more importantly, she was willing to accept the meagre salary and contract terms. I sent her details to Jenny as apparently she also doubled as the human resource officer.

Two weeks passed and I was on my way to see Mr. Daniels to clarify something urgent for a client. As I approached his office, I was surprised to see my PA, Caroline, in what appeared to be a very flustered and distressed state. She refused eye contact with me and sped down the hall to our office.

When I returned, there was an envelope on my desk. It was her resignation. There was no explanation, but it was a very definite departure.

A further two weeks passed. I'd been to see Caroline at her home. I had also visited all my biggest suppliers and clients. I enjoyed both interesting and illuminating chats with them all.

Sally and I had been to dinner a few times and I was getting a good feel for the business and the workers. Of course, Sally tipped the wink as to who were good hard workers and who were loyal, from both the oldest members of staff to the newest.

It was about one month after joining the company workforce, I sent an email from my home computer. It would arrive on the same day a letter from Mother's solicitors. It informed Mr. Daniels regarding my father's immediate retirement and the imminent arrival of their son, Henry Colquhoun-Smyth, Jnr., who would take over from his father on the 1st of the month.

April dawned, sunny and bright, a good omen I thought as I left home that morning.

I sat in my vintage Daimler sports, and waited until everyone had arrived, including Mother. I stepped quickly across to the imposing double doors at the main entrance to the company building, not my usual entry point. The foyer was being used as a reception hall to welcome the new boss.

As the doors swung open, Mr. Daniels spotted me. He swiftly excused himself from my mother's side and bore down like a missile, scowling at me all the way.

"What do you think you are doing, Hal? Get out and back where you belong."

I smiled slowly and said, "But Mr. Daniels, I do believe you are expecting me. Your email certainly said so!"

He was confused and flustered. "Get out! I'll deal with you later!" he growled.

Over his shoulder, I watched Mother approach, "Ah, Mr. Daniels, I see you've found Henry for me," she cooed, offering one of her most beguiling of smiles.

"What?!?" he spluttered!

"Let me introduce my son, Henry Colquhoun-Smyth, Jnr., known professionally as Hal Smith. He was so stubborn about wanting to make it on merit and not his father's reputation that he uses an alias in his working life."

"Mother, do join Sally and me for lunch, I'd like you to meet her. She's rather wonderful and, as of Monday, she will head up the admin offices as my PA."

"Now just a sec, Hal, I hire and fire. It's in my contract," said Daniels, trying to reassert his position."

"Well now, Daniels," I paused and nodded to the two plain clothed police officers. "These gentlemen need to have a chat with you. And just so we're clear, you no longer hire and fire. In fact, you are dismissed. I will be pressing charges and your cohorts are being arrested on the shop floor as we speak."

"Good day Sir," said the CID officer as he led the blustering thief away.

* * * * *

Six months later: Sally has agreed to marry me; the business is thriving again and, much to my surprise, a high percentage of the funds stolen from the firm were recovered from Daniels and his chums.

The 'new arrival' had heralded a new beginning for the factory and me.

Daniels, Lynn, and Jenny were awaiting sentencing. He'd paid them very well to keep two sets of books, as he had the two line managers already away on HM Pleasure.

I love it when a plan comes together.

Unwelcome Visitor

Brodie did so hate it when his sister took it into her head to "cheer him up":

I'd been widowed in my forties. Now in my late fifties, her matchmaking was truly getting old. Surely there couldn't be any other over fifty ladies left. Mercy had scoured the bowling teams, Derby and Jones, dance, and whist club ladies. Surely there could be none left in this small coastal town of Kinsale, Cork, for her to wrangle into meeting me.

My home sat on the high ground near the Spaniard Inn, overlooking the River Brandon which has created a natural bay with Kinsale at its mouth. The elevated position gave stunning views, though the wind fairly blew a hoolie up there come the winter.

I loved it. The fact that there was a grand bar which was always good for the craic just up the road helped tip the balance when I decided to buy it after my Katie had passed.

Mercy had been inappropriately named: At least as far as I was concerned, she had none. She was relentless in her quest to 'save' her wee brother from loneliness. Which, may I say, I do not suffer from.

I enjoy my own company, and the billiards, and shove halfpenny teams have me out twice a week, and the rotary club enjoyed my attendance most weekends.

To be fair, Mercy's insistence this time was irritating me all the more, for reasons nothing to do with her. You see, there was a lovely, new lady who'd turned up at the rotary club.

Her name was Marley. She had a lovely smile, twinkling green eyes and titian red hair that just took my breath away. It hadn't been until yesterday when I saw my mate, Ewan, that I learnt that she was in fact a widow woman.

I had determined then and there to ask this vision to join me for lunch when she came to the club on Saturday. Since she had been there for the last three weeks, I felt it safe to assume she may well be there this Saturday too.

Inevitably, of course, this was when my interfering big sister said that she was coming to me for lunch and was bringing a friend. No matter how I tried to put her off, she was having none of it and ended with the *fait accompli*, announcing she'd already asked the said friend.

My unwelcome sister and her visitor would not be dissuaded.

So, here we are. I had devised a very uninspired menu of quiche, salad, and jacket potatoes, with a cheese board in place of a dessert. My plan was that it wouldn't take too long to devour this and I might just make it to the club before my dream girl disappeared.

Mercy said they'd arrive at twelve-thirty sharp. Like a military operation, on the dot of twelve-thirty, my doorbell rang. When I opened it, Mercy's large frame filled the doorway of my small miner's cottage.

Beaming at me, she leaned forward, and, planting a kiss on my cheek, said, "This is my new friend," and stepping aside revealed the form of my dream girl. "Marley, meet my wee brother Brodie."

Maybe Mercy had finally realised her mission.

I for one was most certainly looking forward to finding out.

The Last to Fall

"You know, being as old as I am is not easy, little one. I've seen so very much, lost so many to whom I've been very attached. I knew your grandparents, and their parents. If I try, I can see the changes in them as their time flew by.

I recall just last year in late March or early April, how vibrant and full of life your parents were. So quickly it seemed that their end came.

I remember you too, in your Easter colours, it was your first outing without them.

I see the loneliness in you since everyone else moved on, and the fear of what comes next. I see it in you now! There is a slight tremble in your being and your voice is but a whisper.

Come now, don't be sad, you've had a glorious life, albeit short, you gave such joy and colour to the world.

There's nothing to be afraid of. It's just the order of things, the circle of life. It's not the end, not really.

Yes, lad, the wind is blowing harder now. I can feel your strength waning. Farewell, my bonnie lad"!

He watched as his last companion fell.

The little boy pulled his father's arm, then cried out, "Oh look, Daddy. How sad. The very last leaf just fell off the tree. Will the tree be cold and sad till spring?"

The great oak sighed and then all was quiet.

The Waiting Room

Jack knew instantly that this was going to be a bad one. His bike slid from under him, robbing him of the last vestiges of control he might have had. Then he was slammed down into the cross hairs of the bridge supports.

The sudden burst of the glorious stag from the wood had caused him to both swerve, and brake, concluding in the loss of control on such a pretty, wood-lined, mountain road. The moment of pain was all consuming, then blessed oblivion.

The whole incident was over in about ninety seconds.

The first sensation he was later aware of was warmth, followed then by such a beautiful, haunting tune playing somewhere nearby. As he forced his eyes open and blinked through the bright golden light, he'd thought to find himself in a hospital bed.

This, however, was not the case. He was neither bandaged nor hooked up to a monitor. Then he realised that he was not alone: quite a few people shared the large room with him. They all seemed well or were sleeping. *"How curious,"* he thought.

He closed his eyes for a moment, then heard a voice calling out some names. Two old men, a woman carrying a baby and two teenage boys stood and were ushered through a door. An old crone and a small boy were heard being told they were going home soon.

Jack called out, "Hello?"

A kindly faced man appeared at his bed. He smiled at Jack.

"Where am I?" asked Jack.

"In the waiting room," replied the man, "the Lord will let you know what is to be done soon. Just rest till then, son."

The light of realisation lit Jack's face. He closed his eyes and laughed – just as he flew into the light.

The Legacy

The Daughter's Story:

Catriona sat at the kitchen window, where she always sat in her mother's kitchen. She ached, knowing that never again would she feel that comfort. The bustle of her mother cooking, her father washing up or getting a bacon sandwich. Or on one of those exceedingly rare occasion, they would share a short oasis and partake of a moment of true contact. Laughter, tears, shared pains, or a snippet of gossip, they were all precious moments to Catriona.

Cat could scarcely absorb the magnitude of change in her world. In only forty-eight hours, she'd recognised that her marriage of less than two years was over. She'd watched her beloved father retreat to a place within himself where nothing, neither comfort, love, cajoling or joy would ever reach again. And her family was broken in a way from which they would never recover.

She had quietly collected the bucket and bass broom and scrubbed, mopped, and rinsed the steps below the kitchen window. She'd found the glasses, brought them in, cleaned them, and set them by the armchair in the sitting room.

She fulfilled her duty as the eldest child, organising everything possible and only quietly consulting her father –

who overnight, had shrunk, become distant and passive — when she absolutely had to.

How, she thought, could the sun be shining so brightly when it should be the greyest darkest of days? She just could not get her head around it.

The next day, as she lay in the hospital bed, the soft gentle voices of the nurses offered condolences for the loss of her tiny precious twelve-week foetus.

"It wasn't meant to be." "Nature's way, not your fault." Their offerings brought no comfort. Her mother's suicide had stripped her of so very much more than just her mother.

The little voice in her head said her mother couldn't take one of the grandchildren already here, so she took this little one with her. She turned her head and let the tears fall.

The Mother's Story:

Loretta sat on the window ledge, the steps and path three floors below looked exactly as they always did. Dark thoughts changed her perception of these familiar facets of what once was her dream home.

That same home that was now her worst nightmare. It had all gone so terribly wrong. She could not comprehend how so much of their life's savings had been frittered away.

336

Pensions and bequests worth thousands and more, so much more, gone!

Sadly, there was nothing to show for it. No expensive cars, no big fancy holidays. They didn't even wear designer labels.

"And that's not the worst of it," she thought sadly. As the instigator of this disaster, the gloriously calamitous title of penury-bringer, belonged to her and her alone!

Single handed, she'd lost every penny they'd accrued and in doing so destroyed her husband and youngest son's future.

He'd given up his career path to become the third partner in the business, the same one that tomorrow morning would cease to exist. Bailiffs, solicitors, and social workers would unveil the full measure of her stubborn stupidity and prideful incompetence.

She wiped the outside glass in the windows, then threw the cloth inside onto the floor, pausing for just a moment. She heard the little voice in her ear mocking her.

She leant back, feeling the sun and sea breeze, then let go.

Her last thoughts cut short as simultaneously a rib pierced her heart and her skull fractured as she hit the concrete steps below the kitchen window.

The coroner said she died instantly. The effect, her legacy, would still be felt decades later by those she left behind.

The Cry of the Mountain

When the world was made, the mountain was pulled from the belly of the earth. She remembered well the pain of her birth. The subsequent surprise at the wonder she felt at the wholly different view of the world she now enjoyed from her newly elevated position. This is her story:

For a long time though, I grieved for the comforting feeling of being enveloped by mother earth's embrace.

Looking back, I remembered my amusement at the development of a creature that finally had stood upright on just two legs. The comedy of their fright upon their first encounter with fire and delight they found in the healing warmth that came and not from the glory of the sun. She let her thoughts drift over the eons of time.

I also saw their fear and suffering when I spit forth the anger of the earth by way of great spouts of fire and brimstone. I wasn't very happy at being used in such a way; these beings had done nothing to my knowledge to warrant such a downpouring of rage.

Had I known then what I know now. Oh then, I would have given all to assist in their total annihilation. I was young and in the way of the young, was idealistic, an ingenue in human parlance.

As they developed, (known now as mankind) they were inventive, creative, exciting to observe. Then came a time of love and joy for me.

They called themselves "the People," they came here with a love for the mother earth, and all her bounties.

They lived in tipis. They honoured the Mother, cared for her. They hunted only what they needed. They cut trees only for survival, for homes, travois, and arrows. They wasted nothing. They cared for the needy and vulnerable and shared what they had.

Later, I watched in horror as numbers grew. Other tribes came, with white skin and a hunger for the yellow metal that runs through my very being.

These two tribes fought each other, until finally the red man was no more. The whites came then in their thousands, like ants upon the land.

They broke my heart then, these men, and caused me such anguish and suffering.

Their need for the yellow metal from my innards caused such pain and destruction. For the longest time I thought I would cease to be, such was the deep and terrible wounds they inflicted upon me.

I cried long days and nights during those times.

Then, these white men had great battles. First, they'd fought the red man; now, they fought each other. They captured and enslaved those peoples they did not understand. Some they decimated in war; others they subjugated and used.

The ancient tribes tried to fight them. I saw some of the battles fought by those who spoke the ancient tongue which I recognised, though I couldn't remember from where, for their language was older than I.

And now, here we are. Some of these complicated people have begun to see that they will destroy themselves with their ignorant and selfish ways. There are those who try to lead their tribes away from disaster. I hope, before I fall into the sea, that they can unite before they destroy us all.

I am old now and long to return to the comforting embrace of my Mother Earth.

For those who follow the ways of "the People," I pray for deliverance.

The Locked Door

As Gerry turned from the bar with a tray of drinks for his pals, one of whom was John, his soon to be best man, he thought, *"Only a fortnight to go till the wedding."* He was beginning to get excited and nervous in equal measure.

This was the first night of his stag weekend in Paris. The weekend had begun well with a French pastry course for all the lads; it had been hilarious. Great muscled brickies and plasterers handling tiny delicacies. Despite much trepidation by the lot of them, it had been a great laugh, the two electricians winning hands down.

They had then showered and changed and headed to the bars. The drinks had been flowing fast and he felt more than a little tipsy. He took himself off to the gents to get some quiet to call Celeste, his French fiancée.

It had been her idea to have the hen and stag parties in Paris, using her family's apartment saving them hotel bills. It was a wonderful place near the *Pigalle*, and had four large rooms, a real bonus for him and his mates. It had enabled them all to afford the trip. The hen night had been last weekend and all the girls had raved about the whole thing.

He and Celeste chatted for about ten minutes and were winding up with their usual "Good night, I love you," when John came in.

He began teasing Gerry about being a soppy git, and being under the thumb already, accusing the laughing Gerry of letting the side down. More of the lads had piled in behind John, wondering where he'd got to.

That was the moment Fate intervened.

The lads were well oiled, and an atmosphere of high jinks surfaced. They unceremoniously shoved Gerry into a vacant stall, cable tied his hands to the pipes, and debagged him, before locking the door with a coin and leaving. They were laughing their heads off as they abandoned him.

The door had barely closed when a huge bang rocked the place. A piece of ceiling hit Gerry's head and he didn't remember anything else till he awoke in hospital.

*　*　*　*　*

For the first couple of days, everyone spoke in whispers and were exceedingly kind. It was the look in their eyes that frightened him, what were they not telling him. Was he a cripple, destined to never to walk again, or was he dying? Come evening on that day, he demanded the doctor come see him. Not even Celeste could calm or comfort him. He had to know whatever it was that they were keeping from him.

As soon as the doctor entered the room, Gerry begged to be told the worst. Whatever it was they were keeping from him he wanted to know, needed to know, and NOW.

The doctor sat in the chair beside his bed and asked if he was sure,

"Yes," Gerry answered.

"Very well. I am deeply sorry to tell you that everyone on the other side of the toilet door was either killed or very seriously injured. You were incredibly lucky, *Monsieur*. If it hadn't been for the cuffs and the locked door, Gerry, you might well be dead now."

Fate is fickle indeed.

PUCCINI
Tosca
PUCCINI
Tosca

The Opera Ticket

Jack heaved the bin up onto his back and grabbed the extra bag. Just as it cleared the ground, the bottom fell out. Instantly, papers were lifted on the wind that scattered the rubbish all over the road. As he systematically worked through the chaos, from one end of the street to the other, gathering it all back up, he pondered the sadness of it all.

Old Mr. Winthrop, who's bin this had been, had neither family nor friend left to come and clear his home after his sudden death last month. The neighbours said he was always polite but distant. Always kept to himself.

He'd apparently lived in this house for over forty years.

It made Jack grateful for his wife Jean, gone five years now, and his two sons, even if they were out in Canada.

As he lifted the last bundle of papers, some fancy print caught Jacks eye. He read: *Teatro di San Carlo, Napoli, presents Puccini's Tosca.* It was a ticket to the opera. The date for the concert a month from now.

Obviously, the old chap had bought the ticket never thinking his health would stop him going, never thinking his heart would stop! At least not at the relatively early age of sixty-eight.

Jack slipped the card in his pocket. Could he go? Should he go?

July 3rd found Jack sitting in a box, in the oldest and continually used theatre in Europe. The Bourbons had been patrons of this beautiful theatre.

He sat upright in his seat, uncomfortable in his new dinner jacket, though less so since the brandy in the lounge of his hotel, which had steadied him a little.

When he left hours later, tears still wet on his cheek, he headed to the hotel bar again.

There, he raised a glass to the man who'd intended to be here, to the man who made it possible for him to be there.

When he got home, he would find out where old Winthrop was buried, and in gratitude for this moving experience, would go visit him now and again. The old man should have someone, deserved someone, who would remember him.

Jack would.

Time Traveller

Robert sat up slowly. His head felt as if he'd taken a kick off one of his Da's old war horses. He looked around and saw he was in the great glen. However, as he stood, he was astonished to see a strange structure nearby.

He thought, *"I must have really cracked ma skull a rare wallop,"* for the sight before him was fantastical.

There were huge glass walls and lights in some magical form hanging from the inner roof beams. He walked gingerly up the slope and sat on a bench of sorts. Beside him lay some paper. They reminded him of the huge proclamation notices usually nailed to the castle door, or to the village green tree.

He was baffled by the form of speech used but impressed by the print quality. It was sharp, neither fuzzy nor smudged as the news sheets usually were.

His eyes lit on the smaller text at the top of the page, February 12th, 2017. He laughed aloud, "What a jape, someone was obviously playing tricks." He threw it down as he spotted a small book.

It carried the colours and pattern of his tartan and an image of the clan crest. The MacDonalds were an ancient and powerful clan, led by their chieftain, Alasdair Ruadh

(Roy) MacIan MacDonald, the 12th of Glencoe, so why did this wee book say it was a clan with its chieftaincy in dispute.

He opened the book, the first chapter was headed, The Massacre? What rot was this? He read on:

"On the morning of Feb 13th, 1692, troops led by Robert Campbell, Earl of Argyll, under orders from King William, attacked and murdered as many MacDonalds as they could. Thirty-eight were murdered by the men who had enjoyed the highland hospitality of Clan MacDonald, a further forty women and bairns were to die from exposure after their homes were torched."

What madness was this? He pondered in confusion.

As Robert sat pondering what was happening to him, a lad of about eight summers came hurtling from the side of the building. He pulled up sharply at the sight of the big highlander but smiled and continued to approach.

"Hello," he said, "are you one of the re-enactors here for tomorrows show?"

"No," Robert grunted in reply. *What drivel was the child spewing?* "Lad, what year is this?"

"I know this," the boy said gleefully, "we learnt this in school today. It's February 12th, 2017." The wee lad was obviously chuffed that he'd remembered.

Robert continued, "So, now we've established that yer a bright fellow, let's see what else you know. Tell me what the story is that this book calls 'the Massacre'."

"That's easy! Everybody kens that one!"

Twenty minutes passed whilst he in childish form told the same story as in the book. Telling of the murder of the clan chief and the decimation of the clan.

No matter how Robert tried to find a different explanation, it seemed the impossible was all with which he was left.

Somehow, he had apparently jumped forward in time, and he now held information and facts about things about to transpire in his own time. *"I must get home,"* he thought.

Robert picked the book up again. On the last page, words caught his eye that almost caused his heart to stop. Scotland's own Lairds would sell us out in 1707 and allow England to create a union of the crowns. Scotland no longer ruled itself.

The name that loomed large in the list of those to betray the country, and to have become rich from his treachery was John Hay.

"It surely cannae be, dear God I need to get hame, I must stop this," he thought.

He began running down the slope towards the mouth of the Glen, leaping over river stones and through the copse that grew alongside the fast-flowing water. Just as he was approaching the spot where he'd wakened, he tripped, sprawling headlong into the side of the river's edge. His last thought before the black took him was, *"Don't let this knock me senseless."*

He came to, hearing his name being called in a voice laced in distress.

"Robert! Robert! Wake up, laddie! Oh, heavens, son, are ye all right?"

The sight that met his eyes was that of his mother bending low over him. "I'm fine mither, but stop bashing ma face. It stings!" Suddenly his mind became clear and everything flooded back. "Mither, whit day, is it?"

"Are ye puddle heided, son?" the woman looked at him, concern etched upon her aging face.

"No, just tell me the day,"

"It's the 12th day of February, in the year of Our Lord 1692. Now if ye're ready, pick yersel' up. Ye bumped yer heid on yon rock. I telt ye no tae run, but wid ye listen? Ye'd think at ten and seven summers ye'd be passed such nonsense."

"Mither, I must speak to the Chief. It's important. I'll take the wood back, but I'm going to run on. The cart will be readied for you when you return. I want you to get Morag and the bairns and go see Aunt Jeannie in Ballachulish, I will meet you there later. I don't want you to argue or ask anything, just for the love of God, do as I bid ye." He took off at a sprint, leaving Ina MacDonald to scowl after him.

By the time he'd finished arguing with Alasdair, his Chieftain, it was near midnight. His Chieftain refused to challenge the Campbell and wouldn't risk offending him by posting guards.

Robert opened the door to the cottage of his father, Rory MacDonald, dead these past five years. To Robert, this was and always would be his Da's cottage.

He intended to be but a minute or two, coming only to gather what meagre belongings he had along with his Da's sword and targe. He was therefore horrified to find his mother asleep in Da's old chair by the now-dying fire.

"What the divil are ye aboot woman, I telt ye tae leave, why did ye defy me?" He choked on the words.

"I'll not be dictated to by the likes o' you, lad. Even yer Da had the decency to explain his orders tae me."

Anger and fear caused his next words to be harsher than he would normally have used to his mother.

"God in heaven, woman, did it never enter yer stubborn heid that it was too important to waste the time explaining? You should have kent I'd not disrespect ye so, had there not been reason."

"Oh Robert," she said. "whit could be that important?"

Such flippancy! Robert wanted to scream.

"Your very life, and that of yer daughter and her wains, now in dire peril. All for your pride woman. God, what have ye done? Get them up now, quietly. Dress in the warmest clothes ye's have and roll the furs. We'll need them more than ever now for we cannae take the trap. Now hurry, and not a word."

Robert slipped out the back of the cottage and scouted the area. Cleverly, his father had built the wee cottage and had backed it in against the tree line at the base of the hill. It was a position that sheltered the house from the worst of the wind and snow in the darkest of winters. *"If the cloud held, and the bairns stayed quiet,"* Robert thought, *"we might make the mouth of the glen before sun-up."*

Talking aloud to himself, Robert said, "We had to! The book said the deed was done, and over as the dawn broke."

His heart was heavy. He knew he'd done all he could, even telling his oldest friend, Ian, who'd laughed and said,

354

"Yer awa wi' the fairies' laddie. Yon fall has coddled yer brains."

He could save only his family today; the coming deaths of those from his clan broke his heart. Campbell will pay, and Hay will be stopped. He'd find a way. He swore it on his father's claymore.

Dawn broke as they reached the home of their friends, the Robertsons. A small clan by comparison to the MacDonald's, but staunch allies. *"We will be safe there,"* he thought. *"We'll use the ancient name of the clan, Donnachaidh, until we can once more be safe, known as The MacDonalds of Glencoe."*

Robert, with his Da's sword and targe, likely lie with the Robertsons or MacDonalds on Culloden Moor, where Robert was last seen in the charge, yelling, *"Alba gu Brath!"*

Bigfoot

Bigfoot had earned kudos from his nickname in 1969, in Vietnam, where he'd been detailed as a scout. He was a Navajo. He could track anything and leave nothing to be tracked by.

It had been another hot, humid day. Every bit of his rotting uniform was wet. In fact, he was wet. His clothes were wet. His socks and boots were wet. He was scared.

Just before sundown, he was, as usual, out ahead of his patrol when a unit of Vietcong passed and was now between him and his comrades.

He'd hidden in the only cover that might save him. He'd crawled into the foul, stinking, carcass of a water buffalo. The stench, he hoped, would deter any of the gooks from getting too close and discovering him.

*　*　*　*　*

His name was really Aaron Snow Eagle, he was the son of a Navajo elder and a white woman. His father, Askii, and Irish Catholic mother, Bridget, had married in the late forties. His father could boast he'd served with the Marines on Iwo Jima. Askii was a Wind Talker.

Aaron was proud of his heritage on both sides. His Irish great grandfather had taken part in the Easter uprising in

Dublin. The aftermath had sent his family to the first boat heading to Boston, USA.

There they would find comfort and support from family and the Irish community.

Aaron was born in the time of melting snow, the spring of 1950. On the reservation at Window Rock, Arizona, outside their small farmstead home, his father had offered up his new-born son to the face of the Great Spirit Father for blessings.

Swooping down to grasp a rabbit caught out in the open, was a snow eagle. Aaron's father knew this to be an auspicious sign. It was from this sacred bird that his ancestors had coined their family name, or so the story went.

His father insisted always, that it was a great omen for his son.

Aaron grew tall, like the trees, and had lean but muscular legs and large hands and feet.

To be perfectly accurate, his nickname was bestowed on him after he'd been called up – on his first day of boot camp. Having finally reached the counter, the Quartermaster at Camp Lejeune had looked him up and down, raised an eyebrow and whistled. He'd then disappeared into the cavernous rear of the stores.

To greenhorn Aaron, the wait felt like it went on for ages. When the Quartermaster returned, he slapped a set of dusty boots on the counter, and joked, "These are Sasquatch's spare pair."

The rest of Aaron's unit heard the jibe, stifled their laughter, but forever after he was "Bigfoot."

*　*　*　*　*

Aaron held his breath and closed his eyes so that he could see only through his long, dark lashes. The wiry, short statured Vietcong soldiers filed past. He let out his breath softly and waited for about five minutes. He then rolled out of his foul embryonic sac of safety. The river was about twenty feet away and he belly-crawled the way his father had taught him as a boy. He'd revisited this ancient martial art in his basic training.

He slid into the river's cool, cleansing flow.

Aaron needed to get back to his unit. He hoped they would not get caught out by the unexpected arrival of 'Cong troops.

Intel had said the area they were in was free of Vietcong! Clearly their intel was off.

It was growing dark now; his friends would have made camp and be expecting him back, but he could not risk encountering the gooks again, so he found a good bit of cover off the track and waited for daylight.

He watched the sun begin its ascent and marvelled at the beauty of mother earth. He began to hide his tracks before making his way back to his comrades. The enemy must find nothing to give him away.

He'd spent about half an hour devouring some dry rations, slowly scouting around, and erasing anything that might have showed a U.S. Marine had passed this way.

He was just finishing his sweep of the area leading back to the carcass when he heard a twig snap. Slowly, he lowered himself on to his belly in the thick of the undergrowth. The sounds that followed suggested a group of five or six men, moving ever closer. Were the gooks back? he held his breath.

Aaron was not afraid to die; no Navajo man is. He knows his spirit will go to join his ancestors, but, by the same token, he was not yet ready to sing in the lodges of his forebears.

Just then he heard a voice he recognised.

"It's gotta be him. No gook has feet that size." It was his Sergeant.

Aaron slowly raised his hand and said, "I'm here."

Sergeant Bill, (Raging Bull) Taylor laughed and shook his hand.

"We lost you just before dark then almost immediately saw multiple signs of Charlie, so we laid low till first light, then came looking."

Sergeant Taylor continued, "Thank God for those big feet. We were surprised, but glad to have found one half boot heel print by the river almost inside that stinking carcass. We knew then that's where you'd taken cover."

You and those size fifteen boots are legend"! They all laughed.

The Dancer

The latter years of WW2

She stood *en avant*, then rose up onto her toes, *en pointe*, then raised her arms and scissor jumped. The *pas de Basque* was a step too far and she crumpled in a heap in front of the long studio mirror. She sat for a little while, then throwing off her self-pitying mood she rose from the floor as elegantly as her 80 year-old frame would allow.

1914

She left the studio and made her way upstairs to her private quarters. The view from her salon offered a stunning view of the *Champs Elysée*. Her apartment was in a building set between *Rue du Colisèe* and *Rue la Boètie*. The honey cream coloured stone with its beautifully crafted balustrades of their balconies gave the look exactly as had been required. Elegance, class, and wealth. It was as stunning inside as it was out. The delicate artistry of French chic was on show in all its finery here. The view from the window down the boulevard of the *Champs Elysée* was just wonderful.

Later in her life she would say she hated it. She had lost her love of the view having twice watched the German invaders goosestep their way down under the *Arc de*

Triomphe. Twice it had heralded the end of the Paris that she loved, and the creation a Paris she no longer could call home.

*   *   *   *   *

Elyse Benoit had, at the height of her career, drawn crowds night after night, month after month, to sold out theatres. She was a *prima donna*, the toast of Paris, Berlin, Vienna, London, and Rome. And one spring at the peak of her career, she was toasted by the rich and famous of New York.

Elyse had returned after a gruelling six-month run and was exhausted, relishing the thought of taking the autumn and winter as an extended holiday. She would, of course, keep up her daily training but refuse any contractual dates until the spring. She had only bought her beautiful apartment late in the previous year. In total, she'd had barely three months in what she referred to as her forever home.

It consisted of two floors; they were the top two floors of the building. She had paid for alterations to accommodate a large dance studio with changing and shower facilities on the lower floor along with a storage room and well-equipped kitchen. The top floor held her private quarters. There was a smaller kitchen, two double bedrooms, a salon with dining area and her master bedroom with *en suite* bathroom and dressing room. Both her bedroom and salon were at the front above the studio.

The view looking right from the terrace outside her bedroom or salon, was the gift that changed throughout the day and night. Always giving something different. A change of pace, the refracted light through the raindrops, the elegance of it in the sunlight, and at sunset, it was different again. She loved it. You could look all the way down the street to the *Arc de Triomphe*. She had loved it from the moment she had first stepped out onto her terrace.

After such a gruelling tour, for now, she just wanted to relax and enjoy being home.

The declaration, on August 3rd, by Germany, stole that wish away.

She survived the *Grand Guerre* in her apartment and had aided where she could the glorious cause against the Kaiser's forces. She delivered messages, rode her bicycle around the streets reporting positions and movements. Attended dinners with the high officers of the Vichy coven and listened carefully to their loosened tongues. For the duration, much of her energy and the bulk of her wealth went to the cause. She would give everything if need be, to keep France free of the Kaiser's boot.

At Easter in 1939, many of her friends had begun whispering about the new regime and their proclamations regarding ethnic groups in Germany, in particular the Jewish community.

The word was, "to get out if you could." Some of her closest family and friends had already left for America, Canada, and England. The news from the offices of the *Republique Francaise* was less than encouraging.

The French forces had been put on alert. On the morning of May 10th the following year, Elyse had risen and as was her custom, had turned on her radiogram. She'd sank into her chair in shock as she'd listened to the news broadcaster declaring Germany had invaded Belgium, the Netherlands, Luxembourg and had crossed the French border. *Herr* Hitler's troops were heading swiftly towards Paris.

"The dogs of war have been let slip again," she thought. *"We beat them before, we shall again,"* and she prayed it would be so.

In the days immediately after this announcement the streets filled with a stream of refugees running ahead of the advancing troops. They told all who would listen of the atrocities and barbarism of the Germans and their attacks on innocent civilians. Elyse was horrified yet resolved she would not join the mass exodus.

From her apartment, the crowds seemed like an ever-flowing river of people and their treasures, the belongings of those who were abandoning her beloved Paris to the Hitlerites.

She saw carts with baths and pianos atop of great shipping trunks. *"As if these things were of any real use in their exodus,"* she thought. It reminded Elyse of her ancestors. These people were fleeing their destruction, just not from the Egyptians this time. But the waves that were held back for her forebears would soon, in the form of a flood of grey uniforms, wash over them all. And their destruction this time would, again be Biblical.

Elyse knew of one friend who had been part of the government, before the traitor Marshal Petain had capitulated.

He was a patriot; on that she would stake her life. And of course, if she were wrong, she would like as not forfeit that life.

She approached him after services the following Saturday morning. He stood with others who all greeted her. Pleasantries were exchanged and speculations on the current situation aired between them all. Finally, all but Elyse and David Crèmieu remained.

They spoke of unimportant things as people dispersed around them until Elyse leaned in to take her leave and kiss his cheeks, she whispered, "I am staying to fight again. How may I aid our country?"

David took her hand. Smiling, he leant to kiss the delicate hand, saying softly in reply, "*Moi aussi*, I'll be in touch." He smiled again, turned, and went to join another group gathered at the café tables opposite the synagogue.

Many of her students no longer attended the dance classes. Some had left in the flight for safety; others, children not of the Jewish faith, had been withdrawn by anxious or bigoted parents who wanted no attention brought by association with the woman. A woman whom they had once adored, a woman whose friendship for which they had vied.

Those people did not want to be caught in the crossfire when the hunters found their prey. The slightest suggestion of empathy or aid for the people of the yellow star could get you killed.

People were afraid. Neighbours, friends, business associates, even family members turned on those with whom they had broken bread, people whose houses they had once visited. It all meant nothing. In the clutch of feral fear, humans turn bestial. Survival is all.

And who could blame them? Humans are a herd species, and in a herd, ostracization means death. Man is not an island, no matter what he might think. And herd animals follow the strongest of them. Right then, it was Hitler's forces that looked like the winning side. The side whose followers would survive.

At first Elyse was asked to look after some boxes put in the back of her storeroom next to the studio. A little later they approached with the request to move her wall of mirrors forward. They wanted to create a void; a space big enough for a person to lie down. It took them two days, but once finished, even she. could see no indication of the alteration, nor the opening device to access the space.

After that, there came a stream of allied and French soldiers, sailors, and pilots. There were a few resistance fighters, too, who needed to disappear out of reach of the Germans. They would stay in her home for a day or two before being spirited away to freedom – or to an appointment with death that had just been delayed.

Sometimes, as she did her daily workout, she was self-conscious, she wondered what the men hidden behind the glass thought of this now-elderly woman. Her body was not the firm nymph like form she once had been. Did they think her sad and ridiculous? She hoped not.

She would have been astonished if she were to have learnt they thought her a heroine, a brave soldier of freedom.

Some children still attended classes. When she was teaching, the men and sometimes women she hid had to lie in that long narrow space. Silent and unmoving as death.

The appearance of normality had to be preserved for their safety. For the sake of the children, too. They needed something, something to anchor them. Her lessons were their only connection to a time when they were not afraid.

It was a cold November day; she had a class and she had two British airmen in her home. One was unwell. The trek to Paris through occupied France, sleeping in woods and walking through winter wind and rain had taken its toll on this young flier. He was full of a very unpleasant cold.

She dare not have him in the void, coughing and spluttering his way to their combined firing squad. She had insisted he stay in one of her bedrooms. There was no reason to suppose it would be unsafe for the duration of the class.

The children arrived; she was surprised to see one of the older boys had returned after a long absence.

Phillipe had been a very promising pupil but had stopped attending when the troops came. He said he had driven his parents mad with his pleading and begging to be allowed to return. How could he be "as good as Vaslav Nijinski if he did not train?"

Elyse patted the boy's shoulder and smiled. "Wise words, Philippe," she said before calling the group to order. At that moment, the boy asked to be excused to use the bathroom.

The session fairly flew by and soon the aging *prima donna* was bidding her pupils good-bye.

Weeks passed in the usual fashion, or what now was accepted as the usual. Men and women arrived in the darkness and left in the darkness. Children came in daylight and left in daylight. The two different worlds inhabited by the two different women that was Elyse, one for the light and one for the dark.

It was a week before Christmas. David had sent a message with the grocer who delivered it to her. Their group was discovered or betrayed; the point was moot. The note said she had to get out.

She could never, would never, abandon her beloved France.

She wore the costume for Swan Lake: she heard their boots on the stairs. The doors to her studio were locked and her music played on the gramophone. It was racked up to full volume. She just about heard their demand to open the door and the threat that they would open fire if she did not comply.

The music was reaching the crescendo when the guns opened fire. She'd never danced more poignantly, nor felt the music stir her soul. Not like this; this moment was exquisite.

When they came through the doors and entered her studio, she was on the floor, in the final position that Anna Pavlova had made iconic. The beautiful costume that she had created herself was of the purest white silk bodice and underskirt, with a white feather overskirt. Her grey hair was up in a chignon and on her head a band of feathers.

All were now tainted by the scarlet of her blood and the miasma of poison, hatred, and bigotry.

Philippe, at first a little unsure, clicked the heels of his new boots, proud in his brown shirt. He stood to attention, saluting "Heil, Hitler," in the uniform of the Hitler Youth. He then turned to go and did not spare a glance at the old woman on the floor.

The Incident

The man in the yellow jacket limped hurriedly along the derelict street past boarded up houses awaiting demolition. The area was scheduled for clearance and many of the houses had been demolished but a number remained. The man headed to one of them that was still more or less undamaged, though its neighbour was already under attack.

Labouring up the two steps to the door, he almost fell as he took a key from his pocket and reached forward to insert it into the lock. Once it had been his haven, his safe house. But, when the decision was taken to clear the slums and modernise, the area residents had all been evacuated and their former homes boarded up. He was unsure why he had kept a key for Number 29, but it had been very useful the past couple of days while he waited for instructions. It had been a close shave a short while ago in the pub where he met his contact.

*   *   *   *   *

I was given a small package which he tucked in a pocket, and we were about to leave when two men entered, one I recognised instantly.

I'd had him in my sights once before, in the seventies, in Crossmaglen, Ireland. I had just missed this IRA member whilst on a "wet ops" mission serving with Her Majesty's troops. Sent, like a wraith, a shadow in the dark, to take the head off the snake. An apt euphemism, for the top provisional leaders in South Armagh.

Following the killing of some squaddies that Spring by a bomb remotely detonated whilst they were on patrol, we'd been tasked to debilitate the effectiveness of this deadly section of the Irish Republican Army by taking out their most deadly leaders.

I'd missed him that day, I wouldn't this time.

The meeting I'd had was to collect the list of the new appointments by the Belfast unit and to get some info from a grass in their ranks.

We'd heard a rumour that two of the "Boyos" were due in town. Now I knew who they were.

Brady and Murphy were two of the Provo's most resolute men. However, Danny, my contact panicked and as you'd expect from men of this rank, they noted the sudden and hurried movements. Danny was obviously known to Murphy, the second man, for he spoke swiftly to Brady, and they split up, one retracing his steps back out one door whilst the other followed in Danny's wake. I feigned oblivion, but wasn't convinced, and wondered if my presence had not been clocked.

And it has proven I was correct to wonder. For after leaving the bar, within minutes, I was keenly aware I was being followed.

I spotted the second in command of the Armagh unit in the reflection of the bus window as I shot across the road. That's how I came to be heading for the old house. A safe house for me, a place I could defend myself from, I knew the layout blindfolded. I would have the advantage.

This was a house I lived in as a lad, years before. Why I'd saved the key on Da's old key fob, I don't know. Maybe it was because it was the last place the family had been a family. Before the divisions, arguments, and alienations.

However, these were no green recruits, and as I tried to get to the only block with little damage, Brady stepped into my path, laughing. I ran a zig zag line and jumped over some concrete blocks with steel rods emerging like burnt skeletal fingers. As I leapt onto a pile of bricks I felt the first bullet find its mark, in my calf, a through and through. Not fatal, but painful, and hard to run on.

Which brings me to where we began this tale, limping, wearing a donkey jacket and high viz vest through a Belfast building site. Still on a black ops mission, still after the Provos, still losing. I had reached the steps to my old home.

The man's next shot caught my left shoulder, spun me around, and took me off my feet.

His foot appeared at my right hand as I tried to get up. I rolled onto my back; Brady smiled.

"Ah, hello, Michael lad."

"Hello, Uncle Pat," I grimaced from the pain.

"Now you should'na have come, laddie. This isn't personal, son, and I'm heart sore to be the one. Make yer peace with the Man, for it's done now, son, God keep your soul."

I'd lost.

Brady squeezed the trigger.

Trapped in Ireland's Shadows

In Ireland's fields so lush and green.

Lay evil; plotting, dark, unseen.

Waiting, like a silent sentinel,

For our gauche, innocent parade.

Just a moment of bawdy banter, fast

consumed in darkness, loss, and pain.

Those poor others, not so fortunate,

Would never smile or laugh again.

An arm, a leg, some so much more,

There's no formula for making sense.

No words, no help,

No love, no recompense.

Tis a place, so few may truly share,

It's post-traumatic stress if you should find you care.

Life is not life, that's caught, and paused in time,

Oh, to travel back, that would suit us all just fine.

We fight, we die, for that we come so well prepared,

But bound now in that moment, we are so brutally
ensnared.

The Painting
Chapters 1-4

1: Molly

Isabella stood at the prow of the ship, her infant pressed to her breast, tears flowing free and fast.

The infant she held was her beloved daughter of only four months. She had but one chance. She prayed the Lord would give her and her child, especially her child, succour, and deliver her, as once he had done for another child.

She laid little Maria Celeste in the currach that had been delivered by the emissary from Escocia, a gift for her christening. There was also a locket of gold, inlaid with beautiful sapphires in the design of the cross of Saint Andrew. Her daughter had received many wonderful gifts, including a stunning Icon, delivered by the Archbishop of Castille upon his return from Russia.

The face of the Madonna shone amidst colours so vivid, gold, Russian blue, and red like blood. It was a valuable piece. Of that, she had no doubt.

Isabella had been delighted and grateful for all the gifts sent for her daughter, but the lowliest of them all, the currach, was the one Isabella was today most grateful for.

As the prow slid beneath the waves, Isabella entrusted their lives to God and pushed away from the disappearing deck. She could swim but knew the weight of her skirts would impede her and would fast drain her strength.

She pushed the currach in front of her, never letting go. She used her one arm and both legs to propel herself towards salvation and the beach.

Dawn began to break and she saw a figure on the shore. He must have seen or heard the explosion that had ripped the hold open to the sea. She did not know what had caused the explosion, but she was very aware of its devastating effect.

With her strength waning, she cried out in desperation for aid. "*Misericordia*, Mercy, *Ayuda*, Help me, *misericordia per favore.*"

She was losing her battle for survival. Her heroic attempt to save herself and her daughter was over. She could feel it. With every ounce of strength her body and soul possessed, she would make one last attempt, one last push.

She saw the figure racing into the surf just as she felt the current below catch her in its grip. Just as she was pulled below the foam, she cried a last soulful message to her baby girl, "*Vaya con Dios, Niña.*"

Jem was a strong swimmer, but the currents off the coast of Cornwall were often so strong that even the strongest of swimmers had great difficulty. He was fast, but not fast enough for the woman. He saw her rise like a siren from the sea and, with a final herculean effort gave a last heave of the currach, desperate and determined to get it closer to him and the shore. Then the woman disappeared beneath the waves.

He reached the currach only moments later and was horrified to discover the contents. He now understood where the woman had found her strength that had miraculously gotten her thus far.

The infant looked up with great warm brown eyes. Cupid lips were tinged with blue. Cornish waters are not warm in winter months.

Jem took the child to his cottage up on the clifftop. His wife heard his frantic shouts as he hurried up the path carrying the currach. She was quick to understand the needs of the child as he laid the infant in her arms.

The currach he left by the door to dry off. Emily went to the fire, and from the pot of water warming there, she poured a goodly measure into a large bowl, she then stripped the babe, discovering the child to be a girl.

She lay the sweet little thing, in the warm water and drizzled handfuls of it over the giggling infant. Soon the baby's lips were pink and she was happily gurgling up at his wife, who looked longingly at the child.

Jem went outside and wiped down the vessel of her deliverance. He considered its shape, determining that if the seat spar were removed it would make an excellent crib that would rock on the stone flagstones of the cottage.

He pulled the contents out layer by layer. First was a quality fur, then a couple of blankets that had been lovingly crocheted in delicate patterns and pastel colours of coral and lemon. Then he lifted out a second fur, again of quality ermine. Beneath that lay a waxed wallet and a leather pouch.

He took it all inside. The furs and blankets were laid near the fire to dry as was the converted currach. She had a bed.

"What have you got there, Jem?" his wife asked.

"They were all in the currach," he replied as he opened the pouch and waxen wallet.

Emily gasped, "Oh, Jem! They're beautiful, she's not from a poor family. They'll come looking for the ship if it carried the likes of her parents."

"Aye, they likely will, but till then she could stay here, eh?" Jem sighed, thinking how hard it might be for his wife to give the child up if it took too long for her to be found.

"Yes, of course," said Emily, distracted as she looked for the bottle Jem had fashioned to feed an orphaned lamb. The child suckled hungrily at the teat.

"Is there anything in her things to tell us her name?" asked Emily softly as the infant dozed off in her arms.

"No, but on a blanket, there are initials stitched, 'M.C.B,' that's all."

"Then I shall call her Molly, till we learn different."

Months passed and it was as if the shipwreck had been a dream. No one came looking, not even the revenue man had been up looking for salvage. The current had not served up much from the ship, either: only a barrel of salt pork and one of fortified wine. Jem had shared the salt pork with his neighbours and sold the wine to the monastery nearby.

As the years passed, Molly grew into a beautiful and intelligent girl with a sunny but quiet disposition. She was loved and loved in return.

The locket lay in the leather pouch where it had been found under the furs. The painting was seen by a local priest. He told Jem that, by the quality, he would wager it would likely fetch a pretty penny. He also said the local monastery might be able to shed some light on its value and origins. It was possibly from a religious source.

Jem did nothing for a long time until after he and Emily had spoken of what could be done to educate the child and honour her heritage. She would not have received the same education as a boy, but an education of some level, she would have had. Both Jem and Emily believed that there should be no discrimination, and so determined to find a way to give her the best they could.

It had broken their hearts when both of Emily's pregnancies had progressed no further than the sixth month. The second loss had devastated Emily.

Jem now delighted in the blossoming of his wife since Molly's deliverance on the crest of a wave. Emily proved a natural mother and she loved Molly as if she'd birthed the girl herself.

They decided that Jem would approach the monastery, inquire about the painting, and also ask how they might find a way to educate the girl that Jem now thought of as his daughter.

After seven years, it seemed as if God himself had taken pity on their broken hearts and gifted the orphan to compensate for their loss and Emily's barren womb.

Life was good.

The painting would mayhap improve their fortunes if the priest were right and would give his daughter the education her true parents would have.

The painting would change their lives in ways they could never have imagined.

2: One Foggy Night

Señora Sanchez's journey here had been long and uncomfortable. Days and weeks filled alternately with fear, despair, desperation, and yet overriding all that, with hope. Hope borne out of a refusal to accept that she, her husband, and their child, were gone, forever lost to her. It was a pain she struggled, even with her faith, to accept. A mother's love dies hard in the maelstrom of grief.

At last, there was some fragment of evidence that gave her hope, a flame of reality.

The painting had been found.

Jem had waited almost three years before deciding to sell the painting.

The change that overtook Jem and Emily's life did not happen overnight. It was a series of events that slowly opened the path to a life they'd never have thought possible.

Emily was cutting the meat and adding a dollop of freshly churned butter to the potatoes she'd mashed in the bowl when the door flew open. Molly tore into the room like a dervish and out of breath.

"Mama, there's a carriage coming, pulled by two exceptionally fine black stallions. They have two outriders and there's a fancy coat of arms on the carriage doors.'

Jem got up from the table and told Emily and Molly to stay inside until he discovered what these folk wanted, saying, they had likely taken a wrong turn in the heavy fog.

The coach pulled to a stop. One of the coachmen leapt down and opened the door next to Jem.

"Are you lost?" asked Jem.

A very impressive-looking woman stepped out.

"No, sir. We are not lost, but I do seek information on something, something I have lost."

She spoke with a foreign accent, which gave Jem pause for thought.

"I'm Jem Nancarrow. How can I help you, m'lady?"

"Mr. Nancarrow, my name is Maria Elena Sanchez, I am here searching for news of my daughter, Isabella, her husband, Ramon Braganza, and their daughter, Maria

Celeste. Eight years ago, they sailed from Spain for London, their ship disappeared during a storm after leaving Calais.”

“And how do you think I may be able to help, m’lady?” Jem was extremely uncomfortable. He would never surrender Molly now. She was his. Emily was her mother, and he was her father, sworn to protect her.

The woman looked into his face, disturbing Jem’s usual calm equilibrium.

He finally spoke, “I don’t recall a shipwreck with survivors, Spanish or otherwise. We do get a fair amount of wrecks, it’s true. The coast here is littered with them. It’s a rugged coastline with deadly currents that are notoriously strong and often fatal. When did you say this happened?” he asked.

“Almost nine years ago, just weeks before Christmas.” Madam Sanchez looked askance at Jem.

“And you’re only now come looking? What age were your daughter and her family?”

Madam Sanchez looked as if she might cry, hurt by his implied accusation.

“I was led to believe their ship had sunk and all hands lost many miles from here. This is not the sea lane route to London. I would have continued to mourn them until my death, but for something that happened recently.”

She continued, "Two months ago, I received word that a gift given to my granddaughter to commemorate her Baptism, was bought by the Spanish Ambassador in London. I am given to believe it was you who sold it to him, through the Abbot of St. Mawgan. Is that not true"?

Jem's heart almost stopped. It was as if he was gripped in the clutches of steely fingers. Icy cold fingers.

"The Madonna and child painting?" he asked.

"Yes, Mr. Nancarrow, the very one."

"I bought that for some meat, milk, and a few coins, from a travelling gypsy. My wife took a liking to it.

"One of the monks from the monastery saw it when he picked up some mutton. He admired it and said he believed it to be a valuable piece. It was he who convinced me to show the Abbott. And it was the Abbott who offered to sell it for me.

"He said a piece like that, should be on the walls of a cathedral or a palace, not a dark farmers cottage. We agreed to let him take it to London to sell for us. That was months ago, and I don't see what it has to do with your search."

Madam Sanchez replied, "Maybe it does not, but I know my daughter would have kept it safe. Its sale gave me hope,

hope that I might get news of what happened to her – and that maybe she yet lived."

"I'm sorry for your loss, Madam Sanchez, but I can be of no further aid. So, unless I can be of any further service, I'll bid you good day."

The elegant, if aging woman, dressed head to toe in expensive black widow weeds, climbed back into her carriage.

She told him, "If you should see the gypsy again, please inform the Abbot, who will get word to me. Find out where I might find the traveller. I will pay him for his time. Please, I must speak with this man."

The coachman cracked his whip and they drove away.

Emily was frantic by the time Jem stepped back into their home. "Jem, what are we going to do? I cannot bear to lose Molly now." She sobbed into his shoulder.

"There now, my lovely, don't you fret. I told her I bought the picture from a travelling gypsy and knew nothing of any Spanish survivors off any shipwreck. She said the ship was bound for London. That storm must have blown it off course; clearly their captain was not familiar with these coastal waters.

"How the explosion occurred I don't know, and it matters not. the ship would have foundered on the rocks and sunk anyway. The result would have been the same, or worse. The infant might have perished, too. Now, my dear, wipe your eyes. All is well." And Jem believed it.

Molly had been listening under the window. Everything made some sense now.

The monk who often came for provisions had said to her last summer that she must have been a throwback. When she asked his meaning he replied," Your colouring and skin tone do not come from Emily or Jem. There has to be a tar brush in your past and no mistake. You have the look of the priests that come from Rome and Castille every so often. Yes, there's a tar brush somewhere."

If she were the Spanish lady's grandchild, it would make sense.

She loved Emily and Jem, and they were her parents, but who was she, really, and did it matter if she was happy?

Days, then weeks and months passed.

Spring was in full bloom. Molly was sitting by the river. It flowed through their pasture then all the way down the hill and into the sea. She had been checking the new lambs, making sure ewes and lambs were all well. She was now hot and sticky.

She removed her stockings and shoes; her feet were cooling in the gurgling flow of the river. She'd also opened her dress at the throat. She was away from the path. *"What harm could it do?"* she thought. *"No one would see me."*

She lay back in the grass, the sun warm on her face. She fingered the locket. It had been a present at Christmas. Her mother had given her the locket and her father had bought her a longer chain than the original. He'd said it was "good Cornish silver."

The original chain lay in the leather pouch that had held it all on Christmas morning. She loved it. She'd been told this was not a thing for the everyday, but maybe to chapel, or special days. It was so pretty, though.

And today, well today, she had it round her neck.

As she lay there, she fancied herself a princess who wore her locket above a fine silk dress. She was dancing with the handsome prince when she became aware of the shadow on her face.

She opened her eyes to find the Spanish lady standing watching her. She was crying, her face ashen.

Maria Elena Sanchez had been watching for a chance to speak to the girl. As Molly had left the cottage and disappeared over the crest down into the meadow, she knew her chance had come.

Molly sat up, "Why do you cry? Are you hurt?" she asked, her kind heart concerned.

The woman shook her head. "Not in the way you think, but I am in some pain." Madam Sanchez lowered herself and sat down beside Molly.

"What is your name?" asked the woman.

"Molly. What's yours?"

Madam Sanchez smiled. "It is Maria Elena Sanchez. You may call me Yaya."

"Are you lost, Yaya?" asked Molly.

"No, *Nieta*, I'm not lost."

"Then why do you cry?" asked the girl.

"I'm just a silly old lady who felt sad. What a beautiful locket you have. Was it a gift?"

"Yes. My mother gave it to me last Christmas. She said a mother's love would protect me forever. Don't you think that is just wonderful?"

"Yes, indeed I do. Your mother must love you very much," said the woman through her heartache.

"Molly, may I ask a favour of you? Might I meet you here once in a while?

"I lost my beloved granddaughter and you and she would have been about the same age. It makes me less sad when I see and speak to you. Would you grant an old lady that kindness?"

Molly looked into the old woman's face. She saw only kindness and traces of sadness in her eyes.

"Yes, Yaya, I'll meet you."

"May it stay a secret between us two?" asked Senora Sanchez.

"I think so," she replied, though Molly thought, definitely! She was sure her parents would forbid it if they knew. She wasn't sure why she believed that, but she did.

Each time they met, Madam Sanchez learnt more of the life of Molly Nancarrow. She was more and more impressed.

Molly's 'parents' had procured her an excellent education. She could read and write. She knew her numbers, could sew, crochet, and cook. She had a private tutor who also taught her Spanish and Latin. Emily and Jem Nancarrow were excellent parents to the child. They were hard-working, honest people with great heart.

The day would come soon when confrontation would be inevitable. She did not want to hurt any of these people, least of all her *Nieta*, her granddaughter. She was fully convinced now: Molly was in fact Maria Celeste Braganza. Daughter of a Spanish aristocrat. She was nobility.

Her Cornish parents, too, were noble; if not by birth, definitely by heart. They had done everything to give the child a good life. They had raised her well.

Clearly, they loved her, and she loved them. They would never allow anyone to hurt the child. And neither would she.

Maria Elena Sanchez had a plan.

3: The Old Man.

The old man trudged up the long, ragged hill to the headland. He stopped to catch his breath as he surveyed the view before him.

The cottage was the first to move into foreground focus. White, with a well thatched roof; it was not a cheap job, he thought. The thatcher's skill was evident in the clean lines, the images of sheaves of corn and *fleur de Lis*, just like on the Kings coaches. The thatcher declared himself a loyal subject with his work. Whoever lived here had done an exceptionally fine job on his roof. Mayhap he'd have a kindly disposition and allow an old man a place to lay his head for the night.

Jacob Belcher tidied himself as best he could and chapped on the stout oak hewn door. He heard a child's voice first calling "Mama, someone is here." Then a woman's voice in reply, telling the child that she was coming and not to open the door. The child had already opened the door before the mother had finished her sentence.

"Hello," said a beautiful girl of about twelve. She may have been a bit older, for she had a small boned, delicate fragility about her that implied a younger, more innocent age.

"Hello," replied the old man, but before another word passed his lips, a woman of around forty appeared.

"Molly, I said not to open the door. Now go finish hanging the washing for me."

"Oh, but Mama, we get so few visitors!" Her pleas were quashed by a timeless look that all mothers manage their rebellious children with a look that brooks no argument. The girl turned and headed away to finish the task for her mother.

"Good day, Mistress. I'm sorry to be a trouble but I've walked far, and my old bones weary faster nowadays. I was hoping I might do a bit of work in return for a night in your barn and mayhap some bread and cheese. That is if you have enough work to set me to earn my sustenance and a straw pallet."

Emily looked the old man over. "There's some wood needs chopping if you're able and the byre could do with a sweep out and new straw laying. Might that suit?" Emily indicated the wood pile and the small barn and byre with a nod of her head.

Jacob smiled, "Thank ye. That would suit me fine. I'm Jacob Belcher," he said offering his hand.

"Emily Nancarrow," Emily smiled and took his weathered and gnarled hand. He had a warm, firm handshake. Both Jem and she put a lot of store in a man's handshake. Jacob had passed muster, though he didn't know he had been tested.

Emily left him to it and sent Molly off to help her father in the fields. Jacob swung his pack roll from his back and removed his outer coat. The coat was one of excellent quality. It was clearly old and well worn, but its origins still declared it a piece of exceptional tailoring.

Emily wondered about Belcher as she prepared some fresh fish for the evening repast. She gathered wild garlic and fennel and, after battering a bowl of dry bread into crumbs she added that to the chopped mushrooms gathered from the meadow just that morning. A little water was mixed with all her collection and a moist but malleable stuffing was ready. She'd cleaned and gutted the fish and had slit from gill to tail. Next, she pushed her stuffing inside and secured it with some string. The fish would be laid atop the fire plate to cook.

Freshly baked cob loaves sat on the table along with a plate of newly patted homemade butter. She hoped Jacob liked fish, for that's all she had to offer. She'd been thinking on who Jacob was and what his story was. She'd be sure to ask at dinner. She smiled at the thought, like she'd need to ask with Jem at the table. He could shame those men in the tower or those inquisitors she'd heard tell of from the inquisition. Her man could wheedle a flea off a wild dog.

Molly came in from the fields with Jem. They'd been fixing a broken fence together. Jem did as he always did on returning home at the end of the day: he went to Emily and kissed her cheek. And, as ever, Emily placed her hand gently on his cheek and smiled her best smile for him.

"So, Molly here tells me you've been entertaining another man whilst I've been working my fingers to the bone for you," he winked at Molly as he waited for Emily's response.

Emily flicked the washcloth at Jem's arm and said, "You should have a care when slandering your wife's good name, else she might start looking for a man who has more trust in his good woman." She, too, winked at Molly who was laughing at the oft repeated teasing that her parents displayed in her company. She knew as she watched them like this that they absolutely loved each other.

Just then, they were interrupted by a knock on the door. "Come in," called Emily. The door opened and Jacob stayed on the threshold. "The wood's cut and the byre swept. I've laid new straw too. Is there a burn or a well that I might wash up?"

Jem stood, "I'll show you." He led Jacob to the rear of the cottage where Emily had made Jem build a covered back porch. There stood an old table with a wash bowl and jug. Since the day they began building their home here, she had insisted there be a place at the back where man or woman might strip and wash the day's toil away in privacy before entering her cosy home.

It was Jacob who spoke first, "I'm right grateful to your good lady for giving me the chance to earn a meal and a spot to lay my head tonight."

"I'm Jem Nancarrow," he held out his hand mentally agreeing with his wife; the man did have a good handshake. "Where are you bound? The road is a hard place for a man no longer in his prime. I've noted your coat: it's a fine piece. I've a mind that you have an interesting tale to tell. I won't press for details, though. To my mind, a man's life is nobody's business but his own. You are welcome to a day or two's rest and feed if you've a mind to tarry and help me with some bits around the place. Let me know later. Let's go eat."

When Jacob and Jem entered, the table was set. The fish smelt so good and moments later Jacob's taste buds attested to the deliciousness of the fish. The bread and butter alone was a mouth-watering feast of flavour.

"You've a fine cook in your wife here," said Jacob as both he and Jem handed Molly their empty and mopped clean plates. "Thank you, Mistress."

"Call me Emily, please, else I'll be looking over my shoulder for the fine lady you might be addressing."

Jem replied first, "You are as fine a lady that ever drew breath, Emily Nancarrow, so quit that. You hear me, woman?"

She laughed as Jacob agreed with her husband; she blushed.

Molly watched her parents. It made her tummy smile to see such obvious an expression of love. She may not understand love completely, but she knew what it felt like. She also knew, even at her tender age, that she had been blessed.

Whether or not these two before her were her true parents, she had been blessed.

Jacob's stay lasted for just over two weeks. On the day he left, he called Jem and asked if he might have a private word with Emily and himself. "Away from young ears, please?" he'd asked.

Emily sent Molly to the chicken coop on an errand. The three sat on the rough-hewn benches under the cottage windows. "What's this about, Jacob?" asked Jem.

"I've not been entirely honest with you both. I've spoken not a word of a lie, but by omission I have deceived. I allowed you both to draw conclusions about me, I doubt either of you got within a mile of the truth."

Jacob continued, "Back in '75, I was a captain of the archers at Schoonhoven. I was with De La Garde and the French troops. I was one of over eight hundred men who finally were forced to surrender to the Spanish."

At the mention of the Spanish, Jem's blood ran cold.

Jacob went on, "One of their commanders bought me from my captor. He was an honourable man and after a few years, he offered me a choice. My freedom, to either go home or I could join the staff of Mariscal de Brigada, the Brigadier Marshal Senior Mateo Braganza, a member of the Spanish aristocracy. 'Home' was a small farm on the Belgian side of the border with France. I joined the French army to escape the alternative, religious orders. He said I could go back if I wished.

"I owed France nothing, nor did I hate the Spanish. The offer to become part of the family's retinue was tempting. He wanted to add a fighting man to his household, and I could fight. I chose to serve in the Braganza house."

Jem could see Emily begin to panic, but he stayed her with a look. They had to know exactly what Jacob wanted. "Go on," said Jem.

"I was with him and his family in France when his son, daughter in law and their child prepared to sail for London. His son was an envoy, sent in the hopes of brokering better relations, to avoid threatened war. Mariscal Braganza however did not trust the safety of his son and family in the English court. He dare not send soldiers, so at the last minute he sent me with them." Jacob paused for a moment, giving his words a chance to sink in.

"I saw Señora Isabella with Maria Celeste in the water. I saw what you did, Jem!"

Jem and Emily's faces were white and drawn with fear. "What do you want?" snarled Jem.

"Jem, please be calm. No-one, not me, not any of Marie Celeste's grandparents want to remove Molly from your care. But they know, as I do, that Molly is Señorita Braganza. Her grandfather, all her family, need you to know, how grateful they are to you both."

"How could this be true?" said Emily, "we were told by a woman called Señora Sanchez that there were no survivors. All had perished," she said.

"And that was true as they knew then. I had been swept along the coast, but I was badly hurt and for a long time I remembered nothing beyond the moment of waking in the convent miles away along the coast. Then early last year I began to get some memories back. As soon as I remembered the ship, the wreck, I sent word to the family, for I, too, had heard that all hands were lost that awful night.

"However, I knew that Isabella Braganza had at least made it off the ship with the child. The family informed me of the painting and the child Señora Sanchez had seen and spoken with. I made enquiries with your neighbours; none could confirm ever seeing Emily in the delicate state of expectancy. Even the monks could not swear that a live child had been carried and delivered by you, Emily, though they were aware of the sadness of lost infants that never survived to term.

"Jem, Emily, the Braganza and Sanchez families want you to come and meet them at the Priory. I swear on the cross of Christ himself that Molly will not be told, nor will she be taken from you. Her happiness is their prime concern, as we all believe is also yours. Will you meet with them?"

Life was about to throw a surprise opportunity into the Nancarrow family's life.

4: The Crystal Glass.

She gazed at the crystal glass that sat close to her right hand. The light from the wall sconces and the array of pillar candles that stood in a uniformed line of light down the centre of the table was mesmerising. The effect transfixed her eyes on the dance of lights with colours exploding like a pyrotechnic display leaping through the facets of the high-quality glass.

Her reverie was broken by a man who asked permission to fill her glass.

She nodded, not really sure what to do. She would have preferred mead or ale but was afraid to offend by asking for it. She nodded and he had poured a good measure of a deep, dark red wine into the fancy glass that her fingers now nervously caressed. It was a journey into another world, and she saw it all through that beautiful glass.

Molly was with a neighbour. Jem and Emily Nancarrow had finally decided that, though it may not be in *their* best interest to accept the invitation brought by Jacob on behalf of the Braganza and Sanchez families, they did it because it may well be in *Molly's* best interest, and they loved their beautiful, kind-hearted daughter, their gift from the waves and a fickle God.

They had donned their Sunday best and gone to the Priory, neutral ground for both parties. The Abbot was a kind soul and squeezed Emily's hand as he welcomed them. He shook Jem's hand and patted his shoulder, too, in reassurance. He led them into his large, comfortable office.

There, the woman who had come to Jem's door sat in a chair near the fire. Opposite her sat another woman who smiled shyly at them in welcome, and behind her chair stood a man. The man was impressive, not in his height or clothes, though they certainly didn't detract from it. It was his demeanour. His bearing was clearly that of a man used to authority, yet with warm and kindly eyes.

It was he who spoke first:

"This is Señora Marie Elena Sanchez, whom I believe you have already met. I am Mateo Braganza and this is my wife, Catalina.

"I will come directly to the point: we believe the child you call Molly, your daughter, is in fact our granddaughter. The child was thought lost in the shipwreck that killed her parents, our son, Ramon," He laid his hand in a comforting gesture on his wife's shoulder before continuing, "and Marie Elena's daughter, Isabella, the woman you tried to save from the sea. The woman Jacob saw push her child's currach towards you as she lost her strength and was taken by the currents to her death."

Jem's memory of that day came flooding back to him. He remembered the vision of the woman, Molly's mother, rising from the sea in a last, desperate push to save her child.

"That woman was my daughter," said Senora Sanchez, "the child, my granddaughter, *our* granddaughter," she gestured to the couple opposite, "she is our Marie Celeste. The locket that Molly secretly wears on the new silver chain was my daughter's. Her father gave it to her the day she was born. Isabella gave it to Marie Celeste on the day of *her* birth. It was on a smaller chain and lay in its own leather pouch, crafted in Spain for my husband.

Emily sobbed. Jem placed his arm around her shoulder, knowing it was not nearly enough to console his wife, gripped in the fear that she was about to lose another child.

"Señor Braganza – "

The man interrupted Jem, "Please, we are family of a sort. Please call me Mateo."

"Very well, Mateo. If this is true, then you must love your grandchild very much to have searched so hard, for so long. We have raised this child. She knows no other mother than

Emily, no other father than I. We have honoured her heritage as best we knew how. She has had the best education we could provide. We would give our lives for her. She is a happy child. Would you tear her from all she knows and those who love her, and whom she loves, too? Surely that would be a cruelty worse than the trauma her true parents' death caused her. Can you truly say you love her and do such a thing to her?"

Jem looked Mateo in the eye. A tear slid down the man's cheek; his own eyes also stung with salty tears.

"Jem, Emily, may we please call you by your Christian names?"

"Of course," replied Emily before Jem was forced to find a voice through his pain.

Mateo began again, "Jem, Emily, we do love her. She is all that is left of our only son and Marie Elena's daughter. And we all agree with you. To tear her from all she knows would be an act of selfish cruelty, yet we cannot abandon her either. Our children's spirits would haunt us forever if we did that. However, we believe there may be a solution."

An hour later, the Abbot declared the meal was being served in his private rooms. It was agreed to continue the discussion of the plans after taking some time over dinner to consider all that it meant. They would return to Abbot

Michael's office after their repast. It was also agreed that nothing definite would be decided tonight.

Emily gazed again into the crystal glass and saw a wonderous future for her daughter, should these people prove to be trustworthy.

Only time would tell she thought, but she had faith in the Lord, and these people too.

FLYING
SCOTSMAN
FLYING
SCOTSMAN

The Empty Chair

Danny sat at the table in Shades Bar. Old habits die hard and he sat, back against the wall facing the door, just like every other visit there since 1975 when he got out of hospital. He was sixty-five now; he'd barely begun to shave back then. A fresh-faced lad still wet behind the ears and not long out of training. He let the wave of memories wash over him.

1969 Edinburgh.

Jack Fraser's Da was yelling out the window at us as we skipped down the steps of his house, two at a time. "Yis look like a pair eh lassies wi yon long curly locks. It'll be lads gein' yis the wolf whistles wi yous done up in they get ups."

We laughed.

"It's the fashion, ya auld dinosaur," Jack called over his shoulder to his da. It was just banter, filled with love. It's what we Scots do!

We hopped aboard a 42 bus and headed down to Porty, that's better known to outlanders as Portobello. There was a dance at the town hall. We were sixteen years-old; we knew it all and were invincible, as only the young believe.

We jumped off the bus as it slowed to a stop outside the Police station and shot across the road. There was a fair queue, and coming from the Musselburgh Road end of the High Street, a large group of lads all loud and brash, like peacocks. If we didn't get to the queue first, we might not get in.

Reaching the foyer to get our tickets, we noticed the recruitment table set up in the corner. The banner declared they were signing up for the Coldstream Guards. Not the oldest regiment in Scotland but the longest continuous serving regiment of the line, in the British Army. They hail from a wee place on the border, not too far from Edinburgh.

The big guy behind the desk was sporting a very impressive moustache, not a trendy Pancho Villa, but impressive none the less. He called, "Over here, lads. Come and have a wee chat."

Half an hour later, we excused ourselves as we'd eyeballed two fine lassies that we'd met here afore, and we didnae want to miss our chance. However, the old soldier had given us a lot to think about. He'd never know it, but he changed our lives that night, it wasn't only that that did, but it was part of it. Our fates had been rewritten.

Jack and I danced and blethered with Mernie and Bridie all through the evening till the last dance was called. It was a Ladies Excuse Me, where a lad can learn if a lassie really likes you or no.

We were heading back to the girls when we saw them heading straight for us.

"Are ye dancin'?" they asked.

"Are ye asking?" we replied, laughing. From that moment, Mernie and Jack, and Bridie and I were going steady. We spent all our time together except for Saturday afternoons, for then we were at Easter Road at the football or climbing aboard a coach to the away pitch.

Twelve months later ,I asked Bridie to marry me. She said yes!

I was so excited I could barely contain myself and couldn't wait to tell Jack. He was late to work, that day of all days. I was burstin'.

As soon as he walked in, I raced over. "You'll never guess what? I asked Bridie to marry me and she said yes!"

He burst out laughing as he dug into his trouser pocked and pulled out a small jeweller's box. He flicked the lid up and revealed a diamond ring. He stopped laughing like a loon and said, "As I walked Mernie home last night, we stopped to look in the jeweller's window. I asked which one she liked. She pointed to this, and I said to her,

"If I buy it for you tomorrow, will you marry me? She said yes, once she stopped leaping up and down and greetin'."

Over the next six months or so, as we planned our joint wedding, lots of things changed. Not all for the good, either. The foundry where we worked was closing and there was nothing nearby like it. All our plans to travel and marry and buy a house were disappearing like sand through our fingers.

Then one night Bridie and I were out for a walk and had jumped the bus up to Princes Street. There was a large crowd gathered at the National War Memorial in the gardens. The Pipes & Drums of the Royal Scots and the Coldstream Guards were playing to commemorate some old battle honours won in the Crimea or somewhere. As they played, I recalled the night at the dance and the old soldier. It brought an idea into play.

Next day in my lunch hour, I went to the recruiting office in Shandwick Place and had a remarkably interesting chat with the captain there. He gave me lots of pamphlets and interesting bits and pieces of information.

That night after my dinner, I was set to meet up with Jack. Hibbs were playing the Heart of Midlothian. It was a real town derby.

In the Artisan bar after celebrating a cracking game, I shared my plans with Jack. If Bridie was game, I was signing up. We sat there for a good two hours; Jack was up for it, too.

Our welding and engineering background was wanted in the army, and the pay was a sight more than the dole or working in the co-op. We left each other at St. Ninians church in Marionville Road.

He headed down Lochend Drive and as I headed on down the road, I shouted, "Jack, I'll meet you and Mernie in the George Hotel Bar at the top of Bath Street on Friday night at seven after I pick Bridie up, okay?"

"Aye, we'll see you there."

I'll not bore you with the minutiae of the following months; both Bridie and Mernie supported our decision to sign up as soon as the foundry shut. Both families had grandfathers and fathers who had served. Some had died on active service, and we were all proud of our service history.

We shared our wedding day, marrying on Aug 28th in St. Ninian of Triduana Parish church. It was a simple affair with close family and friends. The joint families put on a great spread in the church hall, and they'd decorated it with garlands and fresh flowers from both family's allotments. It was a beautiful sunny day and we couldn't have been happier.

We signed up a fortnight later, did our training and were on the Passing Out Parade on Jack's eighteenth birthday, I'd celebrated mine a couple of months prior. We were warriors now, or so we thought.

Our first posting was to Windsor to join the battalion. In early '73, we were allocated our married quarters. Two smashing wee houses next door to each other, the girls were fair thrilled at having such a big home and a garden too. Life was grand.

At Christmas, Jack announced that Mernie was expecting, and not to be left behind, on New year's eve, Bridie passed Mernie the box and me the stick showing that we too were going to be parents. Our bairns were due on Sept 23rd and 29th, the following year.

On Feb 5th we received orders. We were being deployed to Northern Ireland. The girls were devastated.

We were trained soldiers, we told them. Strong, fearless, invincible warriors, and in the way of the young and hopeful, we calmed their whispering fears.

In March, we left barracks in trucks. Next stop, Belfast.

It was to be a harrowing experience. We were such newbies; many there were hardened from time with Mad Mitch in Aden. The troubles were escalating, no thanks to politicians at the time. We lost a few in the first weeks there.

In June, we had five days R&R, (rest & recuperation). We flew home and enjoyed the time together. The girls' anxiety was increasing with the impending birth of our bairns. Scans had shown we were expecting a wee lassie and Jack a laddie. We decorated our nurseries together. Blue in Jack's and lemon in ours. We could for moments forget the horrors that awaited us.

We flew from Brize Norton into Aldergrove Air Force Station. Then, it was full on.

The troubles were fierce and there was a lot of political stuff going on, too, that wasn't helping reduce the tensions. It was a tinder pot.

On Sept 10th Jack was called in to see the Commanding Officer. Just minutes later clutching a three-day pass and wearing a grin set to break his jaw. He was heading to catch a helicopter lift back to Blighty, Mernie had endured a fast onset of labour and delivered their son, hale and hearty, at 4 a.m. that morning.

Two days later, it was my turn. Jack and I had a day's overlap of leave and enjoyed time with our wives and new-born wains. They were both ugly wee bundles of red wrinkled faces, though we'd never admit to the thought. The wee tykes had stolen our hearts, and I don't mind admitting it. I cried like a bairn when I had to kiss them goodbye.

Bridie had Jacqueline in her arms and Mernie held Liam tight as we got in the taxi taking us to the station. As we made our goodbyes, Mernie whispered to me, "Keep a watch on Jack. I've a bad feeling this time."

I promised we'd be fine and I'd look out for him.

A couple of months later, we were on duty down in Crossmaglen. Bandit country, they called it. As we pulled out of the suburbs onto the Newry Road, a large van came through towards us. It came hard and fast and in the middle of the road.

Our driver, wee Shuggie, slewed to avoid collision and we tipped at a precarious angle as the verge sloped sharply. We heard Shuggie say, "Oh, shit!" then bang and darkness.

A culvert milk churn bomb was exactly placed for us to hit, just as the van drivers had anticipated as they ran us off the road.

I have fragmented images in my head, none good. I woke up in Musgrave Park hospital. I'd lost a leg and sustained a serious head injury as well as fragments of shrapnel imbedded in my skull and back. They couldn't be removed.

I'd been in a coma for four days; Bridie was at my bedside.

She'd aged. Her eyes were swollen and red from crying. I managed to croak out, "I'll be fine love, dinnae fret." She laid her head on my hand and wept.

"How's Jack?" I asked a little later. She sobbed even harder then, and I don't know to this day if it was compassion for her distress, or fear that stopped me from pressing her for an answer. It turned out that Jack was in Stoke Mandeville hospital back in Blighty, I'd be joining him there as soon as they were happy that my head wound had stabilised.

I was helicoptered over in the first week of November 1975.

Jack was very poorly. He'd lost both legs and an arm to the elbow on his left side. He was fighting hard to live; He'd be okay if he could survive the infections in the first months. We had never given up on anything, and we sure as hell wouldn't start now,

In the August nine months later, he was in his wheelchair next to me, arm wrestling. We'd spent the morning hearing about our prosthetic parts and how they'd be our next challenge. The banter was fierce, and we had a bet to see who'd be walking first.

Just then, our Commanding Officer and the Families Officer appeared at the ward desk. They were followed by

Bridie with Liam and Jacqueline in a double buggy and the regiment's Padre bringing up the rear. Bridie looked awful!

They called us out to the doctor's office and the door was closed. That's when we learnt that Mernie had taken her life.

She'd dropped baby Liam into Bridie as usual in the morning when she would then go to work, but she hadn't gone to work. Bridie found her at about three p.m. when she failed to collect the bairn.

Her note to Bridie said she was sorry, but she couldn't be the wife Jack needed now. She was ashamed of her cowardice and they'd all be better off without her. I have no idea what she wrote to Jack, but that letter came nearer to killing him than the IED in Ireland ever had.

We finally were discharged early in the following year, me in the January and Jack in the March.

The Army, the British Legion and our combined families all helped to find a house big enough for all of us; Jack and Liam would live with us. They had a job to find one that could be modified to deal with all our needs. The one they found was amazing. On St. John's Lane on the front between Porty and Joppa. It had been a small nursing home for blind veterans; now it would be a home that Jack and I could get around in. A lift had been installed, so nowhere was inaccessible.

The front garden was awesome, walled in but with fine views of the Forth. You could see the ships coming into Leith docks, and at night it was like a navy velvet blanket covered in sparkling jewels of assorted colours as the ship's lights twinkled in the dark evening light. A large garage at the back had direct access to the kitchen and it had been adapted to accommodate our chairs. As had the brilliant big car we'd got with our disability pension.

Every year after, on November 15th, Jack and I would go alone to the War Memorial, then down to Shades Bar in Easter Road. It was owned by Eddie Turnbull, a Hibbs hero, and it was where we went after the game on a Saturday.

We still went to the match; the club gave us lifetime season tickets.

But November was when we let ourselves remember that day, the day the terrorists killed off the lives we'd had planned out. It wasn't about Mernie or us. That day was about Shuggie, Neil, and Rockie, who all died that day. We'd drink to them, get drunk for them. Eddie would always send us home in a cab, no fuss, no foul. We did that every year for thirty years.

Then in 2004, Jack was taken ill with yet another urine infection, or so we'd thought. Within twenty-four hours, it was sepsis, and he was gone. The doctor said his heart gave out.

I think he just lost the will to fight. Liam was with him, as were we all, and he went knowing Liam and Jackie were engaged.

So here I am, fifteen years on in our pub. It's not Eddie's bar now; he's long gone now too. It's not what it was, and I won't be back again.

The IRA have finally felled me too, the shrapnel in my skull is pressing ever harder on my brain stem, the medics say I've maybe six months.

So, I came this last time to tell Jack and the lads to get them in 'up there' ready for me.

Next year, well, there'll be another empty chair.

Walking With Ghosts

I walked with ghosts

in Flanders Fields.

Whose spectral hands threw,

the torch, to me and you.

In Flanders fields,

The wind does blow,

O'er the graves,

Where families go.

So many names,

And all too young!

Their lives over,

before they'd begun.

Great Uncle Gabe,

and Sue's Uncle Bill,

They went to fight,

They lie there still.

In Flanders fields

Where the wind does blow,

Where all descendants,

Really should go.

Lest We Forget

Just Think of Me

Just think of me as having gone...
Into another room.
Now, knowing this, please,
Put away your gloom.

You know I hated being sick,
And always feeling ill.
Look now out the window,
Just beyond the sill.

I am the breeze, that rustles the trees,
And whispers through the flowers.
I am living still, in your memories,
In the joy and love that is ours.

I shall wait now patiently,
Until your inbound flight,
But I will send you kisses,
In the wink of the stars at night.

I'll cross galaxies of time and space,

Just to gaze upon your face.

So, don't despair that I'm not there,

I am, I'm close, I'm everywhere.

From your loving mother

February, 2019

A Message from Your Mother.

You know I didn't want to leave,
and how hard I fought to stay.
But the Lord in his wisdom had his plans,
And those I could not sway.

But just because I can't be seen,
It's not as if I'd never been.
I taught you everything I know,
Before time came, for me to go.

I gave you love,
and tender care;
don't think that now,
I won't be there.

In every tear you shed, and smile.
I'll walk with you, yes, every mile.
Our bond of love, lies unbroken,
And the words of love, were not unspoken.

Until I hold you,
In heaven above,
Just close your eyes
and feel my love.

I taught you all you need to live,
To be generous, and to forgive.
Be only kind, to family and friends,
They are all that matters in the end.

For my children, grandchildren, and friends when the

morning comes that I am no longer here.

Acknowledgments

I want to acknowledge everyone from my life who has walked my path with me. Some for a reason, some for a season, and some a lifetime – not always my lifetime, but theirs.

I received gifts of friendship or love or sometimes lessons. The love sometimes was but for a season, and the lessons always had some reason. Experiences that taught me, and on occasion helped me grow. Sometimes the love was short-lived gifts, but gifts I'd needed at the time. And some people walked long roads with me.

My friends and my family, my stalwart buttresses that ensure I never fall far, or for long.

To all of you, I dedicate this book with grateful thanks.

P. Donoghue
aka G. B. Carmichael